Fay Weldon is a novelist, screenwriter and cultural journalist. Her novels include *The Life and Loves of a She-Devil*, *Puffball*, *The Cloning of Joanna May*, *Big Women* and *Rhode Island Blues*. She lives in Dorset.

For automatic updates on your favourite authors visit harperperennial.co.uk and register for AuthorTracker.

From the reviews of *Mantrapped*:

'This brilliant, innovative book, this rich mix of fact and fiction, is so compelling'   *Independent*

'The ideal platform for Weldon to tease out the delicious ironies of gender difference . . . and there are fascinating insights. There's simply no touching Weldon as a writer'
LIZ LOGGARD, *Observer*

'Witty, outlandish and provocative . . . the puckish fiction has the additional force supplied by its author's concurrent meditations on the overlap between reality and fantasy'
TLS

'There is always much to enjoy in anything Fay Weldon writes because her freewheeling style is so clearly the true voice of an attractive, witty, generous-spirited person'
Literary Review

'As always, she is preoccupied with the peculiar mystery of how to live as a woman. She comes to no conclusions in this rich, sad, life-affirming book; but she has never considered the question so wisely'
t on Sunday

FAY WELDON

Mantrapped

HARPER PERENNIAL
London, New York, Toronto and Sydney

Harper Perennial
An imprint of HarperCollins*Publishers*
77–85 Fulham Palace Road
Hammersmith
London W6 8JB

www.harperperennial.co.uk

This edition published by Harper Perennial 2005
1

First published by Fourth Estate 2004

A catalogue record for this book
is available from the British Library

ISBN 0 00 719452 8

Set in Sabon

Printed and bound in Great Britain by
Clays Ltd, St Ives plc

Trisha leaves home

Trisha had been rich and Trisha had been poor and she knew it was better to be rich. Now she was to be poor again.

The mattress Trisha slept upon was the most expensive on the market: she took consolation from that. Madonna had one like it. Trisha bought it after she won the lottery, nine years back. The claims the manufacturers made for it were true. When she woke in the morning her joints were not stiff and she had no trace of back-pain. She might on occasion wake weeping but she did not wake hurting.

Now she was to ache again. There would be no room in her new abode for so large and lavish a bed as hers. She had thought herself so resolved and steady of purpose, so unsentimental, so unattached to belongings, but now suddenly she felt weak at the knees and wanted to cry. She was alone in the world, without even a decent bed or permanent pillow on which to lay her head. Life once had seemed so easy. You did your best and it worked out all right. The advertisement in the catalogue had shown a young woman sitting alone on a bed with a glass of wine sitting beside her on the pink and gold floral fabric of the mattress. It had passed 'the wine-glass test', proving how the springs adjusted themselves to sudden changes in the distribution of weight.

That was how life ought to be, glossy and properly worked out for those who had the money.

Now, nine years later, when push had come to shove, and the creditors were banging on the door, and everything had to be sold, she looked at the mattress and doubted that it was even saleable. There is not much of a market for used mattresses in a prosperous society. The suspicion is always there that the previous owner has died upon it and that it would be more auspicious to start afresh. And the mattress, Trisha could see, showed all too much evidence of a hard-living, on-going life, far too much for a potential customer's comfort. It was stained with the traces of nine years of care-less living, flecked by blood and semen, marked by the breaking waters of pregnancy; it was impregnated, if she put her nose to it, with the soft fumes of marijuana and the acrid after-scent of cocaine.

People had got so fussy. Not just about things but about their bodies. Once a woman had been happy to look as God decided. Virtue lay in playing a good hand no matter what cards were handed out at birth. Greasy hair, put up with it. Big nose, large bottom, too bad. Smile and be grateful. Now it was off to the cosmetic surgeon to defy God's will. Bodies were kept under better control than once they were. They were thinner, cleaner, better exercised, healthier: people of the New Millennium had the energy and will to keep the corners clean. This was a mattress from the Former Age, the old century, and it showed. If a cover had come with the mattress – and at that price it surely should have – she had never bothered to put it on. The help never spoke English, and Trisha wasn't one to ask and burden servant lives further with extra toil. Sheets were understood in Latvia and Estonia but mattress-covers? She, Trisha, did not have the gift for creating order around her and she was prepared to admit it. In her new life she would try to do better.

In the months after the lottery win she had bought and bought and bought, all the things she had ever done without, to make up for years of too-thin saucepans, too-cheap sheets, badly-stitched clothes, and over-perfumed soap. She had bought the best, and not thought about money, other than to avoid bargains. Now everything had to be sold and would go for a fraction of what she had spent. But the pleasure of the antique Buddha, the double-pile carpets, the cocktail cabinets, the ice-making fridge, the serving table which talked back to you and wiped its own surface clean, the little unauthenticated Picasso sculpture of a bull, had lain in the buying, not the owning. So who cared? The money had run out, and credit too: now she would earn her own living like everyone else. She was not new to penury. She had scraped along for years on benefits and occasional work as an actress. Now she would take a computer course and do temping, forget how much she hated office work, being cooped up. Others managed, so would she. It had been good to win the lottery, good to attract the men who went with it, but it would be good to live honourably once again. The nouveaux riches were lonely; they looked over their shoulders all the time to make sure no one was cheating them, taking advantage, but they tended to look in the wrong direction. Those born rich had it easier, they knew the rules and how to keep them, were trained at their nanny's knee never to break into capital, never to lend money, to stick to their own class, rules devised over centuries for their protection. It was only recently she had realised what capital was. It was the stuff in the bank which others more secure than she lived on.

But she had her assets. People liked her. She was forty-four but could pass for ten years younger: she had good, long, skinny legs: she was plump-bosomed, large-nosed and smiled easily. Her hair was thick and naturally curly, henna-enriched. She was flexible: she could touch her toes with her hands flat on the floor in front of her. She looked available: she knew that: nothing much she could do about it: the truth was inbuilt: she looked as if a man might only give her but a little push, and she would fall easily back upon the bed and not complain about it. Round-heeled, her mother had called her once, when she was thirteen and had started going out with boys. Other girls were somehow stiffer in the middle, not given to bending: they got given presents, jewellery, flowers. Not Trisha – she always seemed to be the one giving things – little gifts, cards and so on, hoping to please. She looked good in little waisted jackets with fake fur collars. Tarty, her mother complained. So what? Wearing high heels with jeans meant there was never any shortage of men around, and a shortage of men was what Trisha most feared. Or had until the last couple of months. Perhaps she was traumatised, more upset by recent events than she realised: whatever it was, the thought of having a man about appalled her, someone telling her what to do, watching her every move, interfering with her decisions. She wanted her body to herself, while she worked out what to do next. The idea of strange male fingers approaching her flesh, which until lately would have had her instant positive attention, now gave her the shivers.

She knelt beside the mattress and the idea of praying occurred to her. She put her hands together and closed her eyes. 'Dear God,' she said, as she hadn't since she was seven. 'Help me now in the hour of my need. Forgive me my sins.' But really she had no idea how she could possibly have sinned. She had only ever done what circumstances required of her, and kept a little back for herself. Wasn't that allowed?

No voice from God came in reply, only that of the auctioneer's young assistant. 'So is the bed to be in the sale or out of it?' he asked. Trisha got to her feet at once. He would assume she had been examining the mattress: it would not occur to anyone these days that people kneeled by beds and prayed. She hoped he noticed the quality, and overlooked the stains. He spoke through his nose, though that was probably not his fault. He was in the habit of despising others, she could tell. It narrowed the nasal passages. Nothing was ever worth as much as people hoped and it gave him a feeling of superiority. He earned his living dealing in other's people's disappointments. He was a tall, pale, stooping young man: how did such a person come to have the job he did? She was in a perpetual state of marvel at the way the new world worked. He had qual-ifications, she supposed, in Art History. He had been trained to tell a Manet from a Monet, no doubt, but she did not think he would make it in the wide world. He had too little generosity of spirit. Too many planets in the lower half of the astrological chart, as hers were, to rise to great heights. Too long spent handling what amounted to repossession sales – *turn up, turn up, knock down prices, everything must go. One person's bargain is another person's loss*. Wrong end of the market, buster, down here among the totters, the knockers, the hearse-chasers, the hungry end of the dealing trade. Up the top end, Bond Street and the antique trade, and at the bottom, the skip; in the middle, eBay and the car boot sale. *Look at this, darling, just right for the baby in a couple of years*. What was sold early morning down the wrong end of the Portobello Road for a fiver went for twenty quid at the top, by evening. In the meanwhile the traders helped themselves to a living. Ordinary punters, idle and ignorant, never knew what they were doing: it was their role in life to be ripped off. While the professionals, the lawyers, the accountants, the designers, not to mention the daily help, helped themselves to what was left, and that was before the taxman got the lion's share. Well, now she didn't have to worry. It could all go. All the stuff now piled up in the garden and the front rooms, the over-shiny repro furniture, the stacks of unopened fashion magazines, the garden roller no gardener could be bothered to use, the frilly swing seats – she always thought she'd conceived little Spencer in that one – and the mirror and glass serving-trolleys with boule decoration, a snip at £7000 – and the only single thing she regretted was the bed, with its used mattress.

'I haven't decided,' she said to the auctioneer. 'It might come with me.'

'It won't fetch much in a sale,' he said. 'Mattresses never do. But I could take it off your hands for a fiver. It would clean up. My girl-friend's only got a futon.'

Perhaps he wasn't so bad. They were all in the survival game together.

Writer's note

So far so good. You can start a novel like this. *Lottery Winner Faces Hard Times*. Rags to riches is better, but riches to rags will do. It is heartening in fiction to watch people making good, but facing up to their just or unjust desserts has its attractions too. I remember thinking this in the days of my frivolity, when I was the BBC's darling, and anything I could think of to write they would produce, without argument or committee meetings or worry about ratings. In the days when script editors were there to make writers happy and bring them cups of tea, and not tell them what to do, and my income was great – by my standards – even though my debts were often greater. That lasted for fifteen years, on and off, and ended in the mid-Eighties.

Trisha and her mattress

The young auctioneer went off to harangue the men who were trying to manoeuvre a pool table from the so-called rumpus room down the stairs, and had already broken the banisters. Trisha went to the linen cupboard where a sign now said *Assorted Linens – £25* and extracted an Egyptian cotton sheet from a packet of six, still wrapped, that had cost her £435 from Harrods, and used it to cover the disgrace of the mattress. Here was a decade's worth of personal history. At least she'd had some. Many didn't. Here was the large red wine stain where she had tried the wineglass trick and it had failed. One of the lovers – was it Gregory or Thomasina? Or one of the husbands – was it Alastair or Rollo? – had lunged at her and that had been that. Spoiled, no longer virgin. The bed had been sold on the premise of comfort and hygiene, not the bonus of sexual activity, so she could not take the manufacturers to court under the Trades Descriptions Act. She noted she had begun to see litigation as a way of raising money. She would like to be able to sue God for making her the way she was. See there, a trail of yellowish stains left by little Spencer who as a one-year-old had liked to climb into her bed and sleep there, rather than in his cot, sucking last night's bottle.

That was in the days before Rollo claimed Trisha was an unfit mother. It was not an accusation easy to refute. She was not fit. Good mothers used mattress-covers which could be easily laundered, they breast fed not bottle fed, did not drink too much, go to bed with women if there were no men available, not even to cure a broken heart. She hoped she was a nice mother, but she knew she was not a good one.

The solution occurred to her. She would leave the bedstead and take the mattress. It was as good a memoir of her life as she was likely to get. She would go easy on herself and not start altogether afresh. The mattress would go with her to her new address in Wilkins Parade, the living room, bedroom and kitchen above a domestic services agency, called for some reason Kleene Machine, where she was now obliged to live. The landlady had promised the flat to her, though there was nothing in writing. The rent was cheap: housing benefit would cover it. The area was just about possible, still with a majority of non-ethnics. She had to face it: nothing was going to turn up in the next couple of hours to save her from the squalor of living above a shop. That kind of thing only happened when you were under forty. No former lover, no knight in shining armour, was going to gallop over the horizon and rescue her. She had no choice but to call up the landlady before she changed her mind, and say, yes, she would take the flat, she would move in at once.

It would be okay. She would make the new place into a love nest, cosy and sweet, she would pick up fabric from charity shops and drape the walls: she would drown the smell of damp and mould with scent. She had at least thirty bottles of expensive scent, all opened, all tried, most discarded. They would come with her in the van in which she would drive away from her old life and begin the new. Of course she would take the mattress; it represented her past. She would live to cavort upon it in style once more. The strength was returning to her legs. They were good legs, not as long as they could be, but shapely. Life after all was a great adventure.

Riches to rags

I came to the riches to rags idea in a taxi on my way to a commissioning meeting at the BBC. That was 1985. I was unprepared. I would have to wing it, and did. 'Well,' I said, 'there was this woman living happily in the country when . . .' and made it up as I went along. Okay, they said. These days I would need to take along a twenty-page synopsis, fully-illustrated, to such a meeting and the life would have gone out of it before I even began. That was *The Heart of the Country*, which ended up as a TV mini-series and which I later novelised. Frivolity can be a great asset to a writer: delinquency is part of the calling. I thought it would only really interest recipients of housing benefit in the Shepton Mallet area of Somerset, where I then lived, but it ended up winning the *LA Times* Fiction Prize. A great many people are very conscious of riches to rags; it is their fear and, more often than you would think, their experience.

There was an auction in that novel, too, when my heroine's belongings were sold up. Bereft of a husband to protect her, and innocent of the ways of the world, she was thoroughly cheated by the local small businessmen, from the antique dealer to the estate agent to the lawyer. First they slept with her, then they profited by her. Trisha will not be so foolish. She knows only too well which side her bread is buttered.

That auction is vivid in my mind because, having written it, I was there at its filming for TV. If you write enough fiction, you can have trouble telling the difference between what you did in real life and what you wrote, and filming makes both more vivid. The rectangle of charred earth where I once fictionally burned down my own home, in a novel called *Worst Fears*, written in 1995, is seared painfully into my mind, and the passing of ten years has not muted the pain. I drove past the house the other day and was astonished to see it still standing and was not at all pleased.

Nearly everything you write about, you realise one day, has its roots somewhere in the past. What, for example, is this preoccupation with mattresses? True, this morning I changed my own. Over, end to top, side to side, heavy work. I did it myself without help. I did not want witnesses. There is no mattress-cover. Perhaps I am piling my own housewifely guilt into poor Trisha. I am reluctant to go out and buy a new one: I don't know what kind of shop stocks such things and I would have to find tape, pen and paper to take the measurements and I am upstairs and they are downstairs – you know how it goes. And besides, I have other more pressing things to think about. Easier to write another paragraph about Trisha's life.

My mattress, like Trisha's, is nine years old and expensive. Unlike Trisha's it is in not too bad a state. But mattresses are not the proper stuff of fiction. Beds are trivial on the page, if not in life. When, after thirty years of marriage, doing what all women are warned not to do (*Wronged wife: 'I want*

10

nothing from you, nothing. All I want is my freedom!) I left the matrimonial home, my then husband at least had the grace to give our brass bed away and not share it with his mistress under what used to be our joint roof. I am grateful for that.

Sometimes I wonder who has the bed now – like in that story *A Day in the Life of a Penny*, which all children used to be required to write and I loved to do and others to my surprise hated. In whose pocket is the penny now? In whose home the bed?

I hope it brought them luck, I daresay it did. Luck stayed with me for perhaps longer than its usual run, and may it do the same for them: I cross my fingers. I also hope that though keeping the bed itself they junked the mattress. It had nearly thirty years of life with us, and heaven knows where it came from before.

We do so much in bed, lying down – if we are lucky, that is – get born, conceive others, die – and if it doesn't happen in a bed that's usually bad. Born in a taxi, conceived in an alley, died in an accident – needs must, but bed is best, safe, familiar and dull. Too dull, perhaps, for novels. Fiction is about the exceptional, not the normal. Fiction is focused real life, with the boring bits cut out. Otherwise, just live life, don't read about it. Let alone write about it. Back to business.

Trisha faces the future

So Trisha calls Kleene Machine and tells Mrs Kovac, who is the owner of the property, that she will take the flat. Kleene

Machine's shop-front has been recently repainted in deep crimson, lettering in gold. It is not unattractive. The firm charges top prices. It used to be a betting shop. Mrs Kovac hires out domestic and office cleaners from Eastern Europe and farms out the dry-cleaning on a commission basis. Kleene Machine's little crimson and gold van, driven by Mr Kovac, beetles around the area and is a familiar sight, if a rather surprising one in this mixed area, in which piss-stained, concrete walls and broken windows are still evident. This particular branch of Kleene Machine, an organisation which has so far made good profits by judging the property market and being the first to arrive in up-and-coming areas, was leased by the Kovacs as a concession two years ago. The neigh-bourhood is becoming popular with the media classes – jour-nalists, film makers, ad men, minor celebrities and so on, who are less frightened of gun crime than the professionals – lawyers, doctors, accountants – and are the foot soldiers of the class war, as they prepare to drive out the riff-raff, ethnics of many varieties, take over and gentrify. The media game in London is to buy property cheap and sell dear by virtue of blessing the area with their presence and their spending power.

The police have gone before, making life uncomfortable for drug-dealers, whores, beggars and the gangs of youths, who, listless at best and depraved at worst, used to hang around Wilkins Square and its environs, bringing down the price of property. Now they cluster a quarter of a mile further out and make life miserable for another set of residents. They're restless, they didn't want to go. Wilkins Square has been the province of the uprooted and dispossessed for hundreds of years. Tradition draws them; they drift back, thwarting the police in their attempt to clean up the area. It is touch and go who wins.

Trisha has to rent: she can't buy. She has no money, other than what she makes from the sale, and that will have to go to pay off the last remaining debts. The auctioneers will want their commission; the tax man will want his last remaining pennies before the benefit agencies take over and pay out what the tax man has brought in. Everything will be recorded on computer and camera. Trisha's face will be studied by security cameras as she stands in line at Job Centres and welfare services. No one will let Trisha go free but no one will let Trisha starve. Trisha, by her careless living, has created quite an amount of work for all kinds of people to do, which is to the greater good, no doubt, and just as well, since the human race is in search of meaningful employment, and caring for others, making a difference, is what it likes to do.

Trisha makes the phone call she has been putting off. 'Hi there, Mrs Kovac,' says Trisha. She uses her mobile: the landline has long since been disconnected, and the instrument added to the others in the pile flagged *Assorted Electronics, £30*. 'Remember me? Trisha?' She speaks cheerfully. No point in dispiriting others. 'I'm the one about the flat. Thanks, I'd love to take it.'

'You're too late,' says Mrs Kovac. 'I told you to ring before midday. It's gone to the next person on the list. Flats round here are like gold dust. I was doing you a favour not wanting a yes or no there and then.'

Some people enjoy the power that owning the roof over others' heads entails: to be able to be kind and offer it, or to be mean and snatch it away at will – yes, that can be rewarding. Mrs Kovac finds it so. Trisha has met all too many of her kind lately, power freaks, the kind that cluster

13

in banks or call centres, or wherever desperate need reveals itself. The officials concerned with her bankruptcy – she had offered them chocolate biscuits out of the generosity of her heart and been told she was buying them at other people's expense; there must henceforth be only digestive – enjoyed her helplessness: so did the social workers, who spoke with the soft, consoling voices of the habitually cruel, which belied hard eyes, and the contempt which seethed within. Sensitised now to the unspoken words: *How have you come to be in this fix? Serve you right! Now you, who thought yourself so grand, are brought as low as us!* Mrs Kovac is another. Trisha realises she had done it wrong. As with landlords, so in doctor's surgeries, as in all places where you depend upon others for help, it is wiser to weep, wail, and show distress than to display good cheer. Allow those in charge to show mercy, and then they will. But first, crawl.

Trisha weeps and snivels on the phone. She tells herself it is planned and calculated. It is not. She weeps real tears. *Oh please, Mrs Kovac, please!* She wants the flat, needs it. It is cheap and dirty and damp but it will do. It smells violently of carbon tetrachloride. Mrs Kovac undertakes 'spotting' – removing the worst stains by hand – in the back of the shop, before sending other people's dirty clothes off and away to the mysterious places where soiled rags are restored and returned crisp and clean and plastic wrapped. But there are worse smells to live with. Carbon tetrachloride at least smells of improvement, renewal, hope.

Mrs Kovac previously imported uneducated girls from the Far East, two a penny in their own land, where girls were on the whole disregarded. They were brought in on cheap flights, and allocated where Western need most lay. The clever ones were whisked off into banks, the pretty ones landed in the sex industry, the careful ones became nannies, the kind ones carers, and the daft and docile ones, Mrs Kovac's speciality, became cleaners. Now she ran Kleene Machine she would trust the most dextrous to do mending and repair work: replace buttons, patch, take up hems, let out seams – there is a lot of such work to be done: these days, with exercise done or neglected, diets working or otherwise, people change their shape rapidly. Fat today, slim tomorrow: wide-muscled shoulders on Saturday night, soft and sloping a week hence. But good mending girls were in short supply: the art of careful, delicate and precise workmanship was dying in the East as it long since had in the West. 'Repairs' were a good little money earner if you got it right but finding the staff was an increasing problem.

A few of Mrs Kovac's best girls had got away to good jobs in the fashion industry in Paris, where they commanded good wages. Now they had learned the route, too many others followed. Lately the bottom had fallen out of the Far East market: girls from Malaysia, Indonesia and Thailand were earning their living at home, their national economies were better. Times were better. Eastern Europe and Russia was the new market for girls. Soon that too would dry up and she would be left with the British, who were too disdainful to exert themselves at such mundane and badly-paid tasks. Poles were hopeless at sewing but good cleaners. It was a Communist upbringing mixed up with Catholic guilt that did it, in Mrs Kovac's opinion. They scrubbed both to cleanse their sins and benefit the community. But she could see that someone like Trisha, who had let slip about her past in embroidery, and was clearly in reduced circumstances, might be persuaded to join the mending army.

15

What Trisha had liked about the flat on her earlier brief inspection of it was that it had its own side entrance. You didn't have to go through the shop to get to it. It was private. She could make it nice. A few throws, some cushions and a scented candle or two and it would be just fine. She'd turn it into a little love nest. The area was marginally worrying. There was a Starbucks just around the corner, true – a sign that the district was going up in the world; but there was also a pile of broken syringes outside Kleene Machine waiting for a street-cleaner who never came to sweep them up in his little machine. Touch and go, Trisha thought, but she wouldn't be there for long. This was just a staging post between one good life and the next – with any luck. First, Mrs Kovac had to be persuaded.

'Please, please,' said Trisha, 'I don't know what I'm going to do; I've got no one to be there for me, nowhere to live. I don't know how my life has come to this but it has.' And so forth.

Mrs Kovac said she couldn't change her mind, she always kept her word, and besides, the new tenant was prepared to do bits and pieces of mending and sewing in part return for rent.
'I can do that!' said Trisha. 'It's just up my street!' and indeed this was true. She had been to the London College of Embroidery for a term, between school and Drama College. She'd written this on the statutory form provided by the Rental Accommodation Office, which she'd given Mrs Kovac, and which gave the life details everyone seemed to want these days.

'If it means all that to you,' said Mrs Kovac, grudgingly, 'I'll put the other person off.' So that was that, arranged. Fate took away with one hand and gave it back with the other, albeit finding the recipient a little more shop-soiled by age and experience each time it happened. Trisha didn't suppose her mending duties would be onerous, since Mrs Kovac was prepared to reduce the rent by only five pounds a week. She would meet that problem when she came to it.

On her way to her new home, riding in the front of the van with the removal man and her bits and pieces behind, she felt exhilarated, if a little as if she were the Fool in the Tarot pack, about to walk jauntily over the cliff edge into thin air. She tried to remember little Spencer's face and somehow couldn't quite envisage it. He belonged to some woman who had won a fortune in a lottery and lost it all in a decade. Through her inattention, drink and gambling, he now belonged to his father. That was justice. Men should remember they are fathers too.

It is easy enough to forget children in their absence. The bonding process works best when the child is within earshot. Birds and humans are designed to go foraging for their young and to return to the nest when the offspring is needy and calls out. If the call can't be heard the parent forgets. Other creatures need proximity of touch. Take a cow from a calf and in a couple of hours the cow forgets and the tormented lowing stops. After half a day the cat without kittens stops prowling. Why should we be different? But sometimes Trisha feels bad because she gives so little thought to her absent child.

The mattress turned out to be bigger than Trisha supposed, or else the bedroom was smaller than she remembered. You had to choose which one you wanted to open properly – the bedroom or the wardrobe door – you couldn't have both. Trisha chose the bedroom door. Clothes were henceforth to be unimportant to her new life. She would take all her little fur-lined jackets to the charity shop: she would go to work in dark skirts and white shirts. She would be plain and useful. She was full of dreams of redemption, of absolution. She would have to clamber over the mattress, no doubt, for the odd feather stole and silky chemise, but at least her back would not hurt, only her pride. She would earn her own money and keep away from men. She would live quietly and lick her wounds until she felt stronger. She would try never again to weep in front of the likes of Mrs Kovac, never to be humiliated, never be reduced to inchoate self-pity.

Trisha's soul was much like her mattress: soiled but comfortable.

Novels are not enough

Novels alone are not enough. Self-revelation is required. Readers these days demand to know the credentials of their writers, and so they should. Too often readers cry out for bread and are given stones: writers fail them, fob them off with thrillers, good guys on the political left, the bad guys on the right, or chick lit, first-person tales in the present tense leavened by wisecracks, feeble emotions if nifty enough plots. Writers have to get published somehow: living in garrets is out of fashion. Who would take them seriously if they did? Once writers alone in all the world had privileged information: they could read the human mind and pass the knowledge on. But these days their USP, their Unique Selling Proposition, is wearing thin. Such knowledge is no longer arcane: everyone knows everything. Freud and Jung and a host of psychotherapists have laid out the road map of the mind for all to see: the mechanics of intellectual and emotional reaction have been made clear. From *Meet Yourself as You Really Are; I'm Okay, You're Okay; Men are from Mars, Women are from Venus; The Cinderella Complex* and their like, to *Help Yourself to Contentment* programmes on TV, everyone is now their own expert. Since Meg Ryan faked an orgasm in public, what is there left to be disclosed? It is not better and it is not worse: it is just different.

We are not short of stories, not at all. We wallow in beginnings, middles and ends: if we grow blasé we are shocked into response. Once a severed finger was alarming, now volleys of decapitated heads fly about our screens and no one flinches. Our whole existence is threaded through with cheapo TV fiction: it is script editors, trained in counselling techniques, not writers, who dictate the lines the actors say, the tears they weep, the homosexual kisses they exchange. Our children grow up as heroes of their own lives, believing there will always be a happy ending. Even those wear thin. We would rather have reality TV.

Fiction drifts backwards into once upon a time: it is an industry, its raw material dug up where the market dictates, hammered into shape by editorial teams and committee, and each writer these days is perforce his own committee – *what will the publisher think, what will my friends think, what do I dare say?* The computer sniffs at swear words and underlines them with red. Thus the Stalinist Within triumphs, the free expression of thought is stifled. The Committee Without is there to pick off stragglers: can this be safely published? Will this make a profit? (*The Satanic Verses* would not stand a snowflake's chance in hell today.) Since the touchstone is what has done well in the past nothing new can happen, or

19

only by accident. But prudence does not pay off. The readers begin to yawn and close their books.

Best put your faith then in the new reality novel. Reality TV is real life lived out in a fictional context (the House): the reality novel threads the life through the fiction. Have my fiction, have me.

That off my chest, on with the story of my own life. Trisha's is going to have to wait a bit. As she wept, pained and humiliated, so did her writer.

Times I have cried in public

I cried when I was fourteen turning fifteen and I left my father on the quayside at Wellington, New Zealand, a tall, dark figure getting smaller and smaller as the ship departed, knowing I would never see him again. Nor did I. I was off, unwillingly, to England with my brave and wilful mother. That was 1946.

I cried when I was sixteen turning seventeen and the headmistress told me that I alone of all the Upper Sixth had not been elected prefect. That was South Hampstead School for Girls and only this morning I had a letter from the current headmistress asking me to address the school on any subject of my choosing. *If My Friends Could See Me Now*. Some could, if they were interested, but too many have died. That was 1948, the year I realised there was no magic to protect me from misfortune.

It was a shock when I realised my school days were five years behind me. The degree of shock, if this is any consolation, remains much the same now the gap amounts to fifty-five years. The terrible realisation that the present is not always with us is a one-time event and not subject, thank God, to perpetual renewal.

Better to be grateful for the time one has, and the time one has had than lament that there is little left. If I look out of the window where I write this early morning I see the sun rising over the pollarded lime trees of what were once the gardens of the most powerful abbey in England. The trees look the same as in the sixteenth-century print someone showed me recently – the old gnarled trunks, the spurt of new, thwarted if determined foliage, like the drawing of an inexpert child. It is autumn, the most colourful autumn for years after a hot, dry summer, and the trees are coming to life with the dawn, in a kind of greeny-pink haze. A woman walks a little dog. It should be on a lead and is not. People, delinquent and otherwise, have walked here for centuries. The monument to the dead of the First World War comes into relief as sunlight breasts the wall of the church and stripes the dark grass withlight. Beyond the trees the ground falls away from the old castle ramparts, and you can see right across a wide landscape to the next ridge of hills and the little airfield which flashes its light as confidently as if it were Canary Wharf.

The Abbey was torn down by Henry VIII, in a fervour of asset-stripping, and the stone parcelled out to nobles in London to build their fine houses. But a lot was stolen in dead of night, and many old houses in these parts have chunks of Abbey stone built into their fabric. And we still

21

have the trees, and the past showing through into the present, if you have a mind to look.

I will put a tree or two in Wilkins Parade and Wilkins Square where the addicts gather, to cheer the place up, to share my good fortune in being able to see what I have seen this morning, the old and the new, the past and the present, all merging into one another. Good fortune must be passed on.

> *Look thy last on all things lovely, every hour*
> *Let no night,*
> *Steal thy sense in deathly slumber*
> *'Til to delight*
> *Thou hast paid thy utmost blessing,*
> *Since that all things thou would'st praise,*
> *Beauty took from those that loved them,*
> *In other days.*

My mother would quote that at the drop of a hat. She never went to school but she had a head full of poetry, and passed the knowledge on to me. Just before she died, at the age of ninety-five, we remembered together at least two consecutive pages of Tennyson's *Lady of Shalott.*

> *Four grey walls and four grey towers,*
> *Overlook a space of flowers . . .*

What else are the Abbey gardens? My grandchildren's heads are full of pop lyrics, in the same way, but I think we had the best of it.

I cried when I was seventeen turning eighteen and my father died. I had just come home from France, where I had been working in a Youth Aliyah camp for Jewish children on their way to what was then known as the Holy Land, and was staying with my aunt and uncle, Mary and Michael Stewart in Amen Court, in the shadow of St Paul's. I was to be there for a week before taking the night train to St Andrews University. Home had vanished in my absence. My mother had left London to live in her Wild Meg cottage on the Cornish moors. Once again, I had only my suitcase and memories I preferred to forget – lost landscapes, lost friends.

Michael and Mary were Labour Party activists and were to end up in the House of Lords, he an ex-Foreign Secretary, she a very worthy Baroness. A telegram came. Mary opened it and said 'Bad news, your father has died' and put it down on the hall stand. She cried a little, my father being her brother, and I cried too, to keep her company. We did not touch; we were not a touching family.

'We have grim news,' say *The Sunday Times* and others when they ring up to tell you some public figure or friend has died, 'we have grim news.' And you reply quickly, 'who?' And they give you the name and it either shocks you to the core or you remain oddly and guiltily indifferent. Sometimes it is those apparently closest to you whose death does not seem to impinge much upon your own life, while the death of those you scarcely know and rarely see can strike you to the quick. Grief comes bidden or unbidden, and there is little you can do about it. It is as if the circles of acquaintance given to one in life are flawed: off-key, they overlap but do not coincide. You can spend a lot of time with others, and take very little notice. Or spend a little time, and be devastated.

I had not seen my father for three years and I think I had struck him from my psychic address book. We went to *Oklahoma!* that night – we did not cancel, and it was my birthday treat. Life, my aunt said, must not be disturbed by death. That was 1949: there had been a war. Amen Court stood alone amidst rubble. The times were drastic, and still out of joint.

I met my mother a few days later in a Lyons Corner House: brief reference only was made to my father's death. She did say she shouldn't have left him, and he was the only man she had ever loved. She seemed surprised I was disturbed in any way by his death. But then she never reckoned fathers much. And since she didn't see why I should take his loss personally, I tried not to. I did cry on the way back to Amen Court and a lady on the bus asked me if anything was the matter and I remember saying, 'I have no home and now no father.' Then I cheered up. I had a sense of drama, but could not keep self-pity up for long. On the night train up to St Andrews I took off my black armband and that I thought was that. He shouldn't have gone and died if he wanted my love. Fatherless – so what was new anyway?

Black armbands – strips of black satin bought at the haberdashers – had become fashionable in the war, replacing the wearing of black clothes to signify a family bereavement, and my mother, as a concession to the event, had bought them for Jane and me to take to university. Our new friends would treat us more tenderly, or perhaps find a useful way of striking up a conversation. Jane – having left school at fourteen and finished the correspondence courses which were to earn her a matriculation certificate – that wonderful document which qualified you to get to University – and now living in a bed-sitting room – set off for Exeter as I set out for St Andrews. I don't know whether Jane wore her armband, or not. We did not discuss such things, or indeed, ever talk about my mother as if she were not in the room, which precluded discussion of my father's death. And as Jane went South and I went North, my mother went West, to St Ives in Cornwall, having decided all places under the sun were equal, and St Ives was where the pin struck that she had held over a map of the land, and let it fall. Almost off the map, not quite. Which is why it happened that Jane met her husband Guido the artist in St Ives, and they begat Christopher, Rachel and Benjamin, who begat Alexander, Isobel and Imogen, Nat, Jake and Henrietta – and all of them come to Christmas dinner, long after Guido and Jane are gone. And all live in houses which do not vanish under their noses: we work hard at it and keep the gardens nice.

I remember the armband so vividly. 1949. I stepped aboard the train in England wearing it, and off the train in Scotland without it. I remember the act of will it took to take it off. I felt ungrateful and disobedient, but I meant to be a person without a past, only a future. Of course it is not so easy.

To wear black at all – now the mainstay of most wardrobes, and a symbol of smart practicality – was still seen in the Forties and Fifties as unlucky. (As for white lilies, 'funeral flowers' – they should never be brought into a house. The association with coffins was too strong, not to mention the white waxiness of the blooms themselves, too like the corpse itself to be countenanced.) The armband was a kind of half-way house, between the excesses of Victorian mourning and today's way of achieving 'closure' as soon as possible, by way of Bereavement Support Groups. It was an explanatory statement to strangers. *'Forgive me if I'm not as polite or considerate as I should be. If I cry in the street, on the bus, I am not mad. Someone close to me has died.'* It should be revived: I should not have taken it off.

The quad at St Andrews was bleak stone and the green grass formal, and the paths formed like a saltire cross. It was a long way from home but there was no home anyway. Ghosts stalked the town and haunted the long beaches, but we students wore red flannel gowns to keep out the cold, and sat in lecture halls where our predecessors had gathered for five hundred years, bringing sacks of oats to pay for their tuition, and slept as they did from too much wine and debauchery. There were crosses in the cobbles to mark where prelates had been burned to death for their beliefs. All could have recanted and been saved, but they preferred not to. They would rather be right about the transubstantiation of the Virgin Mary. For lack of a family, I daresay, I regained a sense of 'we' which has never left me. 'We' students, in defiance of our teachers, 'we' workers in defiance of the bosses, 'we' writers in defiance of the TV moguls, 'we' women in defiance of men. And in the meanwhile I found friends and chattered on.

I cried when I was twenty-five rising twenty-six and had run away from what I saw as a bad husband (I think in retrospect I was a worse wife than he ever was husband) with my little boy tucked under my arm. Now I needed to get him into a nursery school, so I could be free to work. The husband, headmaster of a secondary school, married to provide a roof over our heads, was the 'no wife of mine works' kind of man, prevalent in the Fifties. I had flung myself into a hostile world with no means of support, not even from the State. My mother was in a sorry state, living

26

as a companion to an elderly woman with whom she did not get on, and had only a single room to her name. I would be no more welcome in that house than my mother had been before I was born, in the hospital where my father, her husband, had found a live-in job as a single man. Lithe single women can be slotted in anywhere, sneak in and out of institutions at night, but not women with children. (No wonder the birth rate falls as women everywhere learn how to look after their own interests.) Somehow, now, I had to earn. Just another runaway Fifties wife, I wept in front of the woman who ran the school, and didn't want to admit my child and so encourage immorality. That was in August, 1957. I was really low, so sorry for myself. 'Somewhere to live', difficult enough today, was even more difficult then, and the State even more reluctant to help.

I was staying with friends, Laura and Stephen Cohen, in Yeoman's Row, in Knightsbridge, in the flat Laura's father, Wells Coates, the Bauhaus architect, had designed. They were good to me in the hour of my need, and took me and Nicolas in without a thought for their own convenience, dreadful cold in the nose and all. It was the kind of cold one gets when relieved from a great pressure and strain, and the body allows itself to give up its defences and descends into welcome illness. It was spectacular.

That day at the nursery school I wept, and sneezed, and sneezed and wept, and the headmistress relented, and Nicolas was allowed in her day care centre. Weep and plead, as a woman, and it shall be given to you. I see I have taught Trisha the same sorry lesson. But sometimes one can't help it: the tears flow unbidden. The first time at the therapist it is normal for the client to cry and cry. The story of one's life, told by oneself to a sympathetic listener, induces great self-pity and indeed childishness. Afterwards one is ashamed.

As it happened I only sent Nicolas to the centre for a single day. The children were so pale and sad, the weather so cold, little stiff arms pushed into winter coats, the weeping when the mothers departed so distressing. I could see that the idea of childcare was fine in theory but appalling in practice: that the interests of children and parent overlapped but as so often did not coincide, and what was good, and indeed necessary, for the mother was not automatically good for the child. Unless of course the parent is so horrible in the first place – and a few are – that being at a distance from them can only be advantageous. I took Nicolas out of his nursery that evening and never took him back. I wanted my freedom: I wanted to live unobserved and uncriticised, I wanted to be free of husbandly and motherly interference and control, but want, I could see, must be my master for a time yet. I wrote to my mother and asked her if she would leave companioning her old lady and help me with Nicolas and she said she would. Of course she did; I knew she would. We might be back to where we'd been before I had been panicked into marriage with the headmaster but at least times were better. The baby was now a child and easier to look after, and I had the promise of a better-paid job, one more fitting my graduate state, found for me by my lover and mentor, the Dane.

I wept and wept when the Dane, a yachtsman copy writer, author of *Bridge That Gap With Cadbury's Snack* and other famous sayings, went on holiday with his wife on money I lent him for the purpose. That was in 1957. How could I refuse? He had found me the job, that of a trainee copy writer, at Crawfords, a proper big time agency situated in

28

High Holborn. It had the Milk Marketing Board account – *Drinka Pinta Milka Day* – amongst others, and I loved him, and was (minimally) guilty because he was married. 1958, and my mother and I found a flat on the top floor of a house in Earls Court. There were five flights of stairs and no lift, no carpets and almost no furniture, but it was somewhere to live. We still had dark grey army surplus blankets on the beds, under which the Dane would join me, secretly, so as not to upset my mother, and his wife. And at least there was now a little surplus money for me to be able to lend it straight back to him. I had become pregnant, miscarried, and he had wept.

1959, and I was at Crawfords and shared an office with Elizabeth Smart, author of *By Grand Central Station I Sat Down and Wept*. She was a kind and beautiful woman and a fine writer, and I was a great blubbing bulky thing and a panicky one. The Dane had used his influence to get me the job in the first place: now Elizabeth taught me how to write advertising copy. How to forget the verbs and sprinkle adjectives, and try to make them pertinent, and never to use words for the sake of words, that every one has to mean something or you excise it. She taught me the value of exactitude, though I think I had an instinct for it anyway. She loved George Barker the poet, a dysfunctional relationship, in today's terms, and had four brilliant children by him, and when I miscarried the Dane's baby she was sympathetic and did not say 'just as well', though it was. She became the gardening correspondent for *Vogue* and wrote remarkable poetry, and when George wrote *The Dead Seagull* – his answer to *Grand Central Station* – there was a great literary hoo-hah. Elizabeth won on points, because of her prose and the heart-rending nature of the then emotional subjugation of women to men, which she caught on the tide, just as the tsunami which was women's liberation began to gather force. *This misery, this indignity, really cannot go on any more.*

Elizabeth and George's fourth child was called Rosie. She was fourteen when she first came to a party of ours, in the Sixties, precocious – though not by to-day's standards – thoroughly charming and astonishingly beautiful. She was to have a baby which was to be born addicted to heroin – now a common enough occurrence, then it made headlines. Elizabeth looked after the baby, but Rosie died soon after from an overdose, to everyone's distress.

I find I pray for Rosie from time to time: she is on an internal list of the missing and remembered. The grief of parents we know is shared: it is to be borne and faced by all. And Rosie carried with her so focused and vivid a personality – perhaps the shortage of available time to live sharpens the quality of the living – she is not forgotten. No wonder that Shelley gang, with their poetic intensity and their early deaths, are still spoken and written about.

We were all pre-feminists then: it simply did not occur to us that if men misbehaved, the answer was to have nothing more to do with them. That 'love' was a trap not worth falling into. The female response at the time was still to feel more love, have more babies, write more poetry, sink yet further into masochism. My problem was, I could see, that unlike Elizabeth I was not doing it with any style. I lost some weight and put on heels, and after work one day, after as I remember choosing a selection of adjectives for Simpson's store in Piccadilly and naming a women's department 'Young and Gay' – what innocent days they were – I sat on a bench in Holborn and reproached my dead father for leaving me. I made contact with his spirit as he whirled around with the autumn leaves that fell amongst the traffic of New Oxford Street that day. I made a pact with him. It was time he looked after me, I said. He had failed to do so in life – other than sending his mistress Ina to tell me he was turning in his grave – let him do so in his death. He had left me no money, no home, he had not protected me from my mother. Let him see to it. I for my part would stop sulking, stop playing games, stop waiting to be protected from my own folly, stop whining '*Now see what you made me do!*' I acknowledged my part in my own misfortune. I really think my father heard. Whether he was there of course I have no idea: I do know that I spoke to him.

At any rate it was after that my life turned: within days I fell out of love with the Dane, upon his confession of a drunken act of infidelity with a passing Danish tourist, waved goodbye to him as he set out for Ibiza to deliver some rich man's yacht, without dropping a single tear – the girl from Denmark had somehow lifted my moral responsibility to the wife, the miscarriage seemed a boon from heaven. I met Ron Weldon at a party, left my poor mother behind me, acquired a house and a home and a man of my own, and finally unafraid, grew rich and famous.

I wept in public fifteen years later on the steps of White Centre at BBC TV when Graeme MacDonald told me that *Smoke Screen*, my just-screened *Play for Today* – Wednesday nights, an audience of some thirteen or fourteen million – had not been a success with the audience and the BBC weren't going to commission me to do another. Not for a time. That was in 1969. The first reports into the link between smoking and lung cancer were emerging. The play had been successful enough with the audience, but not with BBC management. Their feeling was that I was causing trouble, stirring up unpleasantness, frightening the audience. I should stick to writing about women, not venture out into the great male world of important matters. *Smoke Screen* was about an advertising man, working on a cigarette account, who dies of lung cancer. My hero, puffing away, had a family to support, and insurance premiums to meet before he died, and felt that his duty to his family was higher than his duty to the public. And so by and large it is. What can a man, or indeed a woman, do in the face of necessity? What was I doing in advertising myself? The necessity of so doing was fast fading. I could keep myself in other ways.

The ad agency, no doubt irritated by my lack of loyalty, my intransigency, called my bluff after *Smoke Screen* and asked me to work on the Players account. It was a challenge, and I declined it. My boss Douglas Haines, the handsomest man in advertising and a good friend ever since, told me my duty was to my employers rather than society. Docile though I thought I was, I found this difficult to accept. My employers' enthusiasm for me dwindled, as well it might, and eventually I was 'let go'. That, and no doubt my habit of filling in my hourly time sheets as a consultant so that I earned what I thought I deserved, rather than the ceiling limit suggested by an eight-hour a day week, finally drove my employers to action. I was filling in 30 or 50 hours a day, out of the available 24, and they took no notice, or pretended not to, until finally I went too far.

'*Be bold, be bold, but not too bold!*' as the girl who marries Bluebeard in the fairy story is warned. I was too bold. Not only was there trouble at the office, but on the mythical BBC Honours Board my name was now in black, not gold, which meant '*Don't use her: trouble*' and I hadn't even been trying. Disgrace, at the BBC, usually lasted for two years or so; after that time everyone up and down the corridors had been promoted or changed jobs, and had forgotten, and when your name came up again at a meeting there was no one who remembered the awful things you had done to speak against you.

Morality, for all of us, tends to be what we can afford. Nobody wanted to believe what had to be believed. Smoking was nice, and natural, and had a gentle tonic and hygienic effect, and we all went round in a cloud of smoke and since we all smelt like old ashtrays it didn't bother anyone. The only people who didn't smoke were those who couldn't afford to, which for many years had included me.

Graeme MacDonald professed himself very surprised that I should cry. He said I did not seem the crying sort. I think I must have exuded an air of infinite good cheer, infinite resilience.

Television was always only a transitory medium, of course, that was its point. Flickers on a screen in the corner of a room. I shouldn't have wept, and it was humiliating. But somehow Graeme MacDonald, now dead and gone, still lingers on the steps, palely grey, intense and handsome, gay at a time when no one was meant to be, standing there, grave and confused and embarrassed by me, caught up in time and preserved, like Rosie Smart at the party. It is extremely difficult to believe in mortality while people live on in these acute snapshots of themselves. Graeme MacDonald, Rosie, dead? I don't believe it. Death is non-existent: it is just some peculiar and aggravating wrinkle in time, our false perception of the nature of past, present and future, which insists that one has to be over before the next can begin.

And then I didn't weep for ages, not really weep, other than everyday and unmemorable tears of petulance and anger, of course, until 1991 when I wept for a whole two years because after thirty years my life with my husband Ron was over, and by his doing, not mine. That took me down a peg or two. At that juncture my new husband-in-waiting took me down to the Embankment and made me look at Boadicea with the knives on her chariot wheels and said 'That's what your readers think you're like,' so I pulled myself together and stopped crying. God knows what fate has in store next: today is all ancient Abbey grounds and morning sunlight, tomorrow it may be Wilkins Parade and Mrs Kovac, and day by day time is running out.

Trisha's mistakes

Trisha had been playing Polly Peachum at the Lyric Theatre the day she won three million pounds in the lottery. The notices for the show had been good. This had been her big break after years of small parts, temping and bar-maiding. If she had known then what she knew now – the things she would not have done when it came to winning the lottery! She would have remembered to tick the no-publicity box. She would not have consented to a public ceremony when she went to collect her cheque. She would not have replied, when a journalist thrust a microphone in front of her and asked what she was going to do with the rest of her life, 'Spend, spend, spend.' And then added, almost as an after-thought, 'and fuck, fuck, fuck.' She had thought it was only radio but there were TV cameras there too. The clips were excerpted into the opening credits of a successful girlie TV show, and ran for a month before anyone told her, turning her into a kind of mini-celebrity until the public got bored. She sued and won another £50,000. To them that hath, etc. It also ruined her chances of being taken seriously ever again in the acting profession. When the show transferred to the West End she was not asked to go with it.

Other things Trisha should not have done: she should not have had a baby by a humble stunt man. She should have chosen a bank manager. She had gone for looks, not income, thinking she had more than enough of the latter. But of course she had not. Once pregnant, she should not have married the father. As it happened Rollo had his own stroke of good fortune and soon became the face of a range of men's toiletries. Now that he could pick and choose amongst women, he thought he could do better than Trisha. Within six weeks of their marriage being written up in *Hello* and three days after discovering Trisha was eight weeks pregnant, he left her for a Page 3 girl with a degree in economics, famous for having once allegedly slapped Elizabeth Hurley's face. He divorced Trisha, married her successor the day Spencer was born, and disappeared from her life.

Trisha was brave publicly, and cried privately, and gave birth to Spencer with only her mother in attendance. People came to visit her to drink free drink and eat free food and use her pool but she thought they did not care about the real her. Men would use and abuse her and demand presents. She thought women might be kinder than men and took up with Thomasina Deverill, and gave money away to lesbian causes. Thomasina was a success at the Edinburgh Fringe with a one-woman cabaret show about the awfulness of men, and when she came back had taken against little Spencer, mostly on the grounds that he was male. Thomasina wanted Trisha to have Spencer adopted and have a female test-tube baby by a gay friend instead. Trisha refused, Thomasina left.

A year later, when Spencer was four, Rollo turned up again. He had been converted to born-again Christianity, and wanted to claim custody of his child and bring him up in decent surroundings, by which he meant free from lesbian taint. In vain for Trisha to say that had been just a passing phase. By then Trisha also had a well-documented drink and drugs problem, and though that too was over – drugs now made her dizzy and alcohol made her sick – the court found against her, and Rollo – with his wife the economist now in government – was given care and control of Spencer. And Trisha, though she should have been upset, found that she was not. Spencer was a hyperactive child who yet had a weight problem, and she knew she failed him.

Trisha tried to be angry with Rollo. Her friends thought she should be, and she tried, but when she looked inside she found a rageless hollow. She lost quite a few friends this way. *Why didn't she fight the bastard? What sort of unnatural mother was she?* (This from friends who would no more dream of getting pregnant than they would look after their old mothers.) The fact was she was a man's woman even though the man had left her. She was just instinctively on her enemy's side.

And Rollo was so very convincing and charming in court, and such a good actor, that she was quite persuaded by him along with everyone else of her own unfitness to rear a child, and clapped when the judgement against her was given. She had to be stopped by her own lawyer. His name was, fetchingly enough, Hardy Acre, but there are more than enough names already for you to focus on.

To wit: **Trisha** and her six-year-old son **Spencer**, her husband **Rollo**, and her lover **Thomasina**. No doubt there have been more and other transient relationships: Trisha is, after all, a thespian, and thespians have a kind of life fluency, a need to be all things to all people; they are prone to sudden mood swings, fits of irresponsibility and changing fortunes. They are the playthings of writers, and whom the writers love they destroy. In the parallel real life there is **Fay, the Dane,** two **Rons,** my mother **Margaret,** my aunt and uncle **Mary** and **Michael**, my father **Frank** and his ghost, **Graeme MacDonald, Elizabeth Smart, George Barker** and **Rosie**. All were prone to self-destruction, without need of writers.

Trisha was reared in the confident days before herpes, AIDS, and fear of secondary smoking swept the Western world; the days when we could drift through our lives, taking what came along on trust. We assumed that politicians were wise, that food was safe, that pension companies paid up and scientists knew what they were doing. But there can be no more drifting: today's world punishes those who do not take care to look after their future. It is increasingly difficult to know how this is to be done.

Trisha has certainly not looked lively enough. She has met her come-uppance, and the credit has run out. The day the cashpoint refused to give her any more money she put the house on the market. It stayed stubbornly unsold for a year. What she thought was a desirable residence to too many others apparently looked like a supermarket, all false gables and unseasoned wood. The swimming pool grew an unusual sort of mould, which turned the water murky grey within hours of filling. Her creditors moved in and forced a sale. The house filled up with little men with weasel faces who claimed to be bankruptcy advisers.

It was found that in some mysterious way the deeds had Rollo's name upon them, and not a mention of her own. She had a recollection of promising one evening to look after Rollo for life and he must have taken her seriously and she have signed a document in a fit of drunken sentiment. That was when he had sprained his ankle in a fake car crash and was depressed, thinking he would never be an effective stuntman again, and then became the official face of the sensitive man about town, and had only to worry about his looks, not his survival.

Drinking made Trisha effusive and emotional, given to absurd gestures, giving things away to friends: *'Take this, and this, darling, and this, because you need it. Take this holiday, this camera, this house. By all means borrow my Valentino suit, it suits you better than me.'*

Trisha spends many days in front of the judges of the family court: the house is to be Rollo's, they decide, though she can keep the contents. It seems fair enough. Rollo has little Spencer to bring up. What with one thing and another the £3 million has simply dissolved away and now Trisha has to live like other people, worse than other people. The papers have lost interest in her. She must interpret herself now from her face in the mirror, not the one in the newspapers, from the words on her lips, not the ones in the headlines. She is an ex-celebrity, and what can be worse?

Also to blame in my opinion are Trisha's lawyer **Hardy Acre** – she has told him so often not to pursue her interests through the courts he has come to believe her. There is also Trisha's accountant **Vera Thicket,** who, while holding a few hundred thousands of Trisha's money in her client's account, ran off to Chile with a conman and all the money. Easy come, easy go: Trisha of course blames no one but herself. Trisha chose

38

both her accountant and her lawyer because their names appealed to her. Some would say in that case she deserves what she gets, but your author is very fond of Trisha.

Trisha is valiant, defiant, and uncomplaining. Drink may make her forgetful and silly but she is never nasty-drunk. Your writer does not have a drink problem, in case you're wondering. She is far too sober most of the time for her own good. Nor does she smoke, not because she has given up like so many through nobility and strength of purpose, but because she never got the habit in the first place.

On the anger of mothers

Later on in our lives, whenever I could wrench my socialist mother out of the council houses and flats where she was determined to live to be at one with the people, I would house her in what (to me) were more suitable surroundings. Instead of being harassed by the guard dogs of her neighbours, alarmed by the noise of domestic violence through thin walls, and distressed by the backbiting of neighbours, I would deliver her into rose-covered cottages and pretty houses where she would have a garden and neighbours to appreciate her wit and style. She was very wise in everything other than her own life. Here she could enjoy her guilt to the full and feel free to exclaim in horror every time I took a glass of wine (*such a waste of money, save it and give it to the poor, if you don't need it yourself*) or served anything other than plain food. (*Such a waste of time: you should be reading and writing: nothing nicer than cabbage, fast cooked, with pepper and butter: it only takes five minutes.*) I did not doubt my love for her or hers for me.

But there was a time when she was really fed up with me, and my sister Jane too. Mama had tried to escape us; she had put a pin in a map and fled to St Ives: she had given us twenty years of her life and that was enough. Or so she thought. But we would not let it rest at that.

She'd launched us into the world as bright girls with student grants, and then gone off to leave us to our own devices. (My annual grant was £167, over £3 a week, which my mother saw as great wealth. She gasped in admiration at the generosity of governments. The whole family, grandmother included, had managed on far less from time to time.) We were well-brought up, sensible, clever, friendly girls, but not good at thinking for ourselves. Our mother had done that for us. I'd been reared in an all-female household, gone to an all-girls school, and had scarcely talked to a man in my life, let alone 'dated'. I had no idea how to conduct myself. Soon enough I was pregnant. Jane had at least the grace to marry Guido Morris, a man respectable in the world of the arts – a member of the St Ives set, his work now in the Tate – albeit penniless and irresponsible with several families to his name already and twenty-five years her senior. The father of my child was a penniless orphan, once a boy bandsman in the army, now a singer of folk songs in the Mandrake Club in Soho. I think Jane and I both assumed our mother would save us from disaster, and when she did not we resented this backsliding on her part. Not that I can remember Jane and I ever discussing our mother. She was too much part of us to be seen as a separate entity.

Other girls at least managed to fall in love with possible partners. Jane and I courted disaster. Perhaps we felt the need to fill the space in our mother's life, to compensate for the exhiliration we had felt in at last leaving home. At any rate we felt obliged to bring her our babies back, for her to look after, to fill the vacuum we had left behind us.

Mama had no visible means of support, either, at the time. She had run an advertising agency in New Zealand in the war, but had hated every minute of it, and had turned down all suitors out of pride and the determination that she would never, never rely on the support of a man again. So now, since she had to eat, she wove reed baskets on the moors outside St Ives. She'd pluck the reeds, weave the baskets, walk to Penzance, sell the baskets, buy the week's food with it, and commune with nature to her heart's content. Larks and sunsets bought her real delight.

> Old Meg she was a gypsy,
> And lived upon the moors:
> Her bed it was the brown heath turf,
> And her house was out of doors.

But still we trusted her to look after us when it came to the crunch, and she did. (*You thought you could do this to us, mother: but we are your problem not our own! Look after us!*) She left the moors and joined us in London, and then moved us all to Saffron Walden, a place chosen because she liked the sound of the name, and we would be amongst strangers, without witnesses to our disgrace, where she hoped our delinquencies would go unnoticed, but of course they were not. On the contrary. To have relied upon the anonymity of London would have been more sensible. My poor mother. She would wake early in a state of anxiety, brood for an hour or two, come to an unnecessarily complex solution to a simple problem by breakfast time, and put it into action by lunchtime. Her solution this time had been that I was to change my name by dead poll to that of the baby's father, tell my friends and colleagues I had married, and then give up my job, move out of London where I was not known, and start my life afresh. That it was ten times more difficult to earn a living in the country than in the city, that I could have stayed where I was in the Foreign Office and fought my way up to higher grades and better wages (they could only fire you for immorality, I later found, if you were unmarried and had three babies by more than two different fathers), and was far too talkative and indiscreet to start again anywhere with a secret past, and was not likely to forswear my friends, did not occur to her. It did occur to me but she had a powerful personality and I assumed she knew best. I did as she suggested. I was horrified to be then sent a wedding present to my new Saffron Walden address by my Foreign Office colleagues: surely this was taking gifts on false pretences? I ought to return it at once with apologies for misleading them. But my mother was against it. I must stick by the story, she said. Say the marriage had been called off, anything. I imagine what I did do was simply put off writing the thank-you note until the time to do so decently had passed and I was so pregnant nothing seemed to matter other than what was going on inside my own body. But I cannot remember. It remains on my conscience. A bad patch. A bad girl. How terrible children can be. Bad behaviour is not a one way street. And certainly, if the mother leaves early, the children linger longer. But we had no such overview at the time, of course not. Those were the pre-Freudian days.

March 1954, and there I was with a baby, the dramas of pregnancy and childbirth over, with the reality of a small child to face. Guido came to claim Jane and her new baby

Christopher, and installed them in a cottage in deepest Sussex and brought marrow bones home every weekend. '*Lots of nourishment in these, my dear. I am going to theological college so must be away most of the time. They don't know I'm married, so don't tell them.*' My friend Belinda, who had come to join Jane and me in our sibling pregnancies, was rescued by the father of her child, who very soon married her. I remained unmarried and unrescued, and, dreams of self-sufficiency over, let alone the hope of running a little cake shop (mother's idea, but no customers came), commuted to London every day, by train, to Fleet Street, where I answered readers' questions on Hire Purchase problems for the *Daily Mirror*. My stepmother had sent me a cheque for £200 from my father's estate, and I had spent £100 on a typewriter and used it to write job applications. Now I worked and earned in a world still not properly adjusted to the fact that some women did not have men to support them and with a wage structure that echoed that fact. This meant leaving at 6.30 in the morning and coming back at 8.30 at night, to be finally driven out, along with my mother, by a ghost who wept up and down the twisted corridors of our 17th century house, and fleeing to London. But at least at Liverpoool Street station I had been able to afford and buy weekly copies of *Amazing* magazine. 'Alienation in time and space,' as my psychoanalyst Miss Rowlands was later to describe my passion for the science fiction of the time, 'and no doubt a comfort.' Those were the great mid-Fifties days of science fiction – Heinlein, Azimov, Frederick Pohl, Philip K. Dick – philosophers and sociologists all. I came across them by accident, in search of a cheap, fast read, tearing off the lurid covers so as not to be observed reading rubbish in the train, and this was my good fortune.

My mother was not happy in London: our tiny rented flat in Chiswick, all I could afford, was too dull to have so much as a ghost. Landladies were reluctant to rent rooms to women with children and no husband or visible means of support. You took what you could get, especially if you had no deposit, no three months' rent in advance. My mother chafed. Granted I was going out to work, but if she had to stay home and be bored, why did I feel entitled to go to parties in the evenings? Why did I need these friends of mine, with their chattery, frivolous ways? Should I not stay home of an evening and keep her company? Couldn't I just settle down?

I found another job in London in a tiny ad agency in Dover Street, Scott-Turner, which paid minimally more than the *Mirror*. *'Did you know you have 200 bones in your foot? No wonder sometimes they hurt!'* But still the job only barely paid the rent: and all I wanted to do was go to parties and meet men and fall in love like anyone else, but I couldn't. My mother's disapproval was too strong. I had made my bed: now it behoved me, she thought, to lie upon it. I ate plentiful cheese rolls bought from the shop next door to the office. There was a brothel above the sandwich shop – the bad girls, dressed up to the nines, came and went through the Mayfair streets around. (The sex industry at that time was booming: provenance of Maltese gangs.) I had to take my shoes to the menders, unable to afford new. There was no television – too early in the world's history for possession of such a thing to be normal. What could I do in the evenings but cook and eat? I grew fat and then what was the point of parties anyway? I stayed home with my mother and the baby. The commuting days in Saffron Walden, ghost and all, now seemed in retrospect like heaven.

Little Nicolas was robust, energetic and now two years old. Babies are easy enough to deal with when they lie there and smile at you, or at anyone who comes in sight. But then they grow older and cry when you leave them, and wrap their little arms around your legs to make you stay with them, and resolution collapses. He had rosy cheeks and pale blond hair: he was beautiful but exhausting. He cried noisily and bitterly when I set off in the mornings, and my mother's face was like stone. My best friend Judy Anderson met and married my colleague at Scott-Turner's, Michael Birmingham, with whom I had had many a depressed if interesting conversation and after that I had to work alone, in silence. *'Did you know your foot has 200 tiny bones in it'* – and all the sorry things that could happen to them unless you took care. True, the Institute of Contemporary Art had the floor beneath our offices and naked girls bounced upon trampolines in the name of art – 'happenings', they were called – but it might as well have happened a thousand miles away. None of it seemed to have anything to do with me. I was depressed, and fat. I was being courted by the headmaster of a technical school in Acton, Mr Bateman, a maths graduate, twenty-five years older than myself. He asked me to marry him.

I could see the many advantages. Anything would be better than life as it was. Marriage would make him happy, and my mother too: she could escape, and I could ease over to lie in a respectable bed, free from the disgrace of unmarried motherhood. Not, frankly, that my status bothered me. The disgrace of being married to an elderly headmaster, and having to introduce him to my college friends, seemed worse. *'What, can she do no better than this?'* But I would have housekeeping money; I would have my soul back, I would no longer be for ever worried that the State would turn up, declare me an unfit mother, and send Nicolas off to Barnardo's. True, the headmaster had also warned m: '*No wife of mine works*' and said I could not join the Labour Party. '*I must be seen in my position to be above politics*'. Though indeed it turned out later that he was writing reports about any untoward political activity observed or communist sentiments uttered on the part of his staff. (But that was par for the cold-war course. The war for hearts and minds was on and if those Fifties writers took to science fiction it was because, after the McCarthy witch-hunts, they were nervous of making political statements which related to the present, or so I have heard it said.) In 1968 Nicolas was to be thrown out of his grammar school for staging a political protest. His headmaster of the time had been discovered doing much the same thing as Mr Bateman a decade earlier – only writing reports on students, not staff, warning admission secretaries not to take certain pupils, whom he saw as troublemakers and activists. Whatever changes?

I said yes to the headmaster and waited for my mother to say '*But you can't possibly!*' She said nothing, so I married him, in Ealing Registry Office, in a too-tight blue dress, to the barely disguised winces of my friends. And I was as unsuitable a wife for him as he was a husband for me.

It was during the time of my marriage to Mr Bateman in the late Fifties that I met my mother by chance on my way up to town. It was on the platform of South Kensington Underground Station. I was travelling north from Acton, the sorry suburb where I now lived with my new husband and my child, having exchanged one small flat for another – albeit owned not rented – and a restless mother for a grizzled husband. But I was full of resolutions; I distinctly remember my determination that not a month of my life would go by in which I was entirely celibate. Oh, I was a monster! It would not be my husband: he had voyeuristic tendencies but no interest in actual sex. This kind of thing one found out in those days only after the wedding ceremony.

On South Kensington Station my mother Margaret looked me in the eye, and turned away, expressionless. She cut me dead. My cry of greeting died away. I was devastated. Margaret wore a navy greatcoat, staff issue, London Underground. It drowned her. She was a little thing to contain so much intelligence, fanaticism and fierce morality. They ate her away, that was the trouble. I clouded my body with fat: she was thin, bare to the winds of tragedy. Had I reduced her to this? Surely it was the other way round, and it was all her doing? I always did what she said, didn't I? She had encouraged me to marry the headmaster, and that puzzled me. It was such a stupid, desperate, death-welcoming thing for a daughter to do, and just a word from her and I would not have done it, but she would not say the word. She wanted her life back too badly.

Until that moment at South Kensington Station I had not realised that I existed in any kind of reality at all, or any that impinged on others. I had thought I was a figment of my own imagination, at the very best my parents' bright idea, gone sour. Most realise this at about twelve: I took rather longer.

Margaret had celebrated her new freedom by getting a job on the London Underground, saying in effect, '*Now see what you've made me do!*' Jane and I had let her down. I was turning into a lower middle-class housewife, a kind of Jerry Springer case, and her elder child, Jane, the poet, had taken up with a penniless artist, and had two small children and nowhere to live. Was this what the sacrifice of Mama's youth had come to? She could have been a writer, should have been a writer, had been a writer – and then she'd had two daughters and they had ruined her life. And for what?

The job wasn't all bad. She even liked it. There are advantages to being a public servant: at least you are doing something useful. The posters of the time, luring people into the tunnels, advised, '*It's Warmer Underground,*' and they were right. It was. At least underground, my mother said, she was never cold. She was a good and conscientious employee, the one to approach the snarling dog, pick up the fluttering bird, face the mugger, step forward and brave danger when others drew back. I think she rather fancied the foreman, one of the West Indian immigrants the London Transport Executive shipped over from Jamaica to solve the staffing problems of the day, though nothing came of it. Men always fancied my mother, so witty and bright and kind, but she would have nothing to do with them: principle got in the way, or perhaps it was that she could not endure too much emotional pain.

We will not see her like again. We have learned prudence, and what is right behaviour and proper thinking, and what is not: we understand the mechanisms of our own behaviour: we are cursed by therapy even as we are saved by it: it de-natures us. We can't be forgiven because we know only too well what we do, and forgive ourselves in advance. My mother, born 1907, seeing her century out, thought and felt from first principles. Cut dead by her, in 1957, I stumbled back home to my peculiar husband and my crowded home and rethought my life. 'Tough love' they would call it nowadays, and it is not nice to be on the sharp end of it.

But see how the very existence of the phrase 'tough love' cheapens and weakens the very concept it stands for? We know how to explain ourselves to ourselves well enough, but with every handy phrase, every useful shorthand, we lessen the complexity and interest of our lives. If every young woman in every bank looks alike, every TV presenter seems to have the same face, one young man at a party is indistinguishable from the next, if as we think alike, so we look alike, who can be surprised. Our everyday language has become too skilled, too dismissive of complexity, for our own good. We like things nailed and certain. The cleverer we get, the more stupid.

I see the platform in my head: South Kensington, open air, not my mother's base station, Gloucester Road. She must have been transferred for the day. Jane's husband Guido was to get a job announcing at Victoria – he had a beautiful, plangent, actor's voice. He enunciated beautifully, in the fashion of his parson forebears. Jobs were easier to come by then: in the days of high employment no one wanted GCSE certificates, proof of residence or bank references, wages came in a brown envelope, no questions asked: just a ridiculously high proportion taken away by the tax man to pay for pensions which were never to materialise except in benefit form, and doff your cap while asking.

The event stays sealed in my memory. I had always liked South Kensington Station where the train emerges from the tunnel before burrowing into it again. Now I see my mother in her uniform on the platform, doing whatever platform staff do, and I hop off the train in excitement, and she sees me, quite clearly she sees me, and whatever she sees she does not like, and she turns her face away, in calculated indifference. We were never to mention the episode again, either of us.

At the time of this maternal rebuff I was sharing my marital home with Jane and her two small children. They crowded into the living room, leaving us the rest of the house. It was in fact only half a small terrace house in Acton, the ground floor having already been let off to Doreen, a very fussy woman who wore her curlers until five each evening, complained about the noise of stomping children above her, and who regarded me as no better than I should be. She was accustomed to tall, thin, quiet, lonely, stooping, respectable Mr Bateman upstairs, and he had suddenly acquired, and was allegedly married to, a vigorous, poshly-spoken young woman with a small child of uncertain origins, and now her sister and two more children under five had come along too. Doreen complained with perfect reason, and if she was without sympathy what was she to know of the complexities of my life? What were we all up to? Sometimes I would leave the house in the evenings – driven by my husband in his souped-up little pale blue Ford Popular – dressed up to the nines, low-cut dress, very high heels, net stockings and tightly belted waist. (The difference between bad girls and good girls, so far as their dress went, was in those days clearly delineated. Good girls dressed so as not to be noticed: bad girls drew attention to their assets.) And Doreen must have noticed when I went out dressed for Ladies' Night at the local posh hotel. My husband that year was Grand Master of his Masonic Lodge. I was Lady of the Lodge. I hired a kind of evening dress in mauve tulle for the occasion and the masons and the wives looked at me oddly. (Was it that the marriage itself seemed strange to others, or was it the dress? I will never know.) Sometimes I went out as wife to the Musical Director of the local Operatic Society, wearing some scruffy skirt and laddered tights. And all the while, by day, the thump, thump, thump of little children racing across floors.

Doreen was confused, but no more confused than I. How had I come to this pretty pass?

I tried to engage Doreen in a scheme by which all the households down the road would serve dinner from a central cooking pot – it pained me that every day twenty housewives prepared meat and two veg from the same butcher and the same greengrocer, it seemed such a waste of time. We could make enough for everyone and they would run down the road to us for their portion, and we would share costs. She looked at me as if I was mad and I daresay I was. I had yet to learn that other people do not necessarily want to do what is in their best interests. I was properly chastened.

Twenty years later, on holiday with the children in the Gambia, visiting a Muslim household where there were four wives and four cooking pots over four separate fires, one in each corner of the same cooking hut, all cooking rice in a room temperature well over 100 degrees, I suggested to the husband that they could surely take turns to cook the rice, and do it over one fire in one big pot. He said, '*But each wife competes to please the husband.*' I daresay those women felt the same way as the women of Acton. It is all just a matter of degree.

We were oddly happy, Jane and I, living together with the children for those few months, and it was good of the headmaster to give her shelter – Jane and Guido never had the money to pay for any fixed abode: he loved her but was not a good provider. There was no doubt however but that we were crowded, even by 1957 standards. Guido made it a condition of his joining Jane that we shelved the living room (we would pay) so that he had room for his books. I at that stage owned one book: Wyndham Lewis's *The Apes of God*, of which I had bought a first edition for two-and-six, stolen from the housekeeping money, a book I kept under the bed. I still have it – the only possession left from my young woman-hood I did manage to keep.

Fed up with my chaste first marriage as I was, I had taken to sleeping on the sofa in the living room, where I was racked by a bronchitic cough ('*Cough it up, girl, cough it up, what ails you?*'), but now with Jane's arrival I had to return to the marital bedroom and get up to cough in the loo. I wrote a television play in that loo, I remember (those were pencil and paper days, not computer), about a prostitute, in which I explained to an uninterested and easily shocked world how easy it was for a girl to come to such a pass. It was returned from the BBC with a note saying they could not contemplate dramas on such a subject, 'no matter how well written'. I treasured that phrase but wrote no more: I did not want to 'be' a writer; I just wanted to earn enough money so I could live other than by the kindness of men. Men were frequently kind, but they could also be very odd.

It was shortly after this that I determined to run away from home. I was not five but twenty-five, or more, but you would not have thought it. I would leave my sister to fill my place. She could look after my husband, cook his boiled beef and carrots, iron his shirts. I felt my father egging me on. Had he not just sent Ina to trace Jane and me to Acton, and declare herself horrified in his name? '*If your father could see you now, he'd turn in his grave.*' And she didn't know the half of it. I was moved to take action. I resolved to leave secretly in the middle of the night, telling no one, not even my sister. In retrospect there was no need at all for secrecy, but women who feel they are behaving badly often fear the violence of men. Mr Bateman had shown absolutely no signs of violent behaviour heretofore. And later he was to sound genuinely confused, rather than angry, at my leaving him thus. *'But why didn't you tell me you were unhappy. I would have helped you leave.'*

Be all that as it may, I tucked my child under my arm and ran away in the middle of the night, stealing four pounds from his wallet, and took grateful refuge in Laura and Stephen's snazzy flat in South Kensington. If your mother fails you, and your father is dead enough to turn in his grave, you have no option but to look after yourself.

There were, of course, other reasons for my feeling justified in leaving home. As so much that happens in this life is, it was a matter of convergent dynamics, rather than a simple answer as required in murder cases. *'But why did you do this?'* *'Because, your honour, because . . .'* The *because* is never single-stranded, it is a whole tassel of factors: you have to extract the brightly-coloured one and offer that as explanation. My *becauses* in this case included it seeming wrong to me to live with one man while being in love with another – the Dane, that is to say, the sailor ad-man. My father sending a messenger from the grave. My husband's averring that after we were dead we would live together in the hereafter, just him and me, in a little cottage on a mossy bank by a river. Forever. *'I saw it in a vision, darling.'* You could play grandmother's footsteps with fate as much as you liked, but when the music stops and you are playing pass the parcel you must on no account be caught with the wrong man. Or they might be with you for eternity. That too was a very bright thread in what I would refer to as the knotted tassel of reasoning that leads to action.

Young women are beyond belief. I wish I could report less superstitious nonsense on my part but I can't – not and still speak the truth of my experience.

Trisha starts a new life

The stairs which led up from the dry-cleaners to Trisha's new living quarters were very narrow. It is unlucky to pass another person on the stairs, for fear that in brushing up against them your souls will be exchanged, and you will reach the top of the stairs, or the bottom, a different person. That day Trisha Perle crossed on the stairs with a stranger to her, **Peter Watson**, whom you have yet to meet. Both, at the time, were in a bad, ungenial mood.

Well-behaved, handsome, de-natured Peter Watson, thirty-six, lived as it so happened with Doralee Thicket, journalist. They had been together for six years. *'This is Peter Watson, you know, Doralee's feller?'* Not that Doralee was particularly famous, or rich, or in any way unusual, just that somehow she seemed more vivid than he. Once upon a time women were indignant to be introduced as someone's wife, daughter or sister, as if they had no identity of their own – these days the insult is more likely to be offered to men. Women are so vivid and mettlesome these days, so vigorous in their being, even when like Trisha down on their luck, I am surprised they do not subsume the whole male race.

If I describe Peter Watson as de-natured, as one describes a piece of much-laundered fabric, it is because one has the sense that once there was more stuffing to him. Yet he has a handsome enough, thinking, empathic, executive face, is over six foot and goes to the gym religiously, as does Doralee. He does not look unlike Russell Crowe but wears glasses. He seems to have a promising future before him and one feels life has gone comfortably enough so far, but that perhaps his mother, or someone, has made him anxious and a little jumpy in childhood, and over anxious to please. But you would be glad enough if he had the window seat in the aircraft, the one given to an able-bodied man so he can open the door in case of an emergency and a chute landing. The barber uses a number two clipper on his hair, so it is short-cropped in the modern style, and his clothes are smart and clean. His hands, unlike Trisha's, are not nicotine stained.

Peter Watson works for a daily newspaper: indeed he is deputy head of its research department, and sees himself as being 'in the loop'. He goes to senior editorial meetings. It is not as exciting as being in features or on the news desk, but the whole place so pounds with energy the job is more than good enough for him for the time being. He is the one who knows the facts behind the facts, and the detail behind the sweeping statements newspapers love to make: he is consulted on international affairs, the mood in the Congo, the state of the Albanian Air Force, whither Europe, and why Gibraltar. If he does not know he will find out. He is relied upon and trusted, and the Editor does not shout at him.

Peter's partner Doralee is pretty and smart, and more ambitious than he. You could accuse both of smugness, but that would be unkind. They have both had parents who loved them, and no reason to believe the world won't go in the way they have experienced it to date: they love the nanny state and feel that nanny is perfectly well suited to looking after them, and that so long as they behave like everyone else all will be well. They talk out any emotional problems that might arise, and look after their health. They drink bottled water, and choose flat not fizzy: bubbles seeming to the young couple to be somehow chemical, trivial and false. Tap water was to be avoided: it had been recycled through other people's bodies too many times for comfort, and was full of their hormones.

It is true that Doralee sometimes swigged a glass of tap water in secret, in desperation, having read that over-chlorinated water contributes to the current rise in infertility. It wasn't that she didn't want a baby, she did, indeed, she was 'trying', like so many of her colleagues at *Oracle*, the woman's magazine for which she worked. It was just that sometimes courage failed her, and she would like to put motherhood off for a year or so, while seeing herself as the kind of person who never goes back on a decision, and not wanting her partner to see her as a ditherer. The occasional glass of tap water seemed to take the responsibility of choice away. Anyone is entitled to an off day, and to have doubts about the wisdom of procreation, let alone its expense, and act upon these doubts. And sometimes when the water from the shower was blue from excess chlorine, she'd wonder what kind of unhealthy chemical world was this to bring children into, anyway? She did not tell Peter of these concerns: he wanted a baby even more than she did, and would only quote statistics at her to demonstrate that this was an ever-improving world, and not even overcrowded. Indeed, the latest demographic trends showed a falling population rather than a rising one – except in China – and they had a duty to spread their genes as plentifully as possible. Then Doralee would think, *'but we aren't living in China*' and mutinously swig some more tap water. She would leave it to chance.

Trisha's world scarcely extended beyond what she could see around her, let alone encompass the problems of China. She thought that so long as she was happy she would be healthy, forgetting it was a long time now since she had been happy. She dieted furiously from time to time but not for long. One glass of wine and she forgot about the future and lived in the present – and what is dieting but living for the future and declining to enjoy the present – and the diets she chose were always ones which allowed her to drink alcohol. She smoked dope on occasion, and drank Chablis in the years when she could afford it. One can always remember the name and vintages are not a bother. She seldom took cocaine – as Peter and Doralee would occasionally, and in moderation, the better to keep up with their smart friends. Trisha preferred to be soothed, cooled out, rather than speeded up.

Both Peter and Doralee were very aware of the dangers of stress, and did what they could to avoid it. Peter had learned deep-breathing techniques and Doralee always meant to go back to yoga classes though actually the thought of the boredom entailed was in itself stressful. Trisha on the other hand, by the manner of her living, the general messiness of her life, seemed to invite stress in. If nothing happened she panicked: perhaps nothing would ever happen again. So naturally her life was full of untoward events. When what happened, happened, Trisha was the one to face it with greater equanimity.

A selection of antecedents

My suspicion is this – that just as one day Peter and Trisha cross on the stairs, so one day there is bound to be an actual crossover between the novelist's actual life and the alternative reality as presented by that novelist. That the times have finally and sadly come to this, that a novel simply no longer feels meaty enough without the input of the writer's life and sorrows. All my writing life I have argued that fiction and autobiography are separate. '*Good Lord*,' I have been in the habit of saying at literary festivals and in interviews, where writers are so frequently these days required to bare their souls, '*if any of what I wrote was true I would be in prison or dead.*' Now I can see that I ought to have been in prison or dead, if I were to get my just desserts, that is to say if to lust in your heart is as sinful as the act itself, as St Matthew reports. All these monstrous acts I have written, all the murders, crimes I have conceived, are as good as done. I who was accustomed to saying earnestly to my audience, 'If you want to write a novel you must lose your good opinion of yourself', should repent. It is a terrible thing to say. I have been urging others to be as bad as their characters. Late-Victorian novelists felt obliged to present noble characters capable of good deeds, Soviet writers would only be published if they provided worthy role-models for their readers, the Chinese to find excitement in the fulfilling of the factory quota. Our writers fostered discontent and rebellion. Those women who read my novels in the Seventies and come up to me at literary gatherings still and say, '*But your novels changed our lives. It was you who gave me the courage to leave my husband,*' in fact bear witness against me. But what I wrote was all true, true, true. I never slept with my father, as Praxis does in the novel of that name, written in 1977, but I daresay that if like her I met him in a bar and he picked me up, and I didn't know who he was, I would not hesitate. Like would surely call to like. Think it and it's done.

It has not been the habit of writers to show their hand too clearly. Flaubert writes about his own father when in *Madame Bovary* he describes the good Doctor Bovary's disastrous attempt to cure a club foot by breaking all the bones in it and stretching it until the foot gets gangrene and all but drops off. Flaubert couldn't bear to keep the incident out, though it meant Dr Bovary had to behave out of character for a whole chapter. '*Madame Bovary, c'est moi,*' Flaubert famously says, giving the game away. I daresay Chaucer had an affair with the Wife of Bath, gat teeth and all. But Chaucer's not going to declare that, either.

Just as the world of screen and airwaves blends and melds into real life, so too, today, must the creations of the printed page. There are elements of me in Trisha, and parts of Rollo and Peter in every man I have ever known. Mind you, men of the Newer Age have to be learned: they are not the ones I grew up with. Men of the Former Age tended to be without emotional conscience, like George Barker, or Ted Hughes or my husband of many years Ron, but at least they produced art.

If Rollo, the ex-stuntman now born-again Christian and conscientious father, or Peter, the bottled drinking water (*still, please*) newspaper man were to write a poem, you'd know in advance it would be fairly terrible – mealy-mouthed, sentimental and commonplace. When it comes to the reformation of the world, Rollo believes in the efficacy of the new overarching social-worker-Jesus, Peter in the Power of Purchasing. Both are victims of the Pelagian Heresy: that we are all nice people at heart, really, so it's only others who come along and muck things up. George Barker and the Dane, of an earlier generation, knew only too well about Original Sin: they revelled in it, and were loved the more because of it.

Charlotte Brontë, dealing with men of the Former Age, did not attempt Mr Rochester from the inside out: she observed him from the outside in, and very erotic the result is. That was when men and women were differently reared. Far easier these days to write about men from the inside out. Now they are just more people, it is rather disappointing. So they were like us all the time.

Mind you, some things don't change. Good behaviour never gets a woman anywhere: bad behaviour gets a man everywhere. I say this from long experience of husbands, lovers, sons, both of the Former and the Newer Ages. But then I would, wouldn't I. If I were a man I would no doubt reverse the genders.

Life in the slow lane

The day before Trisha's worldly goods went under the auctioneer's hammer, Doralee Thicket allowed a vase of water to spill onto the foam mattress she shared with her partner of long standing Peter Watson. This may not have been a good omen. It was six thirty in the morning, and high summer, but there was quite a wind, the unexpected kind that blows up sometimes in the early morning of a day in which thunder is expected, and gives you a glimpse of the intentions nature has for a globally-warmed humanity.

Doralee and Peter lived in High View, in Wilkins Close, just around the corner from the Wilkins Parade branch of the dry-cleaners Kleene Machine. Money has been spent on Wilkins Close – the council has beautified the street, putting in cobbles, fancy street lights and decorative railings, and will get round to the Parade and eventually to Wilkins Square, if the intransigency of the locals allows. But the area is, as they say, 'mixed' and the council may change their mind about the ability, and indeed the willingness, of suffi-cient of those living around to pay tax, and withdraw supportive funding at any moment, and then windows will start to get broken as the Goths and Vandals sweep in, and the barbarians take back what was so long theirs.

But from the outside High View looks solid and grand enough. It has recently been converted from the factory it once was to luxury apartments, but keeps many of the orig-inal features, including its large windows, and interior corri-dors still in the original small red brick. There is a doorman, George, who lives on the premises. Doralee and Peter are lucky enough to have the penthouse flat – a mere five floors up, but still giving them a view to the west of the city and an expanse of sky, from which they can observe the brilliant sunsets of the last days of Empire. They do not see it like this, of course, though Doralee's father Graham sometimes gloomily mutters words to this effect. Rather they see them-selves as living on the brink of a bright new world, in which all will be fair, and the nations of the earth glad and wise, and as one.

61

When Doralee flung open the window to air the room, the edge of the curtain blew in and caught the vase – long red roses given to her by Peter when he came back from work the previous evening – and toppled it.

The bed would have to be stripped and the mattress exposed to the air to dry: she would be late for her Pilates class. She felt vaguely vengeful: the vase would have to go down to Age Concern. There was no time in her life for the agents of misrule; for accidents or inefficiencies, or cheap vases with not sufficient weighting at the base. *Everything has to go.* She sponged the mattress down, first unbuttoning the cover and removing it, but a water stain would undoubtedly be left. Fortunately the roses, though perfect, long stemmed and without thorns, seemed to have very little to do with nature and had not clouded or coloured the water at all. She asked Peter to drop the cover down to Kleene Machine round the corner in Wilkins Parade, together with her once worn black dress with the thin satin straps, on which some idiot had dropped champagne, and a couple of Peter's shirts.

Kleene Machine offered a next-day delivery service. Doralee suspected she paid over the odds for it, but completed work could be left downstairs with George the doorman, and that was convenient. If he wasn't at his desk in the lobby, as sometimes happened, you just opened his cupboard yourself and took the clothes from the rack. The other tenants – there were eight flats in the building, a new conversion of what had been originally a children's home, then a sweet factory, then a makeshift warehouse, and was now a much-sought-after apartment block – had so far shown themselves respectable and honest. Someone had once taken her Armani white blouse with the frilled cuffs but she accepted it had been a genuine error and George had been able to run the culprit to earth. Sometimes on a hot day you got a waft of a sweet spicy warm smell that seemed to permeate the corridors. Doralee worried about the drains but George said that was only the Indian sweet factory asserting itself and perfectly pleasant. Once she swore she could hear children playing up and down the corridors, and complained to George, but he said that was just sound waves still drifting in from the time when it was a children's home. He had an explanation for everything, Peter remarked, so long as it enabled him to do as little as possible and go back to sleep.

The instructions that had come with Doralee and Peter's foam mattress claimed that unlike the products of old-fashioned competitors this mattress did not have to be turned. Doralee turned it nevertheless, every Saturday morning before she went to the supermarket, just to be on the safe side. Peterloo – her pet name for her partner Peter – would help her. They'd turn the mattress together, loving the thump it made as it bounced after falling onto the wooden base, and the little spurt of dust which followed, which proved the claims of the manufacturer to be in error. Foam rubber does attract and absorb dust – not to the extent that upholstered mattresses do, of course, but perhaps, as Doralee feared, more than enough to harbour the mites and other tiny creatures which settled around all larger ones. By such small shared pleasures are good marriages made. True, this was not a marriage, but a close and even harmonious partnership, albeit unblessed by higher powers.

If Doralee was a stickler for efficiency and hygiene, it was perhaps because her mother Ruby had been the opposite. These things are meant to go in sequence, each generation

63

over-compensating in the interests of a balance which never arrives. Ruby, the mother, had been generous-hearted and affectionate to her children and, after her husband had gone, to a number of men, all of whom Doralee detested.

Ruby, born a bright and wilful girl in Liverpool, had married the son of a country parson and come to live in the country in her thirties. She had embraced county life with enthusiasm, even as her husband learned to eschew it. She rode to hounds while Graham joined anti-vivisection movements, and she turned litter louts of travellers from her land as he fought for the human rights of nomads. She became high church as he declared his faith in socialism and humanity, and ran the parish council as he turned his vision to the outside world and non-governmental organisations. Graham worried about population density while Ruby had baby after baby. Her energy was extraordinary and her goodwill too: she battered through opposition and hostility, to be accepted in the end by both village and gentry, who asked her to their cocktail parties if not always their dinners.

'Ruby and I both do good works, but our idea of Good is very different,' as Graham explained to Eve, the yoga teacher with whom he eventually ran off.

Ruby now lived in the vicarage in which Graham – who had a surprising eye for the main chance for one so technically virtuous – had been reared, and which Graham had been prudent enough to buy in the Seventies, when the Church Commissioners rather unwisely sold off all their properties at rock bottom prices.

Graham, in Ruby's eyes, had left home babbling of true love and leaving five children. In his own eyes he had left home to save his soul and the world. Ruby, in Doralee's eyes, was guilty of sins of commission and Graham of sins of omission. Mother shouldn't have done this and that; Father should have done that and this. Doralee herself simply wanted to get things right. She could not understand why balance was so hard to achieve.

Peter seemed better able to accept his family. Although his mother was Jewish, he felt unburdened by his past. Two generations since her family had given up practising their religion, and Holocaust guilt had barely touched him. He was one of two brothers: their father had died of cancer when he was seven but he had been well insured, not particularly close to his family and his mother Adrienne was a competent woman. She had not encouraged grief or self-pity, and had put both boys into boarding schools and got on with her life. Now she worked for a property company, and it was through her good offices that Doralee and Peter had acquired the loft apartment at a good price. It was a neighbourhood which could go up or could go down, his mother had warned, but her firm reckoned it was going up – indeed, they were investing pretty heavily in their belief that it would – and Peter's mother seldom got that kind of thing wrong. She had friends in the Planning Department.

Doralee was neat and small, and conventionally pretty, other than that she had wild frizzy pre-Raphaelite hair, which burst plentifully from her head as if all her bottled-up subversive energy was determined to get out. Usually such hair is red, but Doralee's was straw coloured. She had to colour in her eyebrows to seem to have any at all. She was notable for her shapely behind, once publicly compared by Peter's editor at the newspaper's Christmas party to that of Kylie Minogue. It had been touch and go whether Peter's female colleagues would enter a complaint against Peter's editor for sexual harassment in the workplace, but since Doralee was not actually an employee of the newspaper, merely an employee's partner, the matter had been dropped, to Peter's relief. He just wanted to get on with his work, which he liked: he didn't want to make a fuss. He was well informed and well-educated: his mother had got him to a good public school, though this was not something he thanked her for. He kept quiet about it: best in the new world to have risen from the ranks in the face of adversity, but it could not be helped. He would rise above the disadvantage.

He went hand in hand with Doralee through a sensible and controllable life, and thought her bum was better than Kylie Minogue's and had not in the least minded the editor saying so, but kept quiet about that too.

Doralee, who took her degree in pharmacology, had worked for a few years as a freelance journalist in the medical press, and then eighteen months ago had become a commissioning editor for *Oracle* – a monthly health and lifestyle glossy magazine. Life itself was now glossy, and even leisurely, in comparison to what had gone before. She and Peter liked nothing better than the thought of money piling up unspent in the bank, and pension funds accumulating, and the value of the apartment rising faster than interest rates. They glowed with the pleasure of it, but were prudent. They lived well but not extravagantly.

In theory Doralee and Peter shared the housework equally, but in practice Doralee did more than he. (Research tells us this is often the case.) She cleaned the loos, changed the

66

cat litter and plumped the cushions, long after Peter, the meal microwaved and cleared up after, had turned on the TV and given up for the day. But then she liked doing housework and he did not. Not only was her threshold of domestic competence higher than his but she seemed to have more surplus energy than he; she walked briskly here and there in high-heeled shoes about the house, stacking the dishwasher, cleaning behind the taps, and so on. From time to time Peter would stir himself to catch her round the waist and bear her down on bed or sofa, while she protested ritually that she had so much to do, that she had to get on, that she would miss her course or whatever. They were happy together and it was unjust that the finger of fate should point at them in the way it was to do.

Fate announced its attentions, one might say, by spilling the vase of roses; such minor untoward events are often precedents of worse to follow.

Doralee and Peter's courtship had been conducted in the early Nineties, when fear of sexual disease and disaster was at its height. She had had only one lover before she met Peter, and no one else but him since. Peter had had four girlfriends, but two at a time twice, as it were, each secret from the other, he juggling dates and parties and beds, so he reckoned that only counted as two. He didn't behave like that now, and was ashamed of himself for having done so in the past. Doralee aimed, at least in theory, to have a baby before she was thirty-five, and was currently, if sporadically, doing what she could to conceive one. She found she liked sex without protection so much better than safe sex. It ceased to be a matter of mere sensation, as if there was something complicated and unlikely, loaded with vague possibilities, lurking behind the surface. It was, she'd told

Peter, as if you'd entered the lottery of life and were waiting for the draw and had no idea what the prize could be.

'You should put that in an article,' Peter had said, admiringly. That was when Doralee was still working at *Health Professional Weekly*, and thinking she would die of boredom. 'Call it: *Enter the lottery of life!*' So Doralee had done just that, and had forthwith sold the piece to *Vogue*. It had been very well received, striking a chord with readers and *Oracle* had asked her to join them. She had become their spokesperson for all things spiritual and mysterious, to do with fertility, Gaia, resonance, the inner life and so forth. Starting with the *meantness* of pregnancy: which she did feel, though it went against her training and the general drift of her thinking, now she wrote about the efficacy of prayer, the value of crystals in the search for inner truth, of the relationship between the state of the complexion and the state of the soul. Really there was no end to the things one could write about, and she now had the language of otherworldliness at her fingertips as they flew over the keyboard, without doubt or delay. It was thanks to Doralee that the word 'soul' was drifting back into public consciousness.

After eighteen months trying, off and on, she was still not pregnant, but she did not let that bother her. She was optimistic enough to know that fate would look kindly upon her, eventually, and the later it happened, frankly, the better. God would bless them; they would have a beautiful baby girl. Female was the gender of choice in the Newer World. She would have every scan and test going to confirm that the baby was okay. She might resort to sperm-sorting to ensure the gender, but probably not. It was too calculating, and probably horribly messy and painful, though they never tell you these things.

And if she never conceived, that too would be tolerable. She would be saved the total loss of control which having a baby seemed to entail – the inexorable growing of the alien thing inside, the change to the figure afterwards, a bum too skinny if she dieted and too heavy if she didn't, the general messiness of attitude and behaviour which mothers back from pregnancy leave seemed to develop – and always the awful fear that in the end she would turn into her own mother. After Ruby's twins were born Doralee had seen sick down both shoulders on the back of her mother's jumper. It was revolting, and she didn't even seem to have the will to put on a clean one. Both shoulders! No wonder her father had left, which he did when the twins were barely two months old.

Peter knew well enough, rationally at any rate, that the world was not as entirely benign as Doralee's articles suggested. But they made good money and he was proud of her. His speciality on the research desk was warfare and weapons; he knew everything any journalist could be expected to know about depleted uranium and star-wars defence shields. He knew the map of the Middle East by heart. He had a side interest in epidemiology and the mathematics of catastrophe theory. He suspected that the only way to be saved was to be lucky. He had 20/20 vision but wore clear glass spectacles; partly because he felt they gave him gravitas and partly as an extra defence against the world. It was a point of neurosis in him and Doralee thought it was stupid. His father had apparently done exactly the same. Could such a personality defect be inherited? She feared it might be, though always when she wrote for *Oracle* she stressed that nurture won ever nature. It was magazine policy.

Doralee wrote an article on how men had to be allowed their irrationalities, citing Peter's spectacles as an example, and contrasting their upbringings. Both Adrienne, Peter's mother, and Ruby, her own, had taken exception to what they saw as an intrusion into family privacy. 'But the truth is the truth!' Doralee had objected. Was one never to be free, reckoned grown-up, allowed to go uninspected? What was the matter with writing about one's own life in the papers? Everyone did it. Life was to be shared, not lived locked up in a little private box of one's own. That would suggest one was ashamed of something.

What upset Ruby most was the part of the article which referred to the manner of Doralee's upbringing. Doralee had implied for all the world to see that it was chaotic. Doralee had been the eldest of six, and Ruby was proud that they had all turned out satisfactorily, especially the girls. It had not been achieved without effort.

'You hold me up to ridicule, Doralee,' Ruby had phoned to say. 'You always had matching socks when you went to school, why do you deny it? I know Marylou was once sent home for having holes in her school jumper – she would hold the hamster to her chest and she knew the little fucker chewed wool. Nothing would stop Glorianne from wearing those bloody earrings, and there was that fuss when Rex really did eat one of you girls' homework and no one believed her. I think it was Claudette's geography. But odd socks, no. You have humiliated me in public. Why do you do it, Doralee? Why do I always get the feeling from you that I'm not good enough as a mother?' That had hurt. You expected more support than that.

'You should not have given us those ridiculous names,' said Doralee. 'As if we were trailer-park trash. You lost the right to be taken seriously.'

'They were very pretty names,' said Ruby. 'Surely a mother

has a right to give her children names she likes? How sharper than a serpent's tooth, et cetera. God knows I did not bring you up to be snobby.'

'I am a journalist. I have to earn a living. Do you begrudge me even that?' asked Doralee. 'You have no idea what it's like to be me, or how competitive it is out there. You have to sell yourself as well as your work. You've never even been out to work, you've lazed about at home all your life. And anyway it's true, you didn't have to have so many children. And you never did any housework if you could help it.'

'So not content with holding your family up to public ridicule,' said Ruby, 'you now wish your brothers and sisters out of existence.'

It was quite a spat. Doralee knew well enough that earning a living was not the reason for this betrayal, for betrayal it was and she knew it. She did it because she wanted the world to know how she had suffered, from a partner who wore clear glass spectacles which had caused her friends to snigger, and from a mother who refused to keep a low profile, brought her family into ridicule, failed to keep a husband, and whose general sloppiness had all but ruined her daughter's life.

Doralee then accused Ruby of being a churchgoer, prone to idle superstition and stuck in the past, and it had been quite a difficult row to patch up, and had left Doralee quite upset.

Then Doralee had to put up with Adrienne calling from the office to say in the nicest possible way that Peter was not the kind to enjoy being made mock of in the press, and that she, Adrienne, had done the best she could to bring up her boys, but that if they inherited some of their deceased father's neuroses it was hardly her fault. She had been blamed because Peter's brother Maurice could not pass water in

71

public, but his father had been just the same. Why was everything always the mother's fault? Now this. Doralee should remember that she was not married to Peter, and what was overlooked in a wife was not necessarily forgiven in a partner, and she should be careful.

Doralee bit back the retort that since she wasn't married the least Adrienne could do was not behave like a mother-in-law – this was precisely why she and Peter hadn't married – and managed to cool Adrienne out. But later, chafing, Doralee suggested to Peter that his mother resented her for not being Jewish, and had always hoped that Doralee would fade out of the picture so Peter could marry a proper Jewish girl. Peter bristled and said that was an absurd accusation, almost a racist one. Doralee should certainly not put anything even vaguely like that in the next article she wrote. It was one thing for her to milk her own experiences, but she should leave him and his family out of it. Anyway, as he pointed out, Adrienne had not been in a synagogue since she was five.

It was true, Peter said, that she'd probably argue for circumcision if the baby was a boy, to which Doralee said if it was a boy Adrienne could keep it, since she, Doralee, only wanted a girl. If it was a boy she would abort it anyway so who was worrying? It was the first row they ever had and so shook both of them they went to bed and vowed never to quarrel again. Both were amazed to find they were capable of harbouring such vile thoughts. Peter even had a word with the newspaper's therapist, who suggested he apologise, and Peter did, and went further and told Doralee that of course she could write about what she wanted: she was the creative one in the relationship and he did not want to stand in her way.

Peter stepped on his glasses soon after that and never wore them again, and the families settled down to the fact that they would have to read about themselves in caricature from time to time – or their friends would. Neither Adrienne nor Ruby were great *Oracle* readers. And in the meantime the young people's bank balances got healthier and healthier.

Doralee's mother hoped, of course, that Doralee and Peter would eventually get married. She was, like so many of her generation, waiting for a grandchild that was failing to materialise. Her four daughters were all too clever and accomplished for their own good, and she was fairly sure that the twins were gay. They were for ever going off to some university department where the professor did famous research on homosexuality and identical twins. They could have been part of some control group but she doubted it. Ruby quoted statistics to her daughter – as if Doralee and Peter did not know them off by heart – that the odds for married couples in infertility treatment were better than for 'partnered couples' but it was easy enough to quash Ruby by pointing out that marriage was what both sets of parents had done, and look where it had got them. Lots of children and suddenly no husband just when you had got used to one.

Adrienne was ambivalent about the matter of grandchildren. They were ageing, if people knew about them, and their very existence suggested your life was more in the past than the future. She would have preferred Peter to have taken up with a Jewish girl. She herself had married out, and if asked on street corner polls whether she believed in God would answer briskly 'no'. All the same there was such a thing as tradition and ritual, and as she got older she could see their value. A Jewish wife would bring Peter back properly into the fold, and he would have proper connections within a supportive community. But he seemed happy enough with Doralee, who at least, as she herself did, knew the value of hard work. By and large, she had come round to thinking children by Doralee was the least-worse option.

To recap: **Doralee** has a partner called **Peter** – Peterloo is her pet name for him: he wishes she wouldn't use it, but diminutives come easily to her; it is a matter of family custom on the mother's side. Peter's mother is called **Adrienne.** Her own mother is **Ruby;** the doorman at High View is **George.** She has five siblings, **Marylou, Glorianne** and **Claudette,** called after Country and Western hits, the twins **Bobby** and **Robby,** and a recently deceased dog back home at the Rectory named **Rex.** A high-rise apartment is no place for a dog, and Rex had with age become slothful, overweight and sometimes incontinent. He was better off at home with Ruby.

We also know that Doralee has a good clean foam mattress she turns when it doesn't need turning, and feels older than she need because she wakes stiff in the morning. The fact is the mattress is too hard for someone as light as Doralee. Small, unpadded people need softer mattresses than large, padded people. Also Doralee sleeps an average of only six-and-a-half hours a night, which is far too short a time for proper rest and recuperation. Shortage of sleep makes her a little tense, and increases her partner's levels of anxiety, which are already high. She writes about this in her columns but does not really think the words she writes apply to her. They are for other people.

Sex for Doralee and Peter is frequent at the moment, four or five times a week, once or twice a night, and though sexual activity promotes sound alpha-wave-rich sleep, quality does not necessarily make up for quantity. Peter and Doralee both wake to an alarm clock which is more shocking to the system than they imagine. Best to let morning light wake you – early in the summer, late in winter – but employment imposes an unnatural life rhythm on workers.

Doralee is in her office by nine every morning, and thinks that's late; she tries to do better. It is a competitive world, and employers rule the roost; the employee who is seen to work longest and hardest gets promotion. Doralee gets to a Pilates class at seven thirty three times a week, and will fit in a work-out, a massage, a stint at the hairdresser and the beauty parlour, the better to arrive at work perfectly groomed. (Her mother never even got round to shaving her legs. What man is going to stand for that? And Doralee can remember all too vividly the time she saw her mother's under-arm hair, black disgusting tufts.) Doralee is a size 10 aiming for a size 8 and has the longest legs of any of her sisters: all went into the professions and are high achievers. Bobby and Robby, identical twins, now go to Art College when they are not up at the university being tested, and are performance artists. They earn very little, but have the satisfaction of high principle, which seems to be an inheritable trait, coming down through the male line.

Doralee's father **Graham** left Ruby on what to him were moral grounds, and what to her was an act of gross abandonment. She noisily refused to recycle their household waste, on the spurious grounds that recycling caused more pollution than landfill. This was at a time when he had, in response to the birth of the twins, just taken a new and better paid job as chief environmental officer to the council. '*Building a cleaner countryside*' it said, on the new posters. '*Revive, restore, recycle!*' Frankly, his wife embarrassed him. She had left home when she was seventeen, after changing her name from Kathleen to Ruby in the face of opposition from her parents, who were Seventh Day Adventists, and who disapproved of pop music. In vain for the girl to explain that country music was not pop music. She played her parents '*Ruby, Ruby,*' which moved through her girlish unconscious like a siren call to faraway places and romantic emotions, in the hope that they would understand, because she loved them, but all they heard was '*Don't take your love to town.*'

Despairing of ever pleasing them she had come South and met Graham, and had misunderstood him as he misunderstood her. She had thought he would love her for ever, he had thought she was a sweet and biddable little thing. He had been mildly amused at the way she had changed her name to annoy her parents, and thought she could soon enough grow out of that sort of thing, and change her name back to – perhaps not Kathleen, but something graver and more open, like Catherine. But she never would and when it came to naming her own children the impulse to upset was clearly still there. He did not have the strength of will to restrain her. Doralee, Marylou, Claudette, Glorianne! It did not help the marriage. Graham came from an Anne, Sarah, Jane background, and his mother winced noticeably at the christenings, which were performed, naturally, by Graham's father. But his mother was well mannered and did not otherwise at any time betray her dismay at her son's choice of partner.

And yes, as it happens, Doralee Thicket is related, though distantly, to **Vera Thicket,** Trisha's runaway accountant. This is mere coincidence: a matter of the few degrees of separation which link us to so many unsuitable people. Doralee is Vera's second cousin: her father Graham being a first cousin.

It was obvious to Graham's family from the start that Vera was unscrupulous. As a child she stole: no one's pockets were safe. The rest of the Thicket clan – a moral lot, at least on the male side – were to have little to do with Vera, or she with them. She was known to have stolen someone else's husband, and then qualified in accountancy. Next Vera was to run off with a smooth-talking yuppie from the Lebanon, also married, and was the subject of an unsuccessful Interpol search, during the course of which she emptied her clients' accounts, and went to Brazil. **Trisha's** funds were down to some £6,300 by the time that had happened. **Rollo** and **Thomasina** between them had managed to get through far more than Trisha had ever anticipated. How could other people be so expensive? But Rollo needed a lot of ortho-donty before he got to be the male face of a big cosmetic company and Thomasina's one-woman show in London needed funding. It turned out she needed backing from a rap group, all twelve of whom demanded Musicians' Union rates.

But the connection between Doralee and Vera is, to date at least, no more or less meaningful than two people at the same party happening to share a birthday, which is statisti-cally more likely than most people realise. Doralee is scarcely aware of Vera's existence. Her father Graham once mentioned that there was a criminal in the family, but since he had only seen her once or twice in his life, and had nothing more interesting to say on the matter, Doralee took no notice. Those who have not had children believe in nurture more than nature.

The Thickets bred profusely. Families these days are smaller. The birth rate falls beneath replacement level. Doralee and her Peter will be lucky to have one child between them, and that child will be lucky to have a cousin to its name. And first they have somehow to get over the event which is to bring these two disparate households together, brought about when Peter and Trisha brushed against one another as they passed on the stairs, and their souls were switched.

Who are we to blame for this event? There must be someone, something. Blame the stairs; blame the narrowness of passageways; blame the continuing existence of buildings which should never have been built in the first place. Once Wilkins Parade was a market garden which supplied the City with fruit and vegetables – apples, plums, melons, asparagus, peas. The fields of Wilkins' farm were dug up in the 1880s and became a tenement slum, jerry-built, and now despoiled by graffiti. It was in the 1880s that the High View apartment block was an orphanage. There was a surplus of children then: scuttling around, uncounted and uneducated, dying young. People in those days put their trust in quantity, not quality.

Or blame the fact that the Kleene Machine domestic agency has a history too and the past is never over. In the 1930s it was a fish-and-chip shop for a time, and the smell of poverty and battered fish frying in stale oil still hangs round the old brickwork of the stairs. Before that it was a pawnbroker and perhaps human distress has eaten into its brickwork. Perhaps none of us are as firmly rooted in the here and now as we assume. My son Sam, who has a great sense of fairness, and came into the world, as Wordsworth would have it, 'trailing clouds of glory', asked me when he was three when it was his turn to be a girl. I told him that didn't happen, but I can see that perhaps in some parallel universe down the road gender swap, soul swap, happens all the time. Perhaps Trisha is the bit-part player in some other greater drama, and the Great Scriptwriter in the Sky – the GSWITS, lord of the new fictional religion which I invented in a novella called *The Rules of Life*, has plans for her, which is why she has had to sell up her house and now lives here, with windows which rattle when a truck passes by and floors which slope so that her mattress keeps sliding down towards the door at night.

Better anyway that the conservationists had not interfered, and Wilkins' place been torn down and carted away to some landfill complete with dust, cobwebs and history, and something new, bright and concrete put in its place, and then perhaps the whole thing would never have happened. Blame the Gods of misrule, who are everywhere these days, blame everyone, blame anything, but not yourself.

Fading customs

I received no official training as a writer: I attended no creative writing courses: I did not study English literature at college. Having been so bad at the subject at school, I took up economics instead. My only tuition, and that was informal, happened when Louis Simpson, a poet, critic and Professor of English Literature at Stony Brook in New York, moved into the house next door. That was in 1968.

Time folds and crumples. I have leapt years ahead here from the days with the Dane, who retired to live on the coast and run a sailing school and live happily ever after. I would never have made a sailing woman. It feels dangerous enough to be in a car, let alone a boat.

1968, and I am now living with Ron, and have been for some years. We have a son, the second child for both of us, called Dan. We are still living in Primrose Hill round the corner from the shop, and my life has turned from a disaster area to a bright new development, as has High View Flats in *Mantrapped*. Or at least a very superior and complete internal conversion, if only the smell of the past didn't keep creeping through to the present.

These changes happen so fast. One day there's a derelict makeshift factory: then there's High View. One day there's a derelict runaway headmaster's wife, the next there's Fay Weldon, copy consultant, writer of TV plays, and would-be novelist. Just because she fell in love with a man she met at a party and married him. It hardly bears thinking about.

I had just had my first novel published. Louis was charming, handsome, intense, he knew all there was to know about literature and poetry. He knew how it should be done. I saw his face on the Internet the other day and my heart leapt to my mouth. He was, is, a really good poet. Our conversations were so many years ago he may well have forgotten that he ever knew me. But I have not forgotten him.

Way back then I showed him the novel I had just had published, *The Fat Woman's Joke*. I thought to win his good opinion. I too, the housewife next door, could write, and here was proof of it. I went off daily to work at Ogilvie and Mather, the big advertising agency, but I hoped that somehow Louis hadn't noticed. Advertising was considered a low occupation for persons of any sensibility, shallow and trashy, and anyway a working woman was earning pin money and should stay home and take better care of the children. I also brought shame on my husband by writing a cookery column, an advertisement for the Metal Box Company in disguise, for everyone to see. It appeared every week in a Sunday newspaper, under a former name, Fay Bateman, beneath a picture of myself. *Fay Bateman says.* In my column I advised the public how to cook with cans. '*Just dunk a whole chicken in a can of condensed chicken soup and bung it in the oven,*' I'd write, '*Delicious!*' And in my mother's footsteps, '*Just a little short-cooked cabbage and some butter – what could be better? Serve with a ham soufflé: just add eggs to your can of soup and it's done!*'

At home Ron, a gourmet cook, would spend hours on a cassoulet, or a bouillabaisse, or a *boeuf en daube*, using the garlic and mushrooms which had only recently become available in the shops, and tossing a chicory salad. How he despised my timid habit of peeling mushrooms: what harm did a little dirt do anyone? Our kitchen surfaces were littered with pans and the floor with discarded oyster shells, and I would clean up, and write my no-fuss cookery columns. The pans were copper and never properly tinned. I worried about metal poisoning but was laughed out of court.

All his life Ron fought a bourgeois heritage in which food was meant to be white, pale and bland, and like sex was not to be enjoyed, lest the pleasures of the flesh overwhelm the spirit and lead to dissolution and disgrace.

The tendency to cook fish in parsley sauce, from which Ron's mother, and indeed mine, suffered, the idea that even white pepper was suspect lest it overheat the blood, was to be soon rooted out of society (along with the class system) and the artists, that is to say Ron and company, were to lead the foodie onslaught. And I, one of the wives, was engaging in such careless culinary treachery. '*Cooking with cans – this way the future lies. Just open a can and go out to work!*'

Be that as it may, all that cooking and guilt aside, I had hoped for Louis' approval, but the novel I gave him seemed only to make him angry. 'But this is not a proper novel,' he said, waving *The Fat Woman's Joke* around, 'and what a monstrous jacket!' Indeed, the book had a jacket so terrible – two great rows of chomping shiny white teeth against a staring red background – that I destroyed every one I came across. I would root them out in bookstores and slip the jackets off and trash them every one. I had neglected to do so on this occasion, feeling an urge to present Louis with the truth, warts and all.

These jackets, if in perfect condition, are now in great demand, I am happy to report, I having so rashly destroyed so many of the first edition. The book has never been out of print. I have its current jacket in front of me now; bright pink with a line drawing of a not very fat woman on the front. Once she was all luscious folds of fat. Nothing these days can be extreme. The passage of the years has turned the book from a revolutionary document, first blast in the feminist fusillade, to all but chick lit. The novel now seems to be about a woman with eating problems (a syndrome much spoken of now but un-invented at the time of writing) brought on by a surfeit of domesticity: pleasant enough but not in the least incendiary.

To me these early novels are historical documents, though the publishers say they remain relevant enough. But I suspect they say that because these young persons, not having lived through a pre-feminist world themselves, have no idea of its full horrors.

'If it isn't a novel what is it?' I asked Louis. It is my normal policy to agree wholeheartedly with my detractors, thereby deflating them, but for once I felt defiant. 'My publishers thought that was what it was,' I told Louis. 'It's what they call it in the shops. A novel. People are reading it, and turning the pages. Many even like it.' But I can remember my shock; the terrible feeling that Louis Simpson was right. I was an impostor, an upstart. I had no business dabbling in serious matters.

'Novels have inner form,' he said, practically stamping his foot. 'They have shape, purpose, profundity. They are not constructed like this. This is just and then, and then, and then, as if a child were writing it. Worse, it is written in the present tense, as if it were some film script.'

I had to admit that the book was indeed a TV play of mine I had novelised. Its roots were showing, like Mrs Kovac's on a bad day. It was true that all I had done was move from scene to scene after the fashion of a TV script.

I had been writing TV dramas in my spare time but had become discontented, fed up with having less than total control of what happened on screen. The director had fallen out of love with me, and broken my heart, and the actors would put the wrong expressions on their faces; the designers would unreasonably up-grade the sets, the producer had impertinently taken out a line or two 'because of length'.

It came to me in a flash of light the way not to be interfered with was to rework the play in novel form. I could elaborate as I went along. The characters would now be mine, not what the casting director, on the grounds of cost and practicality, had decided they would be. Their problems were mine, not what the director had inferred that they were.

But the chief reason for my defiance was the simple exhilaration of writing a novel: I had done the play, the skeleton of the plot was sound, from now on what I wrote became almost automatic writing. The muse descended from the skies. The sum added up to more than the sum of the parts, so long as I followed my instinct and tried not to let reason get between me and what I wrote. This conclusion, however wrong-headed, gave me confidence.

I remember writing 'The End' on an A4 pad, wide lined, with a Pentel pen, on the top of a bus going down Regent Street. I was on my way to my office in Brettenham House on Waterloo Bridge. I remember the feeling of exaltation as I wrote those two satisfactory words, 'The End'. This was my *métier*. This was what I was meant to do. This was what I had been born for. This I would do to the end of my days, and there was so much unsaid in the world I could go on saying it for ever.

But looking through *The Fat Woman's Joke*, now so proudly published, Louis Simpson merely groaned. He said this was simply not how novel writing was done. I had a terrible feeling he was right. That the original play had been produced by Granada TV only because the director hoped, not without reason, to get into my knickers. (The euphemism of the time.) He did. The publishers, MacGibbon and Kee, had published the novel version only because they were hoping to amalgamate with Granada and it suited their contract to deliver me up to their new owners. George Melly, musician and art critic, had given the book a rave review in the *Observer*, only because he was friend of Ron's – and hoped to buy antiques from him at a favourable price. Or so Ron told me was the case. The public, I could see, had been thoroughly misled and that was why they were buying the book. It had all been a terrible, humiliating mistake. I had better stick to advertising.

But the next novel, *Down Among the Women*, had already been written, and was at the printers. How was I to avoid the disgrace of fresh exposure? I had been presumptuous. I had stuck my head over a parapet only for it to be shot at. I retreated next door, grateful to still have my domestic life, glad that it was my habit to underplay such small successes I had had so far in the literary world. Grateful that I had children to sing lullabies to, and things I should better spend my time on, such as writing ads and cleaning the burnt copper pans without scratching them yet more, so they didn't leak heavy metal into our food and poison us.

When the proofs of *Down Among the Women* came through the post I almost didn't show them to Louis, though he had relented enough to ask me to, and when I did I was sorry. They seemed to make him even angrier.

'This is just a rip-off of Mary McCarthy's *The Group*,' he complained – a novel which also followed the adventures of a group of feisty college graduates as they disappeared into marriage. I said I didn't think Mary McCarthy could own the idea. Wasn't *The Three Musketeers* much the same, young men off on a mission, learning what life was like? The fruit of a novel was in the execution, surely, not the plot. It sounded okay though I was not sure what it meant. Louis complained that I was argumentative, but was obliged to take my point.

'For another thing,' he said, now on firmer ground, 'there are eight characters on your opening page. This is absurd.

Characters are meant to be introduced slowly, one by one, so readers can get used to them. You just throw them all in and list them. You are meant to be kind to your readers, not defy them.'

This is a conversation thirty-five years old, but I remember its detail, burned into memory.

'Nobody's objected so far,' I said. 'Readers have to do some work too. It can't be all me. Me and my readers are in this together.'

'I and my readers,' he said, but he softened. 'So what you are doing in these novels is engaging in alienation techniques? Is that right?'

'Of course,' I said, boldly. What could he mean?

'Okay,' he said grudgingly. 'It's new but that doesn't mean it works. Eight characters on a page are still too many.'

I took his point. And that is why, though I still tend to introduce characters with abandon, in this novel I re-cap the cast from time to time, putting new characters in heavy type as one does in a film script, to make it easy for readers. Not only Doralee, but all her ill-named sisters and the dog Rex too, and Trisha and her lesbian lover, and the wicked accountant Vera Thicket. And no doubt why now I refer to them as 'the cast', rather than as 'characters'. Over the next year Louis continued to let slip words of remonstration and advice, of which I took good heed, and for which I continue to be grateful.

Thus I remember, though fitfully, Louis' complaints that he had no idea what any of the characters in *Down Among the Women* looked like. I have at least remembered in *Mantrapped* to describe Trisha – but have had to go back to pay the same courtesy to Doralee and Peter. You shall have the cast clear in your mind's eye, as is my responsibility, as clear as if I held a camera, not a pen.

Doralee is, I'll swear, pure invention, but I admit I did have a great aunt Sylvia who lived in a *ménage à trois* with a man known in the family as Willy Beach the Jam King, and another man whose name I cannot recall, but I believe he was a pillar of the community. Sylvia was born in 1867, and when a girl, along with my grandmother Frieda, was a model for Holman Hunt the painter. She and Frieda both had the clouds of fizzy fair hair and the strong jaws the Pre-Raphaelites loved. What's new? Doralee, Sylvia? I have made Doralee look like my great aunt, and she is to end up living with Peter and Trisha in their switched bodies. I met Sylvia only once but she made good scones, as I remember. I'm sure Doralee would too, if only she owned a proper oven and didn't have to make do with a microwave, and convenience food, and wasn't so busy she hardly knew whether she stood on her exuberant tendril-haired head or her nicely defoliated heels.

At the dry-cleaners'

Envisage this. Trisha, the hopeless case of earlier pages, the one who's fallen on hard times after winning the lottery, is now living above the dry-cleaners' in Wilkins Parade. She wonders whether she made a wise choice, whether it might not have been better to put down the phone and accept when Mrs Kovac said she couldn't have the flat, instead of throwing herself upon the woman's mercy. Mrs Kovac's mercies may turn out to be like the gifts of the grateful when dead, not quite what you expect or want. Abandoned needles and nasty bits of cellophane swirl around the recycling centre down the road, and though Harrods vans draw up outside High View Apartments, it is clear to Trisha that the area is fighting a civil war with itself, and both sides are fighting hard. Are property prices going up or down? Not that it matters to her, since she is renting, but she likes to live in a neighbourhood which is improving, not deteriorating. Who doesn't?

Trisha does not mind eking out a living doing odds and ends of mending for Mrs Kovac. Landladies always have to be pacified, in her experience. In return for accommodation they require gratitude as well as rent and she doesn't mind going through the motions. But Mrs Kovac is taking advantage. The day before yesterday Trisha was expected to darn cashmere gloves, which was tricky work, and then Mrs Kovac complained that the darns showed. What did she expect? The physically impossible? She accused Trisha of getting nicotine stains on someone's white lace collar – her fingers were a bit sweaty, it was true; it could get very hot and airless in the flat – and cigarette ash on some guy's jeans who needed a button sewing on. But it was Mrs Kovac's attitude that got up Trisha's nose. There was no respect. She walked in without knocking or piled garments up in a black plastic bag and left them outside the door without comment, which was almost worse. She shouted at Trisha up the stairs as if Trisha was a servant, of no account. She had reduced Trisha's rent by only five pounds a week, and since she set the rent in the first place, who is to say if this amounts to anything at all? Trisha, in fact, is hopping mad, for someone of so normally benign a nature.

Downstairs, Mrs Kovac too is in a state. It is not surprising. Mrs Kovac not only inhales more carbon tetrachloride than is good for her, but is lucky to get six hours sleep a night, and her efficiency and her temper suffer as a result, as is the case with Doralee. Mrs Kovac is now giving a final press to Doralee's mattress-cover, but has set the machine at too high a temperature, under too great a pressure. She hears a slight sizzling sound, and gets a whiff of melting rubber as the old-fashioned buttons which fasten the cover melt and fuse into the fabric below and above. The buttons are now useless, the cover cannot be closed.

Mrs Kovac has various options open to her: she can pretend that all is well, return the cover without comment and hope no one notices; she can offer compensation, or she can replace the buttons at her own expense. She decides to do the latter, and to ask Trisha to do the sewing. Trisha is in no position to dictate terms, Mrs Kovac knows, since Trisha will no doubt be claiming a full rent allowance from the benefits office, whilst not handing the full amount over to her landlady, but paying a proportion in kind.

Mrs Kovac's mistake lies in her decision to hold back the entire delivery for Doralee and Peter – three shirts and a dress as well as the mattress-cover – instead of only the mattress-cover. This means Doralee does not get the little black dress with thin-plaited shoulder straps (which Mrs Kovac hates, because the straps keep slipping from their hanger and must be fixed with a ribbon), in time for Doralee to take the dress with her to the office to wear for Heather's baby shower.

Heather is a colleague who until recently ran *Oracle*'s books page. Doralee likes to change her clothes a lot – Ruby in her time, when the children were small, would drag on the same old skirt and black jumper day after day. The equivalent in Doralee's life is not to bother to change for an office party, and is not a good idea.

The hatred Mrs Kovac feels for the black dress is irrational but sometimes over-familiar garments do invoke paranoia in the hearts of those who service them. Let the bitch wait, thinks Mrs Kovac. Blame the carbon tetrachloride, for making her head achey and her breath sour. Blame Mr Kovac. Blame anyone for her bad temper. She should have been more careful with the ironing machine. Mistakes cost money: that was the first. The second was to try and wring more work out of Trisha than Trisha felt was appropriate.

Trisha loves needlework, or used to at school, when she was in love with her needlework mistress, Miss Little, which is why she offered to help Mrs Kovac out in the first place. It is a pity that such good will and happy memories should be reduced to this sourness, but it happens.

And no doubt about it, Trisha had had a hard time recently, from rags to riches with indecent speed and back again. Vera Thicket used to help Trisha out in these matters but since Vera abandoned her lesbian lifestyle and fled to different loves and other continents, Trisha is on her own.

Now she pulls the bulky linen cover out of the black sack and in so doing tears one of her nails down to the quick, and then another. Seized by a sudden fit of self-pity – not something to which she is prone – she even snivels a little. She has risen above the trials of the last few days well enough, but now suddenly the reality strikes her. She has lost husband, child, lover, lottery, home, career and nearly all her worldly possessions.

She had imagined that at least her long, elegant, crimson, and perfectly manicured nails, a source of pride, a beacon of hope for the future, would always be secure. Now suddenly they are torn and sore, and she sees herself as what she is, not the heroine of her own life, but a woman alone, on benefits, no longer young, with nothing. She weeps. The karma round here is off key today. And anger is boiling up.

Doralee gets back from work and calls Kleene Machine to enquire where (the fuck, by implication, though she doesn't quite use the word) her dry-cleaning is. It is meant to have been left in the porter's lodge for collection and there's no sign of it. Mrs Kovac says she is waiting for the order to be complete, as is her policy. Doralee points out that it is not a coherent or consistent policy as she has often had half orders delivered in the past. Mrs Kovac says the delay is because she is replacing the buttons on the mattress-cover free of charge as a gesture of goodwill. Doralee says she doesn't detect much goodwill in Mrs Kovac's tone. 'I need the dress for tonight,' says Doralee, though it's a lie. 'You've let me down.'

'Your buttons damaged my machines.' It is Mrs Kovac's instinct to attack when faced with criticism. Get in first! 'They're rubber. I could sue.'

'I don't believe this!' protests Doralee, and says she is sending her husband down to collect the cleaning there and then, whether or not the garments have been cleaned. She just wants them back in her possession.

'I only send out orders when they're complete,' says Mrs Kovac, 'and anyway I'm shutting up shop now.'

Today Mr Kovac has fortunately turned up early to help his wife close the steel shutters of the shop. Mr Kovac does not speak a word of English, and was once an illegal immigrant, but now by virtue of marriage and later amnesties is a fully accredited citizen. So far as he knows his wife is a perfectly pleasant woman. At any rate she is a nice plump shape and has blonde hair and all her own teeth, which is more than the wife he left behind ever did. She provides a bed for him to sleep in, sex, and gives him his dinner. He has no idea how old she is, or what her temper is, since she speaks in a monotone and seldom smiles. He takes her tea in the morning. A strange drink, taken with milk. The whole country is a mystery to him. He does not work in the shop but every evening delivers completed orders in his unlicensed, uninsured white van. It is fitted with a GPS device which 'fell off the back of a lorry' in the local terminology, so he can always find his way.

Doralee and Peter live in an ordered world which rubs along cheek by jowl with the disordered one: it is amazing how well everyone gets along with each other, considering. Mr Kovac sleeps with a gun under his pillow, but it would never occur to him to use it on customers, no matter how annoying. He is no criminal, but he has to make his way in the world. Peter has a filing cabinet full of licences, permissions, certificates of competence, prizes: all the divisions in date order, as if he needs proof that he exists. Everything except, as Ruby mourns, a marriage certificate.

Doralee puts her foot down. 'Oh no, you are not closing,' she says to Mrs Kovac. So a Russian countess would have spoken to a peasant, in the days when the gentry could take an idle serf down to the police station for a whipping. 'Not until I have my property in hand or I'll be reporting you to the local Trading Affairs Office. My husband is coming round right now.' She assumes there is a Trading Affairs Office, or that if there is not, someone like Mrs Kovac can

92

be bluffed into thinking there is. She slams down the phone. 'It is too bad,' she says to Peter. 'People like that think they can treat you like shit.' Peter looks startled and murmurs that it's bad policy to make unnecessary enemies. He has been preparing couscous and was just about to stir the grain into the heated oil, but now sees he has no option but to abandon the task and go to fetch Doralee's dress. Her cupboards are full of little black dresses and he personally cannot tell the difference between one and another, but Doralee evidently can. He admires this in her. More, he had been under the impression that Heather's baby shower was the next day, not today, and at the office, and Doralee confirms that this is the case. It is a matter of principle, she says. She simply cannot bear people who say they'll do one thing and then do another. The consumer has to assert their rights. People do not complain enough. Peter puts down his couscous ladle and goes out through the lobby and down to Kleene Machine to help Doralee and the middle classes out. He thinks it will only take a minute, that he will be back to finish the couscous. But it is not to be.

A *lifetime* of keeping clothes clean – three pages the non-domestic reader is free to skip

One of Louis Simpson's strictures was that novels were not meant to be about domestic life, that the kitchen-table novel, written in and around the kitchen, was an egregious, pathetic thing. I chafed against this ruling at the time, I remember:

if subject alone was to be the difference between male and female writing, so be it. So much of life, especially women's lives – shopping, cooking, cleaning, washing – was taken up with the mundane, at least it should be properly honoured in literature. The first novel I wrote, *The Fat Woman's Joke*, being about food, fatness, sex and housework, was seen as revolutionary in its time, though now it is just a pleasant read about things that everyone knows.

I can see my interest as being a little obsessive. There were other things to write about – war, politics, economics, for example – and I did turn my attention to them in due course, but for the first ten years of my writing career, gender and domesticity were my preoccupation. In the early Seventies I wrote a stage play, a dismal and thankfully rather short piece, called *Socks*. Five characters stand around a dying woman's hospital bed, and struggle for dominance, the right to come first in her life. That she is dying, that they have killed her, is of no interest to them. In the end they simply wear her out and she breathes her last. I named the characters Shopping, Washing, Cooking, Cleaning and Socks. I can only suppose that at the time I felt much oppressed by having to keep house. And here the theme is, surfacing again in the form of my preoccupation with the Kleene Machine Cleaners and its management. Peter, fictional successor to the real-life husband Ron, is cooking couscous, which was to be Ron's favourite dish in the Nineties, before death and a mistress carried him off.

My own early experiences with washing were drastic. No wonder Mrs Kovac ends up where she does, married to an illegal with a gun, being rude to clients and exploiting her workers. Laundry, thief of time and energy, exacts an extreme response.

When Nicolas was born, in 1954, the washing machine was a rare and very expensive household object. It was before the age of the launderette. The rich sent their washing off to the laundry to be 'done' by women who had no other option but to work in them, and badly-paid and sickly, steamy work it was, but it was what kept the children fed and out of the orphanages. Dickens's mother, husbandless, was a washer-woman. Yesterday's laundry work is today's call-centre work, where the resentful and the poorly paid cluster, and for the humiliations of the orphanage read the humiliations of being on the dole, with form-filling and loneliness extra.

But ordinary women did the washing in the sink or the tub, wrung the water out of wet clothes with the strength of their hands, such as it was. I have big hands, as did my mother, for all she was a little woman. We spread wet sheets and wool vests to dry over the backs of chairs, first sopping up surplus wetness between dry towels – remembering that the towels in their turn had to be dried – or swung them high from a contraption of rods above the stove, where they picked up cooking smells – cabbage, fish, stew – and became greasy and dusty. So many things, before detergents became commonplace in the Fifties, were filmed with grime.

As laundry and fabric technology arrived, everything changed – yet nothing did. My children count their T-shirts by the dozen and think nothing of putting on whole sets of new clothes within the day, so the washing machine spins without ceasing, whereas the mangle used to turn only once a week. Someone still has to sort garments and bedding, deal with it, think about it, fold it and put it away, but now the task is given little dignity, and is seen as just something to be fitted in along with everything else. The washer-dryer is a godsend, the softener cuts out ironing, the dry-cleaner delivers (mostly) but the drying still sits there for ever, like Cooking, Cleaning, Shopping and Socks, the weight on the dying Emperor's chest, like the nightingale in the Hans Christian Andersen story, clamouring for attention.

To the Novel!

To remind you. **Trisha,** the lottery-winner, has somehow managed to lose a fortune and end up sewing on buttons above Kleene Machine. She is soon to swap souls with **Peter.** Trisha's soul, as we know, is soiled but soft and amiable, her sins more of omission than commission. Such as, forgetting to feed the cat and then overfeeding it in compensation, or forgetting that she has a baby in the pram and leaving it outside the shop, neglecting to pay back money or replace cigarettes, drinking too much, squabbling with neighbours, having round heels (falling too easily backwards into bed, that is) not saving money but giving it away, lying as a child about doing her homework, flirting with her stepfather. Now Trisha's soul inhabits Peter's body. Envisage this soul, normally awash with oestrogen and femaleness, as a bright pink satin heart shape with the bumps and bulges appropriate to its age and experience, becoming little by little younger, more male, smoother, clean of line and curve but duller coloured. Nothing is for nothing: Trisha and Peter are bound to suffer some leakage from one to the other while in each other's bodies. They will not escape unscathed from this experience, if at all.

Doralee is the new woman, who has everything: looks, money, career, brains, self-esteem, the love of a good man.

Note the order in which I have graded these attributes – like the order of ingredients in packet food: the greatest first, the least last. Apart from looks, her mother Ruby would probably have put them in reverse order of the one I do. Looks would still come first in the blessings fate can bestow – then the love of a good man, then confidence (self-esteem is rather a new concept), children, then career, then brains. So much for the changing views of the decades. Her grandmother **Mary** would have seen brains and career as actual handicaps to the good life. It did no woman any good to have a brain – indeed to the Victorians it was seen as a positive cause of unhappiness. Since a woman's destiny was to have children, intellect could only disturb and upset, and her working was an indicator of extreme poverty. Ruby was rumoured to have a brain, which was why she was so difficult, and changed her name so oddly.

Peter – the new man, the perfect partner, non-aggressive, testosterone-lite, is politically correct, a good earner, though not quite as good as Doralee, and a good spender. Their loft apartment in High View, no matter how they try to be smartly minimalist, keeps cluttering up with the plugs and wires of communication extras: flat screens, video phones, whatever's newly out. They look forward to the day when gadgets will be as free of wires as an old battery radio. The times being on their side, the pair is on their way to being what the media describe as a power couple, though are not perhaps so much on the party scene as they ought to be for maximum advancement. Both work long tense hours, and as we know, like Mrs Kovac, do not get enough sleep.

Doralee and Peter bought High View three years ago in a rising market, on the assumption that the neighbourhood was going up in the world. When an Italian deli, a bathroom

97

accessory shop, Kleene Machine and Starbucks opened up, they reckoned they had made the right choice. But a hostel for young male asylum seekers opened in the last six months has changed the nature of the area somewhat, altering the balance of spending power within it. Citizens-in-waiting sit on doorsteps rather than in Starbucks, where there is no smoking, and fan out from its centre, the more buoyant and ambitious marrying such single women as are left available for nuptials. It may be a sexier city, the sum of human happiness may be increased as a result of this influx of non-English speakers, but property prices are faltering. Peter and Doralee are too busy to notice what is happening. No one has mugged them yet, and they feel they are invulnerable.

It is true that I have neglected to give lengthy physical descriptions of Doralee and Peter, of the kind Louis Simpson favoured. But size eight thirty-two-year olds like Doralee, with long legs, working in the media, earning well, and going to Pilates classes tend to look pretty good. You can be sure their features are regular, their hair glossy, their skin clear, their eyes alert and intelligent. To the outsider, such girls who swarm in our workaday cities might all look rather alike, but those that know them well can tell them apart easily enough.

Doralee is the one with the rather too frizzy fly-away hair. She has large blue eyes, and is more intelligent than she is assumed to be. She worries that her bum looks large and her arms are too long, but who doesn't? Look too long in a mirror and anyone's bare arms seem to dangle. Women were bred for carrying burdens, after all, fetching water, getting in the harvest, at the very least lugging children about.

Ruby, Doralee's mother, never had time to worry. She was too busy, or so her critics said, working out annoying names for her children when it would have been simpler to call them Jane, Julia, Bridget, Buffy, Caroline, Anne or any of the more appropriate names available. Her critics, of course, included Eve, who was to be her successor as Graham's wife. Ruby was a size 16 by the time she was twenty; and six children later, a size 22. Ruby felt bad for at least five minutes when she realised that Doralee's pet name for her partner was Peterloo – okay to diminish the seriousness of girl babies while you waited for a boy to be born, but disconcerting if your own daughter did it to a man. But Ruby was too busy organising the amateur dramatic society and training to be a pastor in the local church to worry for long. Now the children were all grown she liked to keep busy. Some said it was the drive and energy with which she met each day that had driven **Graham,** the children's father, from her side and into the arms of the benign and peaceful Eve, who was a size 14.

When Doralee was thirteen and just before the twins had been born – at last, the boy(s) they had been waiting for – Graham met a girl who moved and spoke slowly, and was interested in esoteric religion, and would consent to meditate with him. This was Eve. He had fallen in love with her as they sat side by side in the lotus position and shared their deep breathing. Now you, now me! In and out, in and out, and all of it virtuous, certainly at the beginning. It was Eve who persuaded Graham to abandon local land agenting and become an environmental officer for the council, and then to move on to join a non-governmental organisation, an NGO, which dealt with property matters in war-torn countries overseas. Someone has to own the land where refugee camps are sited, and deal properly with the problems and responsibilities of that ownership. Had he not met Eve, Graham would have still been messing about with local land rentals and change of use certificates for farm land, and still be married to Ruby.

There is no need to describe **Ruby.** You will know her already. She is a middle-aged woman, a size 22, and the high street is full of them. She just moves faster than most, and speaks more loudly.

As for **Peter**, anyone who can trap and set up house with as superior a specimen of womanhood as Doralee is bound to look personable. He has to shave only once every two days. He worries about this sometimes in the night – is he sufficiently masculine? Can the oestrogen in take-away chicken be sapping his virility? He reads and checks the health reports, as well as keeping abreast of weapon development in many countries, and knows all too well how vulnerable the West is to terrorist attack and so on. His is not a reassuring job. He works in a tall office block and the sound of aircraft makes him jump. After the Twin Towers he found his offices moved upstairs to the twenty-sixth floor: others more senior than he were moved down. He worries in case Doralee leaves him, or that like his father he gets cancer. He checks himself for prostate symptoms, even though he is so young, and makes love to Doralee yet again to confirm that he can. Peter's family are in short supply, unlike Doralee's, who have siblings and to spare.

Peter collects his dry-cleaning

Mrs Kovac is left pale with rage and exhaustion after having had words with Doralee. It has been a hard day. But Mr

Kovac, coming by to help his wife put up the new steel shutters, seems to have found his tongue. He speaks twelve words in English in a row. 'Perhaps I see to lady for you,' he suggests. 'She no good to world.' Until now, beyond the occasional 'dinner now,' 'fine day,' 'I go out now,' 'out of petrol,' or 'have no money,' the conversation between them has been minimal.

Mrs Kovac shakes her head, hoping her husband does not mean what she thinks he means, and also that the sudden improvement in his English is not due to too close an association with some young woman. Mr Kovac is a handsome man with merry, twinkling eyes. Mrs Kovac is older than he and doubts her own luck in finding such an affectionate, silent and helpful man. Having resigned herself to the likelihood of his wandering off with some young woman from his own country, wherever that is, she is surprised that a year later he shows no signs of doing so. The idea that he actually wanted to marry her, and that it was not just a marriage of convenience to help with his visa and housing problems, is as much a source of pain as of pleasure. The problem with having something precious is that you can then lose it.

Her husband worries about nothing: she worries about everything. She worries about the business: after a year's trading she is barely in profit. She does not have the volume of trade she had hoped for. Everything looked good on paper; she had a diploma in business management, a bank loan to set up the domestic agency and a small business resource centre has helped with the dry-cleaning start-up, together with ten years of her savings as a call girl, but three recent muggings and two break-ins in the immediate neighbourhood suggest the authorities put more trust in the future of the neighbourhood than perhaps they should. Mrs Kovac is trying to go upmarket but downmarket keeps creeping back. The son of the previous owner got done for dealing drugs, but that has not discouraged his customers – they keep coming back, swirling round her doors like some oily, blackish tide to do their deals outside her door. She notices they melt away when Mr Kovac appears, but he is not always there. She would keep a couple of large dogs but the customers would not like it.

The bathroom accessory shop has closed in the last month, as has the Italian deli. These shops stand empty. Turn your back for a minute and new paint sprouts graffiti, and fancy glass ends up cracked. Vomit, she has discovered, eats away at floor tiles.

'*A learning curve,*' she tries to call it, wrestling what is bad into what is good, as her life-enhancement courses have taught her, but words do not create the world, however much society seems to insist they should. Nothing is what she expected. The up-market crowd, though free with their money, are unhelpful and ungrateful, always wanting more. Down-market types ask about prices and walk out. At least the few old ladies who still totter by have a good word and a thank you when they pick up their best blouse for a funeral, and count out the exact change into her palm. The new lot can't even be bothered to pick up their brown coins.

Mrs Kovac accepts that she is in no position to annoy middle-class customers, of the kind who have mattress-covers and use them, and need buttons replacing – buttons, zips; what's wrong with Velcro? But nor is it in her nature to tolerate rudeness. The most tiring thing about the work, she finds, is not being on her feet all day but the struggle between self-interest and impulse. Self-interest says *smile sweetly and mind your tongue*; nature says *fuck off and die*.

And quite what Mr Kovac did during the day, what it was he delivered from door to door as well as dry-cleaning, who was to say? Mrs Kovac tries to shut her eyes to it. His trouser pockets would be stuffed with bank notes, though she understood if only from his regretful look and gesture that the money was owed to someone other than his wife. Not his to keep, his to pass on, for fear of what might betide if he did not. That was a worry too.

Sometimes she was so busy and tired she would exceed the six weeks' limit she set for the hairdresser, and her dark roots would show through the blonde and she hated that. She was a business woman with a diploma, not a slag with business worries. But there were many compensations, she told herself. Her life was not turning out too badly. Mr Kovac was there every night after ten o'clock, eating his supper, silent and smiling, soft, strong, clean hands searching her body at night. He played the guitar to her, and that was worth a lot, though he slept with a gun beneath his pillow.

Now here was this idiot young man complaining. 'But we pay way over the odds for next-day delivery,' he was saying. His lot affected an accent she would be ashamed of, speaking through their noses and hardly opening their mouths. 'This is unbelievable. My partner's really upset.'

Partner? Couldn't he at least pretend the cow was his wife? But people today were at pains to let the world know they belonged to the new world order. Theirs was not an existence of marriage, domesticity and trouble. Theirs was one in which no one smoked, no one married, and others cleaned the clothes, the better to maximise their lifespan. Mrs Kovac gritted her teeth and repeated that the cover was at the

103

menders, that she never sent out part orders, that the buttons had been of the cheapest sort, and so had melted and damaged her machine, and there had been no need for his wife to have taken the tone she did.

'I was doing your wife a favour,' said Mrs Kovac. 'I am surprised you don't realise that.'

Mr Kovac hovered in the background. All Mrs Kovac had to do was say, '*See to the bitch*' and she suspected he would. But you couldn't go down that path. This was the civilised world, not ancient Rome. You could get anyone bumped off for a tenner, or so they said, by asking around in any pub, and a fiver to crack knees. But there were as many undercover policemen around these days as there were criminals, taking sly pictures and recording conversations. The guy you hired would turn out to be the cop. Besides, first find your pub. They were closing like a field of sunflowers in the dusk, and wine bars taking their place.

'My partner, not my wife,' asserted Peter, and to show his further determination asked for the address of the menders, so he could collect the mattress-cover himself, buttons or no buttons. It was needed urgently at home. He hoped Doralee would take over the couscous. He was hungry and this might take longer than he thought.

Mrs Kovac looked at Peter and laughed. His shirt was a credit to Kleene Machine, but his suit was of the pale, crumpled linen kind, which was high maintenance, of some kind of organic fabric: if you so much as sat on a grassy slope it would pick up a green stain. He was a reed in the undergrowth, too thin for its own good, grown in bad soil, too prone to bending, yet not immune from breaking. Why did he assume he was better than she was? Because she saw to his dirty clothes? The wife, or partner, was having a hissy fit, and everyone was meant to take it seriously?

Mrs Kovac said she supposed she couldn't stop him, he could pick up the cover from the apartment above the shop if that was what he wanted, but she expected payment in full, on his way out, and for the seamstress's time and labour as well, and would his wife kindly put the collection slip in the post to her since she, Mrs Kovac, had to keep her records in order and did not want any further unpleasantness. She would be glad if he took his custom elsewhere.

This would not be the outcome Doralee had wanted, which was a contrite and humbled Mrs Kovac and better service from then on, but it was too late to worry about that. There was some kind of mountain tribesman hovering amongst the garments at the back of the shop, whom Peter would wager was an illegal immigrant, a sinister presence, and Peter was suddenly aware that Wilkins Parade was not necessarily coming up in the world, but could be going down, and that it might be a good idea to sell the High View apartment before other people realised this was the case.

He pushed open the door at the side of the shop while Mrs Kovac made out the bill, and went up the narrow stairs. They smelt of urine, which was hardly surprising, since the side door was not kept locked. He had assumed that the seamstress would be crone-like but the woman who startled him by appearing on the top landing, with his mattress-cover over her arm, was youngish and rather smart, with curly red hair and quite attractive, in a flashy kind of way. He stopped; she stopped. They caught each other's eye briefly – both were in a state of outrage and resentment – and then he went on up and she continued coming down. Neither was prepared to give way to the other. As each brushed past the other, shoulder to shoulder, hip to hip, their souls took the opportunity of jumping. Tradition has it that they can, and now it had happened.

By the top of the stairs, Peter was to be in Trisha's body: by the bottom of the stairs Trisha was to be in Peter's, and the mattress-cover in the Peter body's arms. Trisha would get the best of the deal: if only because her Peter body was younger, and she had access to money in the bank, and could sign the cheques.

On the question of souls

When I was a small child in New Zealand and going to a convent school, there was a lot of talk about souls. Souls had to be kept pure and untarnished, and were always in danger from the devil, who tried to steal them. But they could be sold to him, in an emergency. I had the idea that they hovered over our heads like the proud milky little cloud in Pooh Bear, tethered by a golden cord and rather talkative. I asked the nuns and they said no, souls were inside us, and silent, and I asked where, and they pointed variously to the heart or just above the bridge of the nose. They were real and solid enough. I thought then perhaps they were like the white inner-sole of a slipper – they would have to be thin and flexible. But I was told, no, every soul was different and none of this really mattered, the important thing was to treasure your soul and keep it from harm, or else you went to hell – or if you were me, and un-christened, to a place called Limbo. And if I didn't stop asking questions, such was the implication, I'd be there quicker than I imagined. So I contented myself with visualising the souls of the nuns. Mother Martha's – she was nice – was soft and round and squishy, Sister Alexis's was thin like a rake and dug into her ribs, and yapped for joy like a little dog while she rapped my knuckles.

Mrs Kovac's soul need not concern us too much now, but I think it is a bright pink triangle, waving yellow and black fronds as if it had been too long underwater and developed growths, but otherwise hard edged and crisply configured, like some kind of warning sign at a celestial driving school, fallen into the harbour but undaunted.

You will have noticed the future and predictive tenses which surface every now and then in the previous section. Peter *was to be* in Trisha's body, Doralee *is to fail* to find her little black dress with the shoulder straps, and *is to fly* into – Mrs Kovac is quite right – *a hissy-fit*. I move forward in time, I put the action into the future. I let you know not so much what is going to happen next but what I have decided is to happen next. At least, I am reassuring you, or possibly myself, I *know*.

There is still time to change things, of course: to put everything back into the past, taking out some present tenses, striking out an 's', putting in a 'd'. *'Is to be'* can go back to *'was'*; *'fails'* becomes *'failed'*. It is exhilarating to be able to be so cavalier with time itself. Peter and Trisha can just pass on the stairs, rashly but not fatally, no souls need jump, they may not even need a mention. Life can proceed within its normal limits, without acknowledgement of the existence of the soul. Peter can simply collect the mattress-cover, pay off Trisha, and go home and finish making the couscous.

Or there could be a disturbance down below. Mrs Kovac, finally driven mad by the carbon tetrachloride fumes, could use Mr Kovac's gun upon him, finding him to be unfaithful. Trisha and Peter could get caught up in an ensuing siege. There could be a hostage situation. Peter's mother could have a lesbian relationship with Trisha. Anything. I could weave my own life even more into the text and not acknowledge it, thus saving inventive energy. The field is open just so long as I use the future tense, the '*is to be*' and not the '*was*'.

But I would be left with the feeling of guilt implanted all those years ago by Louis Simpson that there is a proper way of writing a novel, which is to do with recognising the inevitable as it forms in front of you, while not nailing it down too firmly in advance. You will get it wrong if you try. The narrative of the novel is destined, a remedy for the randomness of real life, but hidden – you are Moses on the mountain searching for instructions on tablets of stone, Mohammed in the desert listening out for revelation. To use the '*is to be*' future construction, or the '*is to have been*' future-perfect, is a kind of blasphemy against the gods of fiction. And dangerous. Adrienne to have a lesbian relationship with Trisha? Off the rails entirely.

That GSWITS I was talking about earlier – the Great Screenwriter in the Sky, the one who destroys twin towers as in *The Lord of the Rings*, assassinates Kennedy from a grassy knoll, gets out of a bad plot by sinking the *Titanic* or destroying Pompeii, might do it, of course. His worshippers – of whom I am one – are required to overlook the fact that he is not so hot as a writer – pretty crude, in fact, a B-movie man – and play the part assigned to them with a positive and cheerful disposition. (I, having been assigned *Mantrapped* – a good piece of typecasting, mind you – played

108

the part with gusto. For that I will get credit when the final crits are written.) The whole problem with autobiography is that you know the plot in advance. You are trying to wrest real life into narrative, obliged by 'truth, reality' to stick to the synopsis.

Most writers worth their salt loathe writing synopses for novels, TV series, feature films, anything fictional. Management and marketing insist they do it – it's they who have to fork out the money, after all – and the reluctance is not rational – writers would like to oblige – just very strong. To know in advance, to nail characters and events in place while they are still changing and growing, to wrest the fictional world into shape before it exists, feels like blasphemy. Some even prefer to write the whole work in full and only then offer the synopsis. The dull feeling of *'wrong'* remains.

But all the things which could have happened did; to see the text at proof stage is to believe it. Doralee sent Peter round to fetch the laundry. Mrs Kovac kept the shop open late, Peter and Trisha crossed on the stairs, their souls switched and Doralee waited in vain for Peter to come home that evening.

Opening salvos in a marriage, that is to say, my own

Wilkins Parade in *Mantrapped* is suffering a sea change, just as Primrose Hill did in the Sixties, but then there was no sense of threat in the air, no Twin Towers to fall, no great sense of dispossession or displacement. The bourgeoisie still waited to be *epatée*. Kleene Machine was once called, boringly, the Acme Laundry. But that was when shops were named for simple ease of reference, not for added positive perception. When the Sixties were young and just beginning to be gay (*'Tis gay,'* was chalked up on many a North London street sign, and we puzzled over it; 'gay' still meant 'merry and bright' and was not yet an official gender description) the general feeling was that if there were change why then that was to the good. There was a buzz of expectation in the air, full employment, no yellow lines on the roads, and always a parking place. Or was it perhaps that one was young?

For women, bird's-nest, tortured hair and startled eyes were giving way to caftans, flowing hair and a more natural look: the idea was to seem as if one had just fallen dishevelled out of bed after a lively night; the concept of Europe was not known in the land; there was just abroad and home. We lived in a tall, pretty house in Primrose Hill. It was a time of change and flux in Chalcot Crescent, as it is now in the fictional Wilkins Parade. The immigrant Irish were being driven out and replaced by bohemians – artists, writers, painters, musicians. Houses which had once contained three or four families now housed one or two.

Look out of the window of our Chalcot Crescent house, in the Sixties, and see Primrose Hill, green and pretty, rising steeply from the flat lands around, skirted by railway lines, with its view across inner London to St Paul's. The world of *Down Among the Women* centred here, this demi-paradise. You could hear the lions in London Zoo roaring at night. We could afford to be trusting; we kept the front door key on a string the house side of the letter box. In summer we didn't even bother to close the front door, let alone lock it. When someone nipped in and stole the radio sitting on the hall stand we were most surprised and upset. We had a local fishmonger, cobbler, grocer and hardware shop. We heated the house with anthracite stoves, dusty and fumy. The coal merchant tipped his sackfuls of anthracite into the coal hole in the pavement in front of the house, and I'd carry it up in bucketfuls. In theory the men did it – in practice it was usually the women. Those were good days.

In September 1961 I met Ron Weldon at a party and moved in with him, becoming a householder, and leaving behind for ever, or so I hoped, the poverty and anxiety of being a single mother. Ron was still married to Cynthia Pell, also a painter, but she was no longer with him. His daughter Karen, then aged thirteen, was. I was still legally married to a man much older than myself, a headmaster, who as a result of his own sexual hang-ups had encouraged me to a life of what would then have been called sin, and is now more properly called dysfunctional behaviour. (I notice that Mrs Kovac was a call girl before taking a course and setting up her own small business.) I was no longer with the husband, but living in a fifth-floor walk-up flat in Earls Court with my mother and my son Nicolas, visited by the Dane. I fell out of love with the Dane and into love with Ron. In those days love was such a simple sufficient imperative. You went where it led you.

It took Ron and me two years to get our divorces, and we married in June, 1963 in Camden Town Registry Office – Hetta and William (*Seven Types of Ambiguity*) Empson were our witnesses. (He was to become 'Sir', she was to become 'Lady' – as surprising and welcome an event as when Beryl Bainbridge was to become 'Dame'. Hang around long enough, and anything can happen.) In 1994 I was to marry again in the same place, also in June. (This 'was to' is legitimate. This is autobiography.) On both occasions we had a Chinese meal afterwards. The first time I couldn't manage the chopsticks and was humiliated to have to ask for a fork. The second time I didn't have to ask. Some things you pick up without really trying.

The wedding was a mere formalisation of a relationship that we both assumed was to be life long. I should not really speak for Ron because he died the day our divorce came through in 1994, but I think it to be the case for him and I know it was for me. So fast and sudden, indeed overnight, was the switch in both our lives, after that initial meeting in 1961, so complete and satisfactory the apotheosis from wretchedness to happiness, certainly for me, probably for him, that I assumed fate had a hand in it. All this, though a long time coming, was simply destined. It was a miracle.

When in those early years, by virtue of the fact that I had plays and novels published, could speak in public, sat on committees when asked, and looked okay in photographs, others offered me a degree of admiration and respect, I assumed this too was fate. I must have been very irritating to others. And I was wrong, and a very hard lesson it was. It was happenstance.

Once in bed with Ron there seemed during that decade no reason ever to be out of it, other than what duties the children required and the necessity of earning a living. And of course parties. We were both sociable people, and liked to offer and receive hospitality, so one way and another a noisy and much-peopled household created itself around us. As child succeeded child – Dan, Tom and Sam following on from Karen and Nicolas – and the visiting nephews and nieces, Christopher, Rachel and Ben, the family developed its own traditions and habits of living. But the central premise, as it were, was the marital bed, which was antique, brass, curly, high and wide.

When we married Ron put down his paintbrush and said, 'A man cannot be an artist and a good husband.' I did my best to refute his conviction: I was flattered but I did not want to be responsible for what might come to be seen as a sacrifice. I quoted Rembrandt, Rubens, etc, but he retaliated with Van Gogh, Gauguin and a dozen others and won on points.

After Daniel was born Ron opened an antique shop round the corner from the house in Regent's Park Road. The shop was to become more of a social centre than a serious empo-rium. Here Ron kept open house during shop hours, and partied with his customers. What was sold as junk then are the antique treasures of today. Welsh dressers, ships' mast-heads, Jacobean chests, Georgian commodes, copper saucepans, Dutch tiles, Venetian chandeliers. The week he opened the shop he cleared a truss factory, its contents untouched since 1926. I washed tray after tray of dusty glass eyes. Big, blue veined ones, little, dark piggy ones. They were snapped up and turned into earrings.

The treasure trove from Ron's shop sits well in the houses of those who have grown great and famous over the years; George Melly, David Bailey, Jonathan Miller, Alan Bennett. '*Look,*' people still say to me today, '*that's one of Ron's dressers. It's still missing one brass handle.*' Or, '*That's a Ron clock. It never worked.*' Or, '*you know what I was offered for these six chairs the other day! To think I bought them for ten shillings!*'

Ron preferred potential to fulfilment, but then a painter often does, the vision in the head always outstripping what ends up on the canvas. He kept his respect and reverence for what time had imbued with grace, what some craftsman, long ago, had taken pride in making. His talent was to hypnotise customers into believing, with him, that they had got the most amazing bargain, the most beautiful object in all history, and that it looked better unfixed, unrestored, unfacelifted, than ever it would done up. All things new he despised, except our new golden Volvo Estate, the antique dealer's friend, for which he made an exception. We bought that when I was promoted to Copy Group Head at Ogilvie and Mather.

The morning sun shone into Chalcot Crescent, the music of the Sixties came from every radio down the street. The pleasure of it came to me as a shock. I'd had a patchy acquaintance with music to date, loaded by others' disapproval, brought up as a child with the music of the nineteenth century – anything later was seen as vulgar. My grandmother, trained as a concert pianist, played Beethoven and Chopin, and I loved the former for its energy and hated the latter for what seemed to me as a child to be clinky self-pity. Otherwise there was popular music imported from the States by New Zealand radio, but I was discouraged from listening. No-one forbade me: my mother would just switch the radio off for fear my taste would be debased. 'Swing', 'jazz' were as bad as swear words. But my mother owned a wind-up gramophone – someone's cast-off no doubt – and a single record, *The Wedding of the Painted Doll,* which when I was eight I would play over and over with a thorn needle at the bottom of the garden. *Dum-de-dum-de-dum, de dum, de dum* – presages, in my pre-pubertal state, of some frivolity yet to come. I got through the whole box of thorn needles, and my secret thus revealed, was frowned upon.

My father, divorced from the mother in the days when divorce was a rare thing, lived in comparative splendour in Coromandel in the North, and owned a library of 78's, and had steel needles, and Mozart was eked out in three minute dollops before some one had to get up and turn the record over. But listening to my father's music seemed a disloyalty to my mother, and I preferred to wander off into the garden and eat apricots.

In the Fifties, free at last from maternal control, I listened to the radio non stop, when my schoolmaster husband was out to work – he was a light opera fan and was musical director of the local operatic group in Acton, and I remember dancing round the kitchen with Nicolas, then a very small child, to Doris Day singing *Que Sera, Sera*, in a state of exhilaration, because sometimes a sense of future blessing, an intimation of better things to come, would descend upon the grimness of life in Acton.

Perhaps I caught something of this sense of future from Nicolas himself – because by the Sixties, living in Chalcot Crescent, it was he who took up his guitar and played his new family folk music, Bob Dylan, Leonard Cohen, and took to the piano as naturally and easily as his grandmother. Indeed, he gave up the study of philosophy, at which he excelled, for the piano, and now plays at Ronnie Scott's and suchlike. The other day a taxi driver said to me you're not a relative of Nic Weldon the pianist, are you, and I said yes and he offered to let me off my fare.

Nicolas reports that in his teenage he would get up before everyone was awake to practise the piano only to find me already up, writing on the floor, crouched in front of the Pither stove (before central heating) and as he played would be disconcerted to hear me apparently talking to myself non-stop, but actually just reading scripts aloud. He thinks it was in this way that he developed the narrative sense that all good musicians and composers must have.

That always seemed to me one of the qualities that contemporary music has lost – the sense of narrative, of developing and changing mood, until the piece, be it music, art, or literature, comes to its proper conclusion. Twenty years later, in the Somerset years, Ron too was to return to the trumpet, and to play New Orleans jazz in the West Country pubs, and the story of the band's trip abroad is there to be read, more or less, in the novel *Leader of the Band*. Starlady Sandra, mantrapped by the sax player, leaves her lawyer husband and runs off to France with the leader of the band.

It was a miserable trip, as it happened, and I couldn't think why. But Ron was already in love with the trumpet player's wife, who knew better than me how to tap her foot to the off beat, and who wanted to be a painter, and had no qualms about jazz and its significance or lack of it, though he didn't tell me at the time.

But way back then, in the Sixties, while the good music flowed, I think I was pretty much what Ron wanted, and he me, and we both thought fate had brought us together and between us we could, and would, solve all problems.

All was not simple, of course. Happiness was not unalloyed. Stepchildren were rarer in those days than now: there were few precedents to go by. I was astonished to discover that Karen, then thirteen, resented me. That she would had not occurred to me. But how could she not? I was a newcomer, an upstart. She loved her mother Barbara, Ron's first wife, and she loved his second wife too, Cynthia, but I was a step-mother too far. Cynthia had left in the months before Ron took up with me. The first marriage to Barbara had been brief and impetuous, when he was an art student. The second marriage to Cynthia, a painter too, had been disastrous.

When I arrived, as the third, Karen was living with her mother Barbara and visiting her father at weekends. Cynthia's clothes still hung in the cupboards when I moved in, her plates still stacked the kitchen shelves, her tubes of paint – her cerulean blue, her titanium white – still stood in jars of dried-up turpentine upon the shelf, and Karen mourned her going. Now I had ruthlessly taken Cynthia's place, moved into her very bed and founded a dynasty around it.

I was accustomed to being liked – disapproved of perhaps for the messiness of my ways, both practical and emotional, disconcerting in my inability to conform to the mores of the times – but liked. Forty years on Karen and I get on just fine, indeed with much mutual affection, but it was a long hard road. It took me decades to learn the secret of living peacefully with stepchildren – you must treat them as if they were royalty, and only speak when spoken to. Smile amiably, and try not to catch their eye or draw attention to yourself, and all will be well or at least better.

Cynthia Pell, my predecessor in Ron's affections, was a painter who now enjoys a posthumous reputation. She was a beautiful, full-bodied, full-lipped girl with dark hair and red cheeks, who had gone completely out of her mind. She was a friend of Sheila Fell, Lowry's protégée, another painter of astonishing talent and beauty whose work is much valued. Pell and Fell, Fell and Pell. Pell painted women in distress, Fell painted landscapes. Both women enjoyed to the full the gifts and pleasures of self-destruction. Cynthia took to the knife and Sheila to the bottle. If I diminish them for the sake of a neat phrase I am sorry, but I know no other way of containing them and their troubles in my head. They were both appallingly self-indulgent and destructive but the times gave them no choice. It was as if, in the Fifties, when their work was mostly done, the talent and impulse to paint and the problem of being female formed some kind of corrosive mixture which scoured their insides out and left them raw and bleeding with rage and misery.

Fell, Pell and Plath. Sylvia Plath was the poetic equivalent, vociferous in her distress. I see all these self-destroyers of the Former Age as sacrificial martyrs to the New Feminism. The artists lead the way. This life is *impossible*. Cynthia's scratchy, tormented drawings and haunted paintings are so powerful I can scarcely look at them without wanting to throw open the windows and let the sunlight in. Sheila's landscapes, very different, have a swirling intensity, a lushness about them, but also an anxiety, as if every brush stroke was won with difficulty, and earth and rock were for ever on the verge of flying apart from one another. Evelyn Williams, their contemporary, was another beautiful girl, whose work is now highly sought after, and is hung in the Metropolitan and the Tate. She was not self-destructive, on the contrary; she worked patiently through the decades, with very little acknowledgement until recently, when it has come flooding in. But she had to wait until her seventies to receive it. And her work too is so imbued with tragedy that it can only really be viewed dispassionately from the walls of a great gallery. Get too near and you feel you will never smile again. Yet sometimes when Evie does something cheerful – a child's face or a rising sun – the sense of pleasure left behind is so intense it lingers long after you have left the gallery.

But Cynthia! After leaving the house she shared with Ron, Cynthia lived in a mental hospital for fifteen years, restrained for her own and others' safety, before destroying herself, horribly and graphically, cutting her own throat. I wrote a story about her once, called *In a Dustbin, Darkly*. She lived for a time in real life, and in the story, in a dustbin down an alleyway at the end of the street, while I chirruped gaily about the house, and pretended she did not exist. Ron seldom referred to her. I think he simply did not know what to do about her, either, or how to think of her. This is the problem with the truly mad – their terms of reference and yours do not coincide.

If I am to speak for Ron, Cynthia was perhaps the central tragedy in his life, the person and major life-event around which all other things circled. I was only the bit part player in Ron and Cynthia's life, not Cynthia's in mine. I was deluded in thinking otherwise. The clothes of mine I hung in her wardrobe as I elbowed her out of my life, pushing her waisted jacket with the fur collar (did not Trisha wear something like that?) to the back, could not have brought good karma.

Cynthia turned up in the house once and threw Dan, then a baby, across the room. She snatched him out of his crib and threw. I was shocked and alarmed, but she had at least thrown him onto the sofa. She did not wish him real harm. All the same it seemed some terrible visitation: Mrs Rochester from the attic had erupted into my life. There was a terrible and convincing simplicity with which she accused me of being an insensitive woman and an unfit wife.
'You have stopped Ron painting,' she cried aloud. 'What has he done! Marrying a woman like you! An office worker!' She threw a few shoes about and left.

119

Ron said she would not come again, nor did she. Did he visit her? Sleep with her? I don't know. It became evident to me that 'being a painter' carried far more weight with Ron and his friends than 'being a writer' ever did for me. Writing was something you did, not something you were. The true artist, in the eyes of those talented young people who came out of the Slade, St Martins, Camberwell, in the Forties and Fifties, was bound to be like Van Gogh, mad, bad and tormented. Whereas writing, I would maintain, smiling blandly the while, was if anything restorative; it had a gentle tonic effect. I wrote a story under that name, too, *A Gentle Tonic Effect*, about a young woman who worked for a nuclear power plant, and whose job it was to maintain that radiation was not harmful at all, but gently beneficial.

The more I suspected myself that what I wrote might be explosive, the more I maintained its harmlessness. I think I was quite wilfully disingenuous. I was known in the beginning to his friends as Ron's port and lemon girl: the amiable barmaid type, the provider of money, the washer of dishes. I did not like to disappoint.

Poor Cynthia, in retrospect! It had been her home, her bed, her cupboards to clean and her stepdaughter, not mine, to care for.

But what real attention did I give her? None. I would drink my morning coffee, made sinfully and wastefully strong – now I was out from under my mother's eye I had a taste for excess – from the little brown coffee cups Cynthia's mother had made as her wedding gift to that happy couple. The Pells were wealthy; Cynthia's mother was artistic and able to afford a kiln. I relished the sense of victory. In the

Fifties women were in competition: we had little sense of sisterhood.

So I moved the clothes from her closet, and was glad when Ron took down the painting rack in which both their paintings sat, gathering dust. Friends said – though they seldom mentioned her in my presence – that she painted better than he did. He painted on the backs of her canvases for a while and then gave up altogether.

I wrote a story last year, *A Knife for Cutting Mangos*, about a second wife going through the belongings of the previous one, who ran away, and scorning what she found. Until I wrote the previous paragraph I had not realised to what degree I wrote from experience, and out of guilt. Writing is not in the least therapeutic, but it is how you may perhaps earn the remission of sins, if acknowledging sin is to be excused from it. In writing about an unnatural event, such as the swapping of bodies, I deny myself access to my own past. Notice how the story of Trisha, Doralee and Peter is slowing up? I fear the aridness of having nothing to relate, the desert of non-experience. I will do what I can. I read in the newspapers how ambitious women are taking testosterone to make themselves as bullish as men. Perhaps I should try, the better to know what Trisha feels like when she is Peter.

Writers write about what they once felt and did, painters paint what they see now.

When, twenty years into our marriage, Ron started painting again I would buy him canvases and lug them back on the train from London to Somerset. (We moved out of London in 1975, after various domestic and amatory upsets.) He would thank me politely but did not use them. Artists should

121

stretch their own canvases, not take shortcuts. But he was not good at it: it took more patience than he had, and paintings would crack and peel even as he sold them. And he liked to do flower paintings, but where do you find flowers in the winter? I would buy them from the florist at Harrods and take them home and shove them in a vase and let them fall where they would – I was never sure whether an artist was meant to arrange a composition or take chance as it came and paint what you happened to see: I understand now that the answer is that you do a bit of both.

I was like Madame Bovary: trying to bribe my way into a man's affection with little gifts. I adapted the novel into a stage play only recently: it played to full houses and audiences who got to their feet and clapped, and to terrible reviews. I had altered the story. The critics hated it. The trouble was I knew the woman better than did Flaubert, and I knew the husband too, and the lovers, and what makes you spend too much, why you end up paying for your boyfriend to go on holiday with his wife, 'to make it up'. Forget Flaubert's '*Madame Bovary? C'est moi!*' – c'était moi.

Ron would look at the flowers and their giver with suspicion – as Rodolphe looks at Emma Bovary; where was I coming from? But he would take both canvas and flowers up to his studio and come out weeks later with a painting that brought life and colour to the walls. And I found that he was right. The Van Gogh model was the true one, not the Rembrandt one of my hopes. You could not be an artist and a good husband too. He struggled for recognition and loathed publicity. I had no trouble getting the first, and would talk to a journalist as to my best friend. It was not a recipe for happiness.

I found one of Cynthia's mother's saucers only the other day. It was the only one left of the initial set, used over decades for a pot plant, dark brown and shiny, encrusted with a little circle of built-up lime. It and the pot plant had travelled with me from house to house and marriage to marriage. It brought back strongly the memory of the morning after Ron and I met in bed, breakfasting at the table in Chalcot Crescent, languid-limbed, the cup small but heavy in my hand, the sun shining into the windows and the green city hill just outside, Vivaldi on the gramophone, cream curling into black coffee, and the sense that I was home, finally. As I say, poor Cynthia, poor lost sister.

But how can anyone cut their own throat? What does it take? It does not bear thinking about, and I think about it as little as I can, and envisage it likewise. But it's there. It's in Evie's work, and mine too.

My sister Jane, who wrote poetry, had the same hot line to the appalling infinite as Pell, Fell and Plath, though she did not have the same sense of drama as the other two, and was fortunate enough to have my mother to remind her of the realities of her children. What my sister had was a notion that there was something out there, just beyond vision, which had to be reached no matter what. Trying to grasp it rendered a woman desperate and emotionally fragile. Before people talked so much about 'creativity' as something to be desired, before the jargon of contemporary psychotherapy came so easily to our lips, and we learned to account for ourselves in terms of self-realisation and the need for self-expression, we were left with the vague and painful mystery of ourselves. We had no language for what was wrong. What drives the artist is an urge as powerful as sex and if denied, if the times are against her, if she doesn't find the words, doesn't find her audience, looks inside and find only muddle and misery, why, it's enough to send a woman mad.

It's all swings and roundabouts, as ever. 'Art' for both women and men is less likely these days to drive you insane, but our connection to the source of inspiration is weakened and infantilised by the very self-understanding and self-preoccupation which saves us. Self-consciousness is a sickly thing, saps our strength. Post-modernism, with its *look at me, look at me, see what I've done, guess what I'm going to do next*, has all but destroyed us. The art of our civilisation is not what it was; our songs, books, poetry, paintings, architecture, music, are shadows of what they were. But we don't go mad, we don't end, like Cynthia, in the dustbin. Human sacrifice is rare.

Wedged between Cynthia, the mad ex-wife in the attic and my distracted sister Jane, I was left with the sense of being a dull but very sane person. I was Doralee more than I was Trisha, or hoped to be, more given to the boring foam rubber than the soiled but lively mattress. In Doralee mode I will organise the dry-cleaning and send someone round to get it if it doesn't turn up on the step. Once women ran the errands, now the men do. But I would never decide I want it now, now, now, just to annoy. That is Doralee's temperament, not mine.

Consequences. The past catches up

Trisha hears the steel shutters beginning to descend, then stopping as Mrs Kovac changes her mind about closing

124

up. Trisha has had a hard day: she is emotionally fraught. She has sold up her life in exchange for not enough money. Her eyes are not as good as once they were. She needs a magnifying glass to thread the needle. She feels unjustifiably angry with Mrs Kovac because of it. Soon she will have to get herself some reading glasses: it is the beginning of the end, of the long crumble into old age. What has she come to? When she looks out of the window at Wilkins Parade she can see it is not the posh area she thought it was. Starbucks has a piece of cardboard stuck over a broken window. A stone, or was it done by a bullet? The TV reception is so bad she can hardly get a picture. Mrs Kovac failed to point this out. The stairs, which looked so cute, smell of pee. Cell phone coverage is patchy. She has to stand near the window if she wants to make a call. She can only afford pay-as-you-go. She applied for an account but her application was rejected without explanation. Her credit rating must be minus zero. How has she come to this? Next thing she knows Mrs Kovac is calling up the stairs as if she, Trisha, were some sort of servant. Just because she does the occasional bit of sewing. This arrangement is simply not going to work. Mrs Kovac is in a bad mood.

'Trisha! Bring that cover down right now, will you. I don't suppose you've finished it?'

Too bloody right I haven't, thinks Trisha. What am I, a slave? What did your last one die of?

Trisha pushes open the door to the stairs. She has to ease a half-unpacked box out of the way to get it open. The room is full of cardboard boxes and bin bags: she can hardly get to the cooker to make a cup of tea. Where is she going to put everything? Bin bags are depressing by their very nature, colour, texture. They resemble nothing in the growing, living world. 'I didn't quite catch that,' Trisha calls down to Mrs Kovac, though she can hear well enough.

'Some stupid idiot's coming round to collect the mattress-cover,' shrieks the other. 'I need it down here straight away.'

Trisha goes back into the flat, and finds the mattress-cover. She has already levered off five of the melted buttons and replaced them with new cheap but metal ones; there are five to go. She takes her time. She hears altercations from below. Fury boils up in her. She starts down the stairs and meets Peter on the way up. She thinks he is rather attractive but she doesn't have time for that kind of nonsense any more, and anyway she wants to give Mrs Kovac a piece of her mind. By the time she gets to the bottom of the stairs she is feeling faint.

Trisha sits down on the bottom stair. What is the matter with her? She is staring at a man's shoe. It is on the end of her leg. How did that get there? She can see things very clearly, sharply defined. Her eyes seem to be wider open than normal. She feels different but cannot quite make out how. She has dropped the mattress-cover on to the stairs. It looks ordinary and everyday, a piece of linen fabric of the kind that never folds completely flat and is a nuisance to have around, but nothing remarkable. What a stupid thing, what a stupid piece of fabric, to be the source of such a fuss. The smell of urine is strong, too strong for comfort. She should not be sitting on these filthy stairs. She stands up. The man's shoe is still on the end of her foot. It is a good, expensive shoe. She bends to do up the lace which after the manner of thin, round, expensive laces tends to undo itself. Those are not her hands either: hers are soft and white and tender: these are knobbly and brown and have hairy patches on the knuckles. They couldn't thread a needle. The hands could bring pleasure, she can see that, but they are not hers. So whose hands are they? The fingers move up to touch her chin. She can't stop them. Curiosity seems part of her. The skin she feels is firm but prickly. A young male chin, recently shaved, but now reasserting a beard. Her crotch feels unfamiliar. She feels for it. It's bumpy, something bulky beneath fabric. She snatches the hand away: she is being indelicate. It comes to her that she is a man. The mind is having to work overtime, really hard, to make sense of the signals it is receiving, and as soon as it receives them it rejects them. She shuts her eyes. So long as she does not see she is a man she need not be a man.

In the good days Rollo once took Trisha and Spencer to see a crop circle. There were four circles of squashed corn in the corner of a flourishing field of grain, arranged in a rectangle. One of the branches of the tree above was torn and damaged. Oh yes, she thought without surprise at the time, that's obvious, a flying saucer has landed here. That's what the four engines would do to when they landed, flattening the grain beneath. The broken bit of branch is where it took off again. Only then did she remember there was no such thing as a flying saucer. The mind likes to make sense of what it sees, or else alarm ensues. Wake in the night when there's a bump on the bed: fall asleep as soon as you've told yourself it was only the cat. You don't get up to check. The mind will take risks, but only so many. Two bumps and only one cat, and you're out there with the poker, flailing.

Two male shoes on the end of her feet, and she knows she is a man. But out of whose eyes is she looking? She needs a mirror.

She sees that the other woman now standing at the top of the stairs is perplexed and pale, looking down at her. She has curly, reddish hair, rather inexpertly hennaed. Why so pale? Is she ill? She looks familiar. She could have sworn it was a man who passed her on the stairs, rather young and fanciable. What is going on? Is this an out-of-body experience? Is she dying? The woman on the top of the stairs topples and falls. She has fainted. Her mouth is open. It looks ugly, but at least she has white fillings not the old black kind. When Trisha won the lottery and had money to burn she had all the mercury fillings taken out. All the same, the woman wearing her clothes would look better if she shut her mouth. She badly needs a face-lift, too. Her chin flops into her neck. Trisha goes to the woman's aid but, leaping up the stairs, finds balancing difficult. Her body is weighted wrongly. And why is she wearing chinos? Why are her hands so large? They are definitely not hers. She would have plucked those dark hairs out one by one.

Mrs Kovac calls up the stairs.
'Trisha? He's coming up. I couldn't stop the bastard. Don't give that bloody cover back if he doesn't pay up. I wouldn't put it past him. Twenty-seven pounds seventy-five, or it comes off your wages.'

Hang on a moment, thinks Trisha. Mrs Kovac's charging him twenty-seven pounds seventy-five? Cleaning would be seven pounds seventy-five, okay, but that leaves twenty for the buttons. She pays me two quid. That's just not on. And anyway, Trisha thinks, I won the *lottery*. I cannot be spoken to in this way by this woman.'

Trisha finds her voice.
'Oh shut up you old bag,' she shouts, and the voice from

128

her mouth is deep and powerful. She rather likes it.

The girl who looks like an older version of herself opens her eyes, looks up, and passes out again. Trisha drags her into the flat by her familiar shoes and shuts the door behind her, looks in the mirror without more ado and discovers that she is indeed a man.

Doralee waits

The olive oil in the bottom of the pan grows cold. The couscous, partly cooked, swells and grows stodgy. It will be inedible. A whole hour passes. Peter does not return. Doralee finds a box of chocolates and eats the lot. She feels nervous. It is a long time since Doralee waited like this for a man. On the whole men wait for Doralee. She blames Peter for taking such a long time and driving her to chocolate. It was absurd. She did not want it, did not like it, was not hungry. It was not even organic. It will give her spots and make her fat. Really she should not have chocolates in the house at all. Something like this always happened. Someone bought them for Peter for his last birthday: they would not have had the courage to offer them to Doralee. She would regard it as an attack. One of Doralee's few fears is that she will take after her mother, who was a reasonable size until she had Doralee and then never managed to lose the weight again, if she was ever trying, and just put on more and more and more. Size 22. It is inconceivable. An embarrassment.
'But at least it means she won't get married again,' says Peter.

No one wants mothers to remarry. Besides being rather a

disgusting idea it complicates matters of inheritance. The court gave Ruby the house when Graham ran off with his yoga teacher, as was only reasonable. It is a very pleasant old house, in its own grounds, which was once a rectory. The church next door is not the quaint heritage site it used to be, being topped with a mobile phone aerial, and having had its pews removed, and the bongo drums and the chanting make it a noisy place on a Sunday morning – which is not good for property prices – but the rectory is still worth at least half a million. She can't expect much, of course, since there are six siblings, but she has friends whose mothers have remarried, and the new husband tends to end up with everything if anything dreadful happens. Ruby's layer of insulating fat at least protects her family from this kind of complication. If Ruby ends up in a nursing home and the house has to be sold to pay the fees, and all the money gets used up before the government steps in to pay, so be it. That's life. But the weight Ruby carries at least isn't going to increase her chances of longevity: there may be some inheritance left for the children. Doralee doesn't like thinking in this way about her own mother but you have to be realistic. It is really difficult to save.

Peter's mother Adrienne is thin as a rake and always looks good in little suits and scarves, but has no suitors, which is a relief to her family. She keeps her eyes lowered and does not lift them to meet the eyes of men, other than to stare them out at business meetings, asserting her dominance in decision-making. All her erotic energy and softness got used up in her early twenties when she married Peter's father. When he died there was not much left for anyone else, even the boys. Adrienne had a hysterectomy after a cancer scare and the doctors will not give her hormones and her skin is dry but at least she is thin and wears her clothes well. Adrienne has a lot to be proud of, and was well provided for by her husband's insurance, but that dies when she does. All the more reason for Peter to save.

And where is Peter? Doralee feels sick. It is probably the chocolates. Most were marzipan. She does not like marzipan. Why then did she eat them? She does not understand herself. She hopes she is not pregnant, and catching herself hoping it, feels mean. Peter wants a child, her mother wants a grandchild, so does Adrienne, on balance. Doralee had imagined not getting married would save her from this kind of family pressure, but it hasn't. Another person growing and growing inside her and then bursting out of her? It is an appalling idea, yet how calmly others take it, as if it was the most normal thing in the world. But it isn't, it's primitive and bizarre. Just because it happens in nature doesn't make it right. She is not an animal. It will damage her body and lower her income. She doubts that they can do key-hole caesareans: if she is pregnant she will be left with a scar. It is not pain that frightens her, pain is in the head and leaves no marks, but knives cut flesh. Ruby had a caesarean with the twins, and her wrinkled, stretched, scarred, fat and muscle-less stomach is still a horror. Doralee thinks she will have to go to the bathroom and make herself throw up. But her throat and stomach seem to have gone into a state of stasis. Tickle as much as you like and nothing happens. She coughs and retches but no product is delivered. She weeps.

Tomorrow she must go to Heather's baby shower after work and pretend to envy her. Though already Heather, at seven months, has grown sleepy and vague and vast, and there is nothing whatsoever to envy her for. Heather is indecently proud of the way the baby's movements can be seen under her dress; Doralee thinks the foetus would be better sedated but has too much sense to say so. You are meant to admire insensate growth, for some reason. The blind searching movements remind her of what Peter's penis does sometimes in his sleep at night when he turns towards her and embraces her.

She will wear the black dress with the thin shoulder straps – it rolls up into almost nothing and can be just shaken out and slipped on in a second: she hates the way her colleagues try to party themselves up in the toilets by just putting on a necklace, slapping on more mascara over old and hoping for the best. If Peter manages to get the dress back from the bitch at the dry-cleaners. There seem to be more and more people like that around – rude, unhelpful and offi-cious, with no idea of service, let alone making a profit. The rules of the game more important than the game. Perhaps there was an article in that?

Perhaps she should take over the couscous, but it needs to be made fresh. Leave it to keep warm and it goes to stodge: it ought to come from the pan fluffy and white, the tiny grains separated. Ruby won't have the stuff in the house, saying you can do anything you need by way of carbohy-drate with old cold potatoes. (This is no doubt why Peter and Doralee eat couscous so often.) But she's hungry. She no longer feels pregnant. It will be all right: she can continue to be the heroine of her own life, not share the position with some brat.

She slips down one of her mother's birth-control pills to be on the safe side. She found a store of them, years old, in the third bathroom of the Rectory, the one no one uses because of the old wasps' nest, and stole them. It's like drinking tap-water, a gesture, an act of defiance, nothing more, to show she's her own mistress: of course a glass of water here, a pill there, won't make any real difference. She's just giving fate a little nudge, to make it work for her rather than against her. If she goes on not getting pregnant she and Peter will have to go to the fertility clinic and really concentrate: that will be the time to take the plunge. Peter should have hurried home or at least called her on her mobile. Men are unreliable, even Peter, always led astray by impulse. How they ever win wars she cannot imagine. They'd be leading a bayonet charge and then come across a fossil on a rock and everything would have to stop while they investigated. What does she need a man for anyway? It's just that that blind, stirring, questing, pursuing, sticking-up horrible phallic thing seems to be not just its own imperative, but hers as well.

Gynaecological dreams

Doralee had an abortion once, I write spitefully, telling tales out of school. She was sixteen, and Ruby took her to the doctor who sent her to the hospital where she had a procedure done and was home that afternoon. They did not mention it to the boyfriend, Ken, who was seventeen. He had started work as trainee electrician, there being no low-paid apprenticeships any more, so he earned more than most boys his age still in school. He had a car, which appealed to Doralee. Ruby would rather her daughter had taken up with a medical student or someone with a more ambitious background, but she had always encouraged her children to believe with Jesus that all men were equal, so she could hardly complain. At the same time she did not want her daughter to marry an electrician.

She was relieved when Doralee took up with Peter, who though hardly the county set was at least well-bred North London, the mother from a Jewish family which had apostatised. The county set themselves viewed Ruby and her children with some suspicion. She lived in a good house and was active in proper country pastimes, and a stalwart of the village fête, but she came from the North, and was too unpredictable in her ways to be considered one of them. Ruby did not particularly want to be one of them, but it is always more pleasant to be accepted than not, and for Doralee to have a baby at sixteen by an artisan apprentice would not have been good. Ken was to be a millionaire by the time he was twenty-five, of course, having gone into electrical contracting for the government, but that was not to be known in advance. Ruby took Doralee down to the clinic with reluctance – her worry, even then, was a scarcity of grandchildren. The more you educate girls, the more worldly ambition you inculcate in them, the more you teach them independence from men, the fewer children they have. And the more babies you have, the more you know what is lost when you refuse to let them come into the world. Still, she did it, for her daughter's sake.

Doralee had not told Peter about the early abortion, or termination, as everyone called it. She dreamt about it sometimes; herself lying in a white bed tied up with electrical cords while a welcome sea of blood, whose source was herself, flowed over her. It was a confusing dream, mixed pleasant and unpleasant, both horrible and a relief. Horrible that she should have it at all, that her unconscious, if such a thing there be, was not within her control; a relief because she always woke from the dream happy. It was like bulimia or cutting – making yourself sick or slitting your own skin, scarring yourself – fashions which would sometimes sweep over girls at school

134

as would an epidemic. Doralee had been prone to both in her time – messy and forbidden deeds which yet had to be done, asserting her rights over her own body. The termination had at least put an end to all that, for some reason.

Doralee took the pro-abortion line, the woman's right to choose, as everybody did she had ever met, from her teachers to her colleagues to her partner, but sometimes she resented her mother for making her go to the doctor. It was indeed the slaughter of the innocents, the land was awash with blood; if she'd had a baby then it would be fifteen by now, and a credit to her, and the trouble and fear of raising a child would be in the past, not in the future, and what's more she would probably be married to a millionaire instead of waiting to get some shitty dress back from the cleaners with a partner who couldn't even be bothered to get back to finish the cooking. *Where was he?*

She had told no one about the termination and hoped her mother had forgotten, and that it was so far back in her medical notes it would never be thought of again, but I know. Her writer knows.

A gynaecological history

Lord, what women will do to avoid such a history. All this fecundity and bleeding and womb-centrist behaviour! It's a thing of the past, thank God. I wrote a short story about it once, back in the early-Nineties, called *A Libation of Blood*. Those were the days, when a woman's love life was dictated by her physiology. No longer. You don't have period pains, you carry Nurofen. You don't have premen-strual symptoms, depression, anxiety and black violent rage – unless you're up for murder and the defence wants to enter it as a plea – you have counselling and decline to believe it emanates from you. That the pre-menstrual you is the real you, and the sweet syrupy non-menstrual you just an overlay to help you get and keep your man and keep your children cosy is not easy to accept. Then the real you is too like the cat that kills the bird for comfort, and so best not incorpo-rated into the scheme of things.

Surely, surely, thinks Doralee, in the last week of her hormonal cycle, my own cycle of self-assessment is nothing to do with the time of the month. High self-esteem three weeks of a monthly, moon-dictated cycle? Savage, vengeful, low self-esteem the last? How can it be? Just coincidence. The sanitary pad in the TV ads has wings and seems to fly elegantly through air.

Yet I'll swear that Doralee's basic self, what continues to link us to one another over decades, is not Heather's baby shower, not the baby moving beneath the skin, it is the dream of blood. I am no one to talk – having had an abortion once, between the third and fourth child, wedged between natural miscarriages. I think about the lost child – murdered and thrown away – from time to time, not too often. A girl, perhaps, an ally in a family overwhelmed by males? I will never know. There seemed no other option at the time, nor was there. You destroy another or are yourself destroyed. Nature's way. Cats kill birds, so don't keep a cat, or don't look. We love the cat, we stroke the cat, we feed the cat on anonymous chunks of boiled-up, all-purpose animal flesh from a can with a pretty kitten on it. I know someone who has a vegetarian dog but if you deprive cats they just go and live next door. And you don't want that.

What else could I do? Well? The year, 1971, high summer, pregnant, six months after the last birth, an immediate family of six largely dependent upon my earnings, the new baby due to be born on my sister's birthday, her death still new in my head, her three orphaned children also my responsibility – my mother as well now, she now in her sixties and having no income of her own? As Doralee would say, '*It just wouldn't have worked*.' Sixteen years earlier the first baby had brought its own strength, will, energy and faith with it. This, the fourth, brought doubt and panic. What now would become of me and mine? Ron had already run off once, albeit only temporarily – never one for any reality he found embarrassing, conveniently missing my sister's death and its attendant traumas – and a new baby might drive him away altogether. How was I to keep this family together? I lacked faith in the future. I was no longer convinced there was one rule for me – *everything will be all right in the end* – and another for the rest of creation. So off I went in the taxi to the abortion clinic – it was in Ealing, where I married my first husband, the eccentric schoolmaster. It was a seedy place, a converted suburban house in a genteel district. A stream of depressed girls and women came up its path, a kindly Asian businessman down from the North, bringing with him in his van a little group of eight veiled, terrified and disgraced girls. He paid a single cheque for all of them. How did they get to be in his van, what happened to them next? I will never know. Sometimes I think I write fiction only in order to ensure that I am kept informed as to what happens next.

Here in Ealing I got my certificate of legitimisation from the doctor (on the grounds, in those days, that if I didn't I risked

137

losing my wits altogether, which might have been true enough) and paid over my cheque for £500, and the inconvenient tissue was rooted out. I salute you, baby. I'm sorry. If the doctor hadn't told me you were likely to be born on February 19th, my dear deceased sister Jane's birthday, you might be alive today. I didn't want you to have her fate.

I describe the moment of decision – baby or not – in the short story *Subject to Diary*, set in just such a clinic, when the young career woman, who is complaining in reception that she can never find a window in her diary for giving birth, only for her terminations, is persuaded by the receptionist to just go home and find the window. There was no such person present in real life. The wicked abortionist featured in *The Hearts and Lives of Men*, a novel written in 1987, surfaced fifteen years later. This time his name is Dr Runcorn. Clifford the trendy art-dealer breaks into the abortion clinic and snatches his beloved Helen from the operating table, thus allowing her to give birth to my heroine little Nell. Now there's a fantasy: the damsel rescued! Yet I am so often accused of being mean to men: truly, even in real life they can be heroes.

And there was no discussion with Ron, let alone a daring rescue – other than that I told him I was pregnant, and he said 'You're not going to go through with it, are you!' and I replied to his unvoiced shock, horror and alarm, 'Probably not,' and he nodded. It was before the days when couples 'talked things through'. It was considered a fine thing to conduct a marriage in silence. Now it seems quite outrageous. The question 'Have you been unfaithful to me?' was seldom asked outright, or answered, if it was, by other than by a brief yes or no. Fisticuffs might break out, but not discussion.

Today's Doralee, faced by a termination, would talk the matter over with husband or partner for at least three hours. The decision would only be reached after obligatory counselling for both parties. Then the papers could be signed. It is assumed the father will be present, if not in the room – that's only for living births – at least within call. I do remember my self-pity, waiting for the lonely taxi home – it was not even mooted that I would be collected: Ealing was a long way and Ron had a shop to run – as I watched the girls being herded back into their van, those little silent veiled figures. They at least had each other, and the businessman had enough humanity to help them in tenderly, one by one, murderesses that we all were.

Still waiting

Peter's absence stirs up memories: ghost babies stir in the air. Doralee shivers a little and looks for her pashmina. She shuts the window to keep out the drifting scent of Indian sweetmeats bubbling in the vat. But this was once an orphanage, once a confectionery factory. Time cannot always be kept in its place. The present contains the past. Doralee takes microwave rice and stirs in chopped coriander and prawns and bungs it in the oven. She eats in front of the television, pashmina carefully arranged so she drops nothing on it. Celebrities emote on an island somewhere in a distant ocean. She pretends to despise such programmes but watches when she gets half a chance. Still no Peterloo. She does love him. If he wants a baby she will have one, of course she will. She's just been in a bad mood. She calls him on his mobile. But the thing rings and buzzes and groans on the draining board. He has forgotten to take it with him. He left his front-door key too. He expected to be back.

She calls Kleene Machine. She gets an answerphone. Closed until eight tomorrow morning. Then where is Peter with the cleaning? She feels bad. She didn't really need it in such a hurry. It was mean of her to want to put Heather's nose out of joint by looking terrific while Heather looks bad. It was mean of her to want the shop person to be punished for putting her, a professional woman, to inconvenience.

She nibbles a prawn and worries about Heaven Arkwright. Heaven Arkwright is Doralee's colleague, her career companion; they started a year ago on the same salary on the same day. Now she discovers that Heaven is getting paid two thousand a year more than she is. What a ridiculous name! Heaven is American and was once a cheerleader. She writes little pieces about face-lifts and lipstick, nothing serious, unlike Doralee, and snippets of gossip about celebrities. The freebies which come Doralee's way, though plentiful, are nothing to those that get left at the office for Heaven, or come through the post, in the shape of jars and sachets of face creams and perfumes, little gold slippers, handbags and so on. Heaven has the advantage of not being in a relationship and is happy to person the office on Christmas Day and bank holidays and focus on her work: she doesn't get cystitis – the blight of the sexually active – and is anorexic so doesn't have to worry about period pains or have some man feeding her couscous all the time, or rather failing to – but on the other hand it's hardly a well-rounded life Heaven leads and that's bad for the career in the long run.

'We are looking for well-rounded individuals' say the ads – by which they mean skinny people with big smiles. It's the balancing of all the different requirements that is so difficult. It's quite nice being at home without Peter – if you can stay off the chocolates and stick to the prawns, which are tough, being frozen not fresh, all she could find in the freezer. You just let your thoughts roam. You could end up quite a serious person if you were single. Not that Heaven comes over as all that serious.

She is beginning to get really worried. If Peter doesn't have his cell phone with him what's wrong with a telephone box? But are there telephone boxes any more? She hasn't seen one for ages, come to think of it. Everyone has cell phones. Surely he could borrow one. Or is there something sinister in his absence? He might have left her. Men do that sometimes – walk out of the home and disappear and leave some little fake pile of clothes on the beach so everyone thinks they have committed suicide.

But she's happy with Peter and he's happy with her or there wouldn't be so much sex. Surely? An accident? No, that is not the kind of thing that happens to her and Peter.

She looks out of the window to make sure there are no ambulances or police cars on the corner. There are not. She slips on a coat, all the same, and goes down in the elevator and through the lobby and into the street and looks around. Nothing untoward. She doesn't want to be out here on her own after dark. The muggers will be coming out soon for their drug money. But you mustn't think about that kind of thing or you'd never step out of your home at all and that would be absurd. Heather's mother was run over and killed by a police car answering a call but that was the other side of

London. A police car in this densely built up district would have trouble getting up speed enough to kill. She doesn't suppose Heaven had a mother. She leapt into the world fully formed and perfect, like Athena out of Zeus's head or has Doralee got that muddled? That is how she would like any child of hers to be born. 'If Peter comes back before me,' says Doralee to George the doorman, 'tell him he'll just have to wait. I've got the only key. I suppose you could let him in, but I'd rather you didn't. It won't do him any harm to wait around a bit. He really must remember always to take a key.'

She goes down to Kleene Machine but there is no sign of Peter and there are steel bars over the windows. There is a group of murky young men sauntering towards her so she does not stay for long. There is a light on in the window above, but that seems to have nothing to do with the shop. There is a dark green dirty side door firmly closed which looks as if it is rarely opened. She goes home.

'No sign of hubby?' asks George.

'He is my partner,' says Doralee. 'I don't believe in marriage.'

'I've had four wives,' says George. 'They were all good housekeepers. They all got to keep the house. That's why I work here.'

'Ha-ha,' says Doralee.

'It's not funny,' says George.

An hour-and-a-half has gone by. She calls her father Graham, and Eve answers the phone. Eve is five years older than Doralee. She has a quiet voice and never eats meat. She wears black leggings and cheap High Street tops. She is too fat. She teaches yoga. Doralee hates her.

'Hello, Dora,' says Evelyn.

'Hello Evelyn,' says Doralee. They really don't get on, these two. 'Can I speak to my father?'

'Of course,' says Eve. 'It's very important that Graham keeps in contact with his previous family. It's good for karma.'

'Who's Karma?' asked Doralee. 'Don't tell me you and Daddy have had a secret baby!' Seventeen years since Graham left home but his eldest daughter doesn't give up her resentments easily.

'Graham,' says Eve, coolly, hand ineptly over the mouth-piece, 'It's Dora. One of your daughters.' And she hands the phone to her husband.

'Dora!' says Graham, trying to sound pleased. He has behaved as well as he can to his many children but it is not good enough. He left their mother and only the twins, the boys, the youngest, the males, will ever forgive him. He had hoped that as they reached maturity the girls would opt to rename themselves, as their mother had in her time. But no. As Eve puts it, 'It is more important for them to spite you, I'm sorry to say, than to live good and useful lives.'

'It's Doralee,' says Doralee to her Dad. 'Not Dora. I hate having my name shortened, as I must have told you a hundred times. But I don't want to talk about that, I'm worried about Peterloo. He went out earlier this evening leaving his keys and his mobile behind and he hasn't come back. He doesn't think about me. Supposing I wanted to go out and I had to wait in for him? He's very selfish.'

'You married him, not me,' says Graham. He has switched over to the speaker phone. Now Eve can hear what he is saying. He feels safer with witnesses.

'Daddy, we're not married. Try to remember.'

'I'm sorry. Are you worried because he's gone missing or because he's selfish?'

143

'Because he went out to get the cleaning and he hasn't come back and it's not like him.'

'But your mother said it was a safe area.'

'You and Eve are so, so yesterday,' said Doralee. 'Safe, not safe, it's just human.'

'Have you called the police?' asked Graham.

'Of course not,' said Doralee. 'They never come.'

'I should call them,' said Graham. 'I know they tend to arrest the victim these days, not the criminal, but you could give it a go.'

'You are so cynical, Daddy,' complained his daughter. 'They do their best. But you get through to someone in a call-centre who wants to know your mother's maiden name, and I can never remember it.'

'O'Neill,' said Graham.

'Fancy you remembering that,' says Doralee. 'But it's just in case. It's a nice evening. Peter's probably just gone for a walk.'

'What, down there where you live?'

'It's a mixed area,' said Doralee. 'Very vibrant. We love it. But it's understandable that I'm worried. You walked out on us, after all, without notice: all that was left of you were your keys. It might happen to me.'

'It was a long time ago. You're very much your mother's daughter,' said Graham, and to his astonishment his daughter began to cry and said she loved her Peterloo very much.

'*Peterloo*,' sang Eve, from the back of the room, Abba-like, '*Peterloo, you are my Peterloo*.' Graham hushed her as best he could. But she'd taken all her clothes off and was dancing around naked. When presented with bad karma this was her normal response. She had nice perky little breasts, unlike Ruby's hefty ones, and danced gracefully and slowly, without too much energy, waving this way and that like a poplar. He was very happy with her. She was uncompetitive and

144

had nothing of Ruby's over-active do-gooderiness about her, allowing him to get on with saving the world.

'Doralee,' said Graham, 'I am sure your partner is all right. He's probably just gone to the pub.'

'He hates pubs.'

'Oh, I rather thought he was pub kind of person. Full of information and useful facts.'

'You just don't get him, do you, Daddy. Peter is a private kind of a guy, very reliable, and kind and good.'

'Then he's probably busy doing someone a good turn: taken them to casualty, left his cell phone behind and now can't find an unvandalised telephone box to be in touch. Stop panicking. He may even be trying to get through to you as we speak.' That was over-hopeful.

'We have a call-waiting feature on this phone,' said Doralee. 'But thank you, Daddy, for being there for me.' She even sounded as if she meant it. 'I know I'm over-reacting. It's like, all that past bad stuff in my life.'

All that bad stuff

Doralee's father Graham, although only just into his sixties, still has something about him of that earlier generation of manipulative men, into which I have put Ron and the other artists and poets of that tricky post-war generation. See them clear in Osborne's Jimmy Porter, the one with the gift for invective in *Look Back in Anger*, that seminal drama of the Fifties. When an earning wife was a rare thing, and the husband a meal ticket for life, male resentment against women was rife.

Graham's speciality was a kind of war game of the emotions: the blame game. He left Ruby because she was too active, too busy, too noisy, too beset by crying babies. He craved peace and felt entitled to it. He blamed her for what she was, not for what she did, which is a great cruelty because there is nothing that the accused can do about it.

Ruby, mantrapped, has never fully recovered from the shock of his leaving. She clips curbs when she drives, and forgets things, how many sausage rolls she has ordered for the Church Tea and so forth. It does not stop her driving or organising as she always did. She's just not so good at it. She grits her teeth and achieves her aims, just about, and tries to concentrate but trauma leaves its marks through life, the left-over life which is all the mantrapped and abandoned woman has.

In the days of female powerlessness the male blame game – endearments today, rejection the next – was more frequently played than it is today. It was played out between my husband Ron and me over a period of thirty years. He won hands down. I was an amateur.

Ted Hughes played the same game, as did so many mid-century men of the arts. The poet drove poor Sylvia to suicide (male poet: *you have dared to rival me; I will choose another over you, that'll larn yer!*) and Assia Wevill (male poet: *you have brought down dark cosmic powers to damage me: you have killed my true wife by your presence in my life: I cannot live with you*).

Sylvia was a friend and neighbour in Primrose Hill, so was Assia, her successor in the Hughes' marital bed in Devon. In the eyes of those dinosaur men, woman was the great destroyer; she was Delilah, snipping his hair while he, trusting, slept. His male strength was sapped by the weakness she exploited, as was his capacity for tenderness and love. Ron, for example, artist, musician, man of parts, both loved me (at any rate for a time) and was persecuted by me. With men of his generation – mid-century men one could call them – these things went together. They were reared on George Bernard Shaw (*marriage – woman's meal ticket for life*); Strindberg (*women drive you insane*); Henry Miller (*mock them while you shag them*); Melanie Klein (*good breast, bad breast, and just your luck to have got the bad*); on '*men have art and women have babies*' – and a host of films and books in which woman was the destroyer, the siren, the wanton, the sexual devourer. Every woman, they thought, would turn into their mother given half a chance, and try to tell them what to do. They would do what they could to turn you into her, and once they had succeeded, would be off, to find someone as little like her as possible. Graham's still at it; albeit a shadow of the giants of the past. 'I wish you weren't so noisy, pet,' was all Ruby can remember Graham saying by way of warning, the day before he left. Of course he was going to marry Eve: there was Ruby standing at his mother's sink, using her pots and pans to make the jam from the strawberry bed his mother made. Yet it was he who bought the house. If Eve wants to stay married to him, she had better not make jam, even as he begs her to.

Meanwhile women hung around, the surplus gender, hoping to be chosen, suffering humiliation if they were rejected or abandoned, as a good proportion was going to be, statistically. Today's woman, busying herself demonising the male gender, finds it hard to understand the mewling mindset of yesterday's woman.

Ruby's daughter has vowed never to be mantrapped like her mother. No marriage for Doralee, but of course she is a mantrap in herself, as is Trisha. Good Lord, Trisha trapped a whole male being in passing, soul, body, memories and all. Doralee's an amateur.

Peter is as indoctrinated as his forefathers, of course he is, just in a different direction. Forget the printed page, forget Shaw and Strindberg, Peter and his generation have been reared on a fictional diet of film and TV, in which women are strong, victims are nice, colonialists are bad and the colonised good, fathers are your best buddy and empathy rules. Who cares, wins. The Sermon on the Mount has sunk into male consciousness. Anima triumphs over animus. Blessed are the weak for they shall inherit the earth. A likely tale. But at least dinosaur man is dying out, starved of nourishment in the new age.

And more waiting

Another hour passed. Nothing on TV. Doralee thought she might ring up Heather but no one wants to report their boyfriend is missing. It seems careless, and misfortune is bad for business and prestige. Unwise. She won't use or even think the word 'partner' to Heather: Heather is in a partnership too, not a marriage, but the fact of her pregnancy makes Doralee's relationship seem kind of second class, to do with the free expression of consumerism rather than commitment – so she reverts to boyfriend. She called Ruby. Ruby was making strawberry jam in her big farm-house kitchen in aid of Cancer Research. A local soft-fruit grower had donated his surplus stock, rejected by the supermarkets a week previously as too ripe for the shelves. Irradiation and chilling had failed to control the fruit's overweening tendency to mature. Now Ruby was in a race against time and waste and the kitchen was sticky with sugar, soft fruit and pectin.

'Some people are kind and considerate,' said Ruby. 'They make up for the ones that aren't.'

'Like Daddy,' said Doralee. 'What is that funny noise?'

'Me sucking my fingers, I expect,' said Ruby.

'I expect it was cheaper for the farmer to give you his left overs than destroy them under EC regs.,' said Doralee.

'Now don't be cynical, darling,' said Ruby, 'it doesn't suit you. What's the matter?'

Doralee wept a little and said that Peter was missing. No, she hadn't called the hospitals. She hated hospitals. It wasn't even as if you could ever get through, you just hung on the end of the line listening to some stupid music until you didn't care who was alive and who was dead. Ruby offered to do it for her but Doralee took offence, and said her mother was wishing bad karma on her partner. Of course nothing bad had happened to Peterloo. He was not the kind of person bad things happened to.

Ruby said she had to get back to the jam. She'd left the pan on the Aga and now the sweet sludge was bubbling over onto the stove and burning and caramelising on the hot plate and the smell was dreadful and the stickiness appalling. You were meant to sterilise the jamjars but she thought she'd bypass that stage. She'd rinse them out with the stuff you used for baby's bottles. She had some somewhere. Ruby heard the click as her daughter hung up.

'You care about bloody cancer research more than me,' said Doralee, to the empty air. 'I don't suppose you'll even keep a jar back for us.' Well, she was upset. And for some reason she felt entitled to be horrible to her parents, while being pleasant enough to others, so long as the latter hadn't given her any particular cause for grievance. But in the daughter's eyes her mother was guilty until proved innocent, not otherwise.

Doralee took two of Peter's sleeping pills and went to bed. Everything would seem better in the morning. The pills were of a new generation which meant you were perfectly alert if roused, just got a good night's sleep. She had written an article about the benefits of sound sleep and had done some research into the matter. All the same it was some minutes before she fell asleep. The futon with its strip of foam rubber was uncomfortable. Her head lay uneasily upon its pillow. The curse of the missing mattress-cover, perhaps. She missed Peter. She missed his lean hairy legs besides hers.

It occurred to her that she loved him and that it was more than just a matter of mutual friendship, companionship, shared interests, with sex tagged on. It could become painful, difficult and dangerous, if you were not to pursue self-interest with fixed determination, but allowed yourself to be distracted by random emotion. Perhaps, all unknowing, she had driven Peter away as her mother had driven her father. Her father had just walked out the door one day when asked to relight the Aga for the autumn season. Ruby had been astonished: summer was over: to announce autumn by the Aga ceremony was the man's job. Of course she knew how to light the stove: it was just not her job. Perhaps Peter had similar feelings about couscous but had never voiced them?

Could you do things to others you were not aware of? Be some source of danger to them, sap their strength, steal their being, turn them into something they were not, just by close proximity?

Was she, in fact, bad for Peter? Her sister Claudette said she was; said Peter had changed since he had been with her, become passive, a kind of mini-Doralee. But Claudette was jealous, everyone knew, had always fancied Peter. Doralee slept.

On the villainy of women

As well for the future of the nation that Mr Kovac, new citizen, packs a gun. Someone has to look out for women. True, he's a drug-dealer, and true, in his time he has killed a man or two – but in his own country, not ours, and when young and impetuous and only as custom dictated, in defence of family honour. You could almost believe that all of us, men and women both, left to themselves, and given permission by society, are murderous. Mrs Kovac has had three abortions in her day, Doralee has had one, and Trisha two. Ruby has had none, but simply goes ahead and allows as many little things as come along to live their lifespan out. (She is much criticised for this – *six children! No wonder the husband left.*) Graham makes up for them all by saving lives, distributing grain to starving peoples. By virtue of cutting a corner or two in the past, in far-off, brigand-held lands, and increasing his own profit in ways that are not strictly legal, Graham has managed to salt quite a bit away, which is how Ruby and the children have been able to stay at home in the Rectory, and Eve to dance around the kitchen ethereal and naked for his entertainment. It is all paradox, as Eve observes.

Mr Kovac is a danger only to his enemies. Smile at him and he'll smile at you. No illegal he. He is happy in the city and loves driving and is proud of his van. He delivers drugs and dry-cleaning around the neighbourhood, and collects money owed on behalf of people of many nationalities. He is a pleasant fellow, without apparent guile, and is trusted. His native tongue is Albanian but he has a smattering of Italian, Iranian, even Afghan. He comes home early if he can and helps his wife with the shutters. His compassion extends however, only to the outer limits of self-interest, and Doralee, foolish girl, has placed herself outside it. Doralee has been trained and encouraged to look a long way afield, beyond her circle of acquaintance, to the rights and wrongs of other countries, other races, to such a degree that she's bad at noticing what goes on next door, or indeed inside herself. She goes on anti-war demos with alacrity – blame lies with other nations, just as in her personal life it lies with other individuals – and feels entitled as a consumer to require Mrs Kovac to keep the shop open late, no matter how tired that hard-working woman is. She can kill her unborn child and forget about it within the month, give or take a few nightmares, while still seeing life as innately precious. She has been well trained by her teachers in her rights and in the art of high self-esteem: she sees herself as honest, kind and good.

Yet only last week Doralee sent an e-mail in Heaven Arkwright's name, sneaking into her office at lunchtime to say no but thanks to a request for Heaven to write up a newly-discovered rainforest herb, which when applied to the skin plumped it up and removed wrinkles. That meant the request would then come Doralee's way. Doralee tells herself that natural justice is on her side, this is a grey area: Heaven deals with complexion issues, true, but the herb is also claimed to promote sound natural sleep. She has done nothing criminal, just read an e-mail not meant for her, replied, and then deleted. Doralee is a relativist, though no one ever told her what the word meant, and she believes the moral universe falls into place around her according to her own advantage.

She, the murderess, killer of her unborn baby, is unaccustomed to seeing herself as morally flawed. Mr Kovac has a better sense of original sin. Yet how scrupulous Doralee will be, should she eventually give birth, a better mother than I, three decades back, could ever be. Doralee will bond with her new baby (she will have no choice; the midwife will thrust the infant head to Doralee's reluctant nipple; the mouth will grab and suck and that will be that). And thus bonded, sentenced to a lifetime's anxiety, she will breast-feed for six months as instructed, until the poor little thing is weak and mewly with hunger, and see herself as irresponsible if she shoves a piece of solid food into its mouth, to watch the tiny teeth, already grown, at last find something satisfactory to bite upon.

But us lot, us mothers of the Sixties and Seventies – how good we were at doing what came naturally. We shoved the bottles in the babies' mouths and put up with the guilt which followed. We knew no fear. We saw ourselves as doing the best we could with the material with which we were supplied, and left the rest to chance. We were protected from anxiety by our own ignorance. Three months pregnant with Nicolas, I caught German measles. These days that would be an instant recommendation for termination, there being a possibility of blindness or deafness in the child, but what did I know about that? Upper left arm, we all had a smallpox inoculation scar but that was as far as preventative medicine went. That a baby could be born less than perfect did not occur to us. Nicolas grew up to be a musician and has 20/20 vision. Neglecting to foster our offspring's moral, physical, psychological or intellectual development, we left them alone to grow, and by and large they did.

I watch my grandchildren and pity their parents, as the little ones are woken out of peaceful slumber to develop their hand-eye coordination, their spatial skills, their empathy with others. These infants must work from the moment of birth; they are taught theories of projection at their mother's knee, learn to empathise with their enemy – *darling, if John hits you it's because you hit him first, and poor John, his mother isn't very nice, is she* – must be conscious of their thoughts and feelings from the start, and scarcely a one is theirs alone but has not been fed to them by the kind and well-intentioned. My ambitions for my children were that they should sleep and give me time to write. Mine slept because they were so bored, no doubt, but sleep they did. I loved them and sang them lullabies and pop songs. They could all chant Doris Day's *Que Sera, Sera*, and I tried not to pass on to them the habit of anxiety. And so through rain, hail, love, disappointment, psychoanalysis, notoriety, disgrace, divorce and pregnancies, rehearsals, lost socks, cooking, laundry and plastic bags, I somehow kept the writing coming. Faster, faster, more, more.

Babies were art objects put out into the living world, not the paper world that writers love, but still there for the editing, for the improvement, taking their turn, piling up in the filing tray, sometimes marked 'urgent', sometimes not. I shall give

Doralee a future in which she has a baby. Our personalities are half taken from our parents, half our own. It will have Ruby's eccentricity and Graham's capacity to attract enduring love and partners who dance naked, and Adrienne's liking for little scarves. It will have Doralee's gift for self-interest and Peter's sweetness. It will be just fine. It will have to arrive the other side of the end of this book, in the fictional world, but it's in store for her as a present from me. I hope she's grateful: if she's not at first, I daresay she will be with time.

A good explanation for absence

There was a knocking at the door. Doralee was awake at once. Peter! At last. She would not reproach, she would not ask questions, he was home, that was all that mattered. She would never be snarky again.

They would get married, in a church – or else she would convert to Judaism so as not to upset his mother. She would ask her father to the wedding, she would even invite Eve. She would have a baby. All this between the futon and the door, with a blue pashmina grabbed and flung over the T-shirt she wore to bed. She opened the door eagerly, but it was not Peter, it was a woman of uncertain age, rather over-weight with a lot of red hair which needed a good cut. Doralee arranged the pashmina to give herself more cover.

'Oh thank God, thank God, Doralee!' said the woman. 'You're here. I was so scared you wouldn't be. Anything at all can happen. Nothing's what it seems. It's terrifying.'

There was something sinister about the voice. It was some mad imitation of Peter. Perhaps it was a practical joke on the part of the newspaper? A sort of singing telegram: a bizarre apology for absence. If so it was unforgivable. It was the middle of the night. There must be some other way of doing this sort of thing. It would be a divorceable offence if only they were married.

'Who sent you?' asked Doralee. 'Because I'm tired and need to sleep and I'm not in the mood for jokes. Perhaps you want to speak to my husband? I'm expecting him any minute.'

'Partner,' said the woman. 'Not husband. And I am your partner. I only look like this; try and understand. See me as a hermit crab got into the wrong shell.' Only the previous week Doralee had been writing an article about how not to be a hermit crab, and Peter had provided her with useful details about the lifestyle of these strange creatures. Why was this woman talking about them? Could she be his mistress? But that was absurd. Peter's offices were full of interns whose major ambition was to sleep their way to the top, all in their early twenties with double firsts from Oxford, and they might possibly be a temptation, but men like Peter did not go off with women like this. But then her mother had despised Eve, for all manner of reasons, and it had happened. The other, lesser woman was preferred, just because she was lesser.

'Shut your eyes, Doralee,' said the woman. 'Try just listening and believing. I know the voice is peculiar but I'm pitching it down for you, so it sounds more like the real me.'

Doralee's eyes stayed open and staring. The woman clicked her tongue in annoyance, sounding like Peter when the computer crashed or he found George had failed to bring up the mail. Did Peter perhaps have an older sister he had never acknowledged? The woman pushed past Doralee, and walked as if by right to the desk and straight to the drawer where the pens were kept and took Peter's favourite.

'Doralee,' said the woman, 'try and adjust. This isn't like you.'

'It's the middle of the night,' said Doralee, feebly.

'I'll write it down for you. I know you. You only believe things when you've seen them in black and white. Little Miss Cynical!'

Peter would sometimes call her that when she doubted one of the more extreme conspiracy theories he would bring back from the office. Doralee realised she was gawping, as she tended to do when taken by surprise, and shut her mouth. 'Stop looking like a goldfish,' her mother would sometimes say to her. The woman wrote and studied what she had written.

'Thank God,' she said. 'At least my writing hasn't changed. Or not much. It shouldn't, of course. Individual handwriting is conditioned by personality and muscular movement combined, and no two handwritings are the same, in the same way as fingerprints. Not many people know that.'

Doralee felt cold and wrapped the pashmina more firmly around her. She felt the more vulnerable because her feet were bare.

'You should have bought slippers when I told you,' said the woman. That was the kind of thing men said, not women. Men hid their concern behind reproaches. It was annoying, but forgivable. She was wearing a short suede skirt and a white frilly blouse off which a button had burst and a horrible jacket with fake fur collar. There was a tear in her fishnet tights and black smudges beneath her eyes where her mascara had run. Doralee had the feeling she had just been in some kind of fight.

The woman handed the piece of paper to Doralee. On it was written in capital letters which could be Peter's handwriting or not, 'This is not me. This is Peter. I am in the wrong body.'

'Hang on a moment there,' said Doralee. 'Are you in the wrong body, or is it the right body and the wrong you?'

'Doralee,' said the person, who might or might not be Peter. 'Please don't get metaphysical at this point. It's the middle of the night. We have to do something, and fast. I have a feeling the longer this is allowed to go on the more difficult it's going to be to get back to normal.'

She walked briskly round the room; she was like Peter, anxious and active, making little nervous movements, yet not like Peter. Perhaps this was his mother, a teenager when he was born, and Adrienne only his adoptive mother? That would explain a lot. But why would he send his mother along and get her to pretend she was her own son? Or perhaps she was deluded, insane? Perhaps he visited his mad mother in the loony bin every week and talked to her about hermit crabs and so on. How would one ever know where men really went? They said they were at the office and you couldn't be checking up on them all the time. In the meanwhile the woman was wearing thin stiletto heels which could only be bad for the floorboards.

'If you're going to walk about the room could you kindly take off your shoes to do so?' she asked.

'That's better,' said the woman. 'That's my Doralee.' And she took off her shoes and sat down with a thump. 'I really like heels', she said, 'but you have to get used to them and they don't half pinch. When I come to think of it, she's got far the best of the bargain. My body is fifteen years younger, and see these varicose veins? They're disgusting. And I keep wanting to pee and I hate being so short. I can't reach things. And I have a wrinkly belly. I tried doing a press-

158

up and it was hopeless. At the same time it's kind of cosy in here. But it can't be allowed to go on. Now Doralee, we have to keep this very quiet. I guess we'll both have to take time off work. I don't know who you see about this kind of thing. Doctor? Psychiatrist? Priest? Rabbi? Somehow I think the Rabbi would have the best grasp of what was going on, all those golems and so on. If only I believed in God.' There was a ring on the bell.

'I expect that's the men in white coats,' said Doralee snarkily, 'come to collect you.' She was still angry with Peter. He had left her with uncooked couscous, failed to return with her cleaning, hadn't even bothered to phone, and worried her to pieces. She realised she was now on the verge of accepting that what he said was true, that this was Peter in the wrong body, and it made her crosser still. There was now untold confusion and trouble to look forward to.

'It'll be Trisha,' the woman said. 'I told her to come here. She went back to her flat to collect a few things. But we had to get out of there fast. I would have gone, but she's in the man's body so she can look after herself. At least physically – mentally I reckon she's in a worse state than me.'

'Trisha?' said Doralee. *'Trisha!'*

'Not your type,' said the woman. 'I'm sorry about that, but I wasn't doing any choosing here.'

Doralee went to answer the door.

'It occurs to me,' said the woman, after her, 'it might be some kind of alien attack. There may be hundreds like us out there. We might need the CIA.'

'That is just simply not on,' said Doralee, and opened the door to Peter, His clothes were dusty and looked as if they had been slept in. His nails were broken and his hands were dirty. There was something tentative and empty about him: he looked ripe for throwing away, like a soft toy that had lost its stuffing, or a discarded handbag. But perhaps he just needed a bath and some sleep. He had two black plastic sacks with him, stuffed with God knew what.

'What on earth has happened to you?' asked Doralee. 'And where have you been?'

'Didn't he tell you?' said Peter. 'Men never get to the point, do they. I'm not Peter, I'm Trisha.'

Doralee held the door open and Peter walked in.

'I don't want you to think –' said Peter, '– I mean, there was nothing going on. We were just passing on the stairs. It felt ever so strange.'

'Have you told the police?' asked Doralee. What did he mean, there was nothing going on? Why did he even feel the need to say it? 'Isn't that the first thing to do?'

'Try telling a call centre this kind of thing,' said the Trisha body from the sofa. 'They'll only ask you for your mother's maiden name and send round the social workers.'

'And what is my mother's maiden name?' asked Doralee.

'It's O'Neill, of course,' the Trisha body said. 'One of the Liverpool O'Neills.'

Doralee was finally convinced.

Back to the past

Louis Simpson's advice had borne fruit. He had explained to me how a novel was written. The first two I wrote were written out of ignorance, merely the novels I wanted to read which no one else had yet written, so I'd better get on with it. Others have since caught up with me of course: the unreflective present tense abounds in contemporary fiction: it is appropriate for drama – *she walks across the stage – he lights a cigarette* – but doesn't add much to fiction other than to give a spurious sense of immediacy, limiting the right to overview, to the god-like status of the author, to the moral intervention made possible by the past tense. The stage author, other than by choosing and shaping the subject and writing the dialogue, has no intervening power. It is left to action and event to convey such wisdom as the head of the writer contains. Those early present tense novels of mine were written in the present not because I had thought about it, but because I had started writing in play form and then, novelising what I had written, simply neglected to change the tenses. It worked well enough. So well that in the meanwhile the Gods of the past tense have all but fled. Even history documentaries on TV prefer the immediacies of the present tense to any serious consideration of the past. *'Henry VIII strides through the palace in a temper. His wife is betraying him. "Cut off her head," he yells.'*

Now I started to write *Female Friends*. By this time I was being described by my publishers as a 'feminist' writer. Or as in a TV documentary, *'By this time her publishers describe her as a feminist writer.'* The description comes from them, not her, but she suspects it is in the eye of the beholder. She writes about women in relationship to one another, not to men. This is a shocking divergence from tradition. What she says is disconcerting to others. Friends leave rooms when she comes into them. She is by implication suggesting a revolution: that women need not be men's victims, that men are not automatically objects of adoration, that women are people too. Nobody wants to hear this at the time. To women it suggests that whole lives spent as daughters, sister, wives, mothers, to the abnegation of the self, have been wasted. It denies the past. To men it suggests a terrifying future in which women no longer automatically wash shirts because they are women.

But Fay cannot help what she writes: she describes the world around her; this is not propaganda, simply what she sees. She is bemused by the hostility she meets. She is not trying to change, just to describe. Twenty-five years later, addressing a festival in Chicago, she tries to recant in public, but every time she quotes passages from her early novels which could be fairly said at the time but no longer can, the audience cheer and laugh. '*Men*,' she quotes herself from the platform, '*are like little boys behaving badly at a birthday party. They get away with what they can.*' Such casual generalisations, she murmurs to her audience, are unfair, prejudicial and old-fashioned. She wastes her breath. The triumphant army of women exult too much in victory to understand remorse. Everything turns into an anti-man fest. The way to make an audience laugh is to utter anti-male sentiments, and the men laugh louder and more nervously than anyone.

Fay has a little glass pyramid of a paperweight she keeps on her desk to remind her of the occasion. Engraved in the glass are the words Chicago Humanities Festival III, *From Freedom to Equality*. She loves it dearly, but thinks it would make just as much sense if it read *From Equality to Freedom*. Did women need to be free before they were equal, or equal before they could be free? Abstract nouns get flung about these days any old how. Women are neither free nor equal, of course, but we can be fairly sure these days that it is not men's fault, at least not men in general, though no doubt blame can be attributed to individual men. We will see how Trisha gets on in Peter's body. Who then will she blame for what goes wrong?

The glass pyramid is chipped – perhaps someone flung it across the room once in a temper, but Fay cannot remember, fortunately, who it was who did the flinging, just as Trisha can't remember who it was who spilt the wine upon her mattress.

The third-person present works well enough, I see. Should I continue further with the real-life story of my life in a further book, it could continue in the same vein. '*She does this, they do that: moving swiftly across the room she faces her opponents*' etc. It could be mistaken for a novel. Its predecessor, *Auto da Fay*, was conventional enough, other than – when I could no longer bear to incorporate the reality of certain sections of my past, I slipped over into the third person for a time. This book, *Mantrapped*, is the second volume, and presents novel and autobiography side by side, leaping from one to the other, but related.

Doralee, Trisha and Peter

'I'm truly sorry, Doralee – pretty name, that,' said the Peter body. 'You must have had a really nice mother. Nice mothers give their children nice names. I hope you don't mind me settling in here for a day or two. I'm not one to stay where I'm not wanted. But your husband here, sorry, partner, doesn't think it's wise for us to be separated. And he's right, we don't want to be too far away from one another in case whatever it was that switched on the stairs wanted to hop right back and distance might make a difference. How would one know?'

The voice washed over Doralee. It was strange to hear Peter's voice in this mode, non-stop, hesitant, confiding, nervous and endearing all at once. Had the voice been female she could have ignored it altogether, since it seemed to have so little sensible to say, but being male, and Peter's at that, it kept catching her attention. She was on the Internet, trying to find out some kind of information, any kind of information, about body swaps, and not getting very far. She couldn't concentrate. The Trisha body lay sprawled out on the sofa, taking a nap. The Peter voice burbled on.

'There must be someone we can ask out there. I'm sure you guys know the right kind of people. I tend to know theatricals and racing drivers and in any case I've been rather out of touch lately. If this goes on for any length of time I might consider becoming a male model. I have the contacts. Has your partner ever thought of doing that?'

'It's not quite Peter's scene,' said Doralee.

'I'm not going back to Mrs Kovac's no matter what,' said the Peter body. 'That woman is a toe-rag and a bitch. She was taking advantage. But how am I meant to claim housing benefit if I turn up as a man when I've said on the forms I'm a woman? They're really funny about things like sex change.'

'I'm sure Peter and I can help you out,' said Doralee.

'That's a comfort to know,' said the Peter body. It was studying its nails. 'Look,' it said. 'All perfect. Your partner has very strong nails. That's nice. Mine do tend to go brittle and flake. Well, that's his problem, now. None of this is my fault.'

'I'm sure this won't go on for long,' said Doralee. 'We'll work on it, get it sorted.' She did not know what else to say. She was in uncharted territory. Who could she talk to? She did not trust Peter to be wholly Peter. To confide in Heather would be rash. She couldn't trust her any more than she could Heaven. She was still chafing from her conversations with her family. The Internet, instead of a fountain of wisdom and information, seemed a broken reed.

Dawn was breaking over the city skyline: indeed, an early shaft of sun shone onto her computer screen and made it difficult to read. She had found life swap and spouse swap and surgical sexchange and transsexual and intersexual chat rooms, and TV programmes a-plenty, hermaphrodite counselling, and cross-dressing and troilism and meet your partner here, and porn sites kept breaking through, but nothing relevant that Doralee could find, other than in the witches' Sabbath, where the devil sometimes changed into a woman. And of course Zeus could change into all kinds of things – bulls, swans – but always kept his own gender, even when old. And women in mythology could change into trees or spiders but never anything male. There were cases in psychiatric literature of males who believed they were female, or females male, but they were deluded. She switched off the computer. It took its time fading.

The body Peter sat primly on a stool and chattered on, male knees genteelly together. And the body Trisha sprawled on the sofa, dozing, legs akimbo, knickers actually showing, and then stirred and woke, and Doralee frowned at her, and the Peter body took time to realise what was wrong before moving her legs together. Gender mannerisms took time to kick in, it seemed. But over the next hour, while the Peter body flicked through the glossies, and the Trisha body took a bath, and Doralee waited for offices to open and the fresh day to begin, new habits were quickly learned, so soon the body Trisha was taking little mincing steps and the body Peter beginning to stride about. Doralee worried that the same might happen to their mental habits and personality traits – they would begin to meld into one. She opened a file on her computer, ready to record case notes from time to time. She would turn this into a book, before she was through.

The walls lacked substance. She felt that if she stretched out her hand it might simply pass through them. Yet the Trisha and the Peter bodies seemed more and more substantial, as if they were the real people and she was not. Every imperfection was cruelly magnified. The hairs in the Peter nostrils were long and black and thick, the sides of Trisha's foot beneath the ankles were a mass of blue veins. They were like cartoon figures, in which the artist had drawn in salient points, rather than attempting a realistic model. She felt very little emotional connection with either.

'Peter,' she said to the Trisha body, 'I didn't go to a hypnotist or anything for the magazine? I might be just seeing and hearing everything wrong, and then the memory of the session wiped. If I had been told you were Trisha and Trisha was you this would be what it was like.'

'No such luck,' said the Trisha body in her absurd little pipey, flutey voice. 'There's going to be no clap hands and everyone wake up.'

Doralee took a polaroid of the three of them, but there was nothing unusual to be seen: one man and two women. She did not know what she had been hoping for. She opened a box file and marked it 'Swapped' and put the photograph in it.

She made coffee and ran out for some croissants – both the bodies seemed reluctant to leave the flat, and felt better, almost normal, when she got back. She had coped with problems before. She would again. She had always been good at going into emergency gear when faced with a crisis. Once she'd even dived into the school swimming pool to rescue a drowning pupil – and been made head girl as a result.

The Peter body said he never ate Nutrispread, could he have butter instead, and Doralee explained they never ate butter, it was fattening and clogged up the arteries, and then the Trisha body said she'd really appreciate some butter too, for once. Fuck the arteries. Doralee could see she'd have to be careful they didn't gang up against her – the two freaks against the normal one. Not that they were really freaks: she must not lose her sympathy for them. The Trisha body housed her own dear Peter, the Peter body a woman with whom she had little in common but had done her no harm. But it was difficult.

The Peter body took out a cigarette and thought about lighting it.
'Don't even think about it,' Doralee said. 'This is a no-smoking zone.' It might be that the body Peter was succumbing to stress and taking his first cigarette after three years, or it might be that the soul Trisha was a habitual smoker she was the kind who would be – either way it could not be allowed to happen in her house. The cigarette was stubbed out okay, but Doralee noticed that both the bodies sighed. There really was not much time, if she wanted the unalloyed originals back. It was hard to envisage life without Peter. She was so accustomed to him. He could scarcely be improved upon. He did not annoy her in any way. He was useful to her in her career. He was good to be seen about with. Waitresses tried to chat him up. Other girls looked after him in the street. He made her laugh – not often, but sometimes. They agreed upon nearly everything. The sex was really good. At their 'engagement' party she had found Heather crying in the bathroom: Heather had wanted Peter for herself. She had got over it since, of course, and married

and was now pregnant, but it was nice to know he was seriously in demand. But if he to was to go, she would survive.

She planned to make emergency appointments with a psychiatrist whom she had met at a charity dinner for Aids Awareness and a professor of anthropology she had met at the Alternative Medicine Awards. The Trisha body emphasised that she did not want any of this getting out. Peter was a news-breaker, not a news-maker. It would do Doralee's career no good to be associated with scandal, the Trisha body reminded her. Their employers would not appreciate it if they themselves made headlines. (*Your scandal*, Doralee found herself thinking, *not mine. I am innocent in all this. I am not even married to you*. And then she chided herself for her disloyalty.)

The Peter body rashly murmured that personally she was all for selling the story to the highest bidder, and then relying on the experts – the *Mail* was bound to have them – to bring her and Peter back to normal and then everyone could go back to sleep. 'No such thing as bad publicity,' said the Peter body. 'Not in my book.'

At which the Trisha body protested so strongly the Peter body threw up his hands and said, 'Do what you like. You went to college. I never did. I'm sure you know best,' and sulked for a little.

The Peter body decided he was still hungry and insisted on making scrambled eggs. Doralee pointed out they had already used the allocation of three eggs a week they tried to stick to, because of the cholesterol. But the Peter body said he was a big boy now, and needed sustenance, he was used to more flesh on himself, and was too thin and needed to build his body up. The Trisha body said he wanted to be returned

168

to himself slim and healthy, but at the same time said it was a waste to make scrambled eggs using any less than six eggs, so much was always left on the pan, and went to the fridge and took out a pack of six organic eggs, which he handed to the Trisha body. That made Doralee feel very odd indeed. The woman went to her fridge, Doralee's fridge, as if she owned it, and made free with its contents. But then it was Peter doing it, and he was entitled. Or was he? They'd never had a pre-nuptial agreement because there had never been any nuptials. Should this mess get sorted the first thing to do would be to come to some formal agreement as to who owned what, in case of future disagreements.

The Peter body made the scrambled eggs in a non-stick pan, at Doralee's request, using all six eggs, but he used a metal spoon to scrape the eggs off the bottom as it solidified – taking great scratches of Teflon with it. Doralee didn't have the heart to ask him not to. She was already being made to feel she was a nag and a prude.

It was the Trisha body who intervened and said 'careful of the pan,' replacing the metal spoon with a wooden one and taking over the eggs. The Peter body was happy to let her do it.
'Did you notice that, Doralee?' the Trisha body asked. 'It's the Peter me who's driving the spoon, not the Trisha hand. There must be some kind of leakage going on. You can't put a masculine, right-brain led, testosterone-drenched mind into an oestrogen-soaked body and expect there to be no crossover. I am really worried about this. If I find it interesting what do you think the CIA is going to be? It'll be no fun if Trisha and me end up the object of scientific research. Worse, this probably has military significance: the authorities are bound to want to experiment. The Trisha body is hopeless at spatial relationships, by the way. It's affecting me. I look at the

dishwasher, try to work out how to load it, and I just can't do it. It's catching. You should see the mess she lives in.'

'I haven't had that opportunity,' said Doralee, formally. 'You haven't told me what went on after you crossed on the stairs. There are a few missing hours.' But the Trisha body seemed to lose concentration and, making no attempt at all to clear up after the mess that was breakfast, wandered off to sort through the piles of old clothes she had lugged over in the black bin bags from Wilkins Parade. The Peter body had managed to burn the bottom of the pan, after all that, and had sloshed in milk, which the real Peter never did, and then overcooked, so that the stuff was like a pile of little yellow crumbs threaded through with browny-black worms.

Doralee called the office to tell them she would not be in that day, she was working from home. She called Peter's office to say he had laryngitis – that was clever, if he had to call the office himself at some time he could claim trouble with his vocal cords. She found that she was trembling and crying. Shock seemed to have bypassed her brain and attacked her body. She thought that perhaps Heaven Arkwright had launched some devilish plot the better to be revenged, that her dead baby was paying her back, that Mrs Kovac was responsible for this disaster – had put some kind of Transylvanian curse upon her. Nothing that had happened to her at school or work had seemed so bad as this, everything had had precedents, was meant to have precedents. If all else failed, if you were raped or widowed or orphaned or robbed, or had a child in prison or on drugs, there was a support group. But for this, for the transfer of your partner's being into someone else's shoddy, badly looked-after body, there was nothing. Then she pulled herself together and got on with setting up appointments.

The Trisha body dithered about who to call first. She waved her hands in the air distractedly. She was wearing jeans with high heels: Doralee would ask her to take the heels off and borrow her slippers, and the Trisha body would agree, only five minutes later to be back in the heels, complaining that Doralee's feet were too big.

'I'd say a priest or a rabbi would be most likely to help,' said the Trisha body. 'There is a full moon, this might be some kind of werewolf thing. On the other hand there is this need for discretion. We don't want someone drunk on communion wine to go blathering to his superiors. Or her's, most likely, these days. And I don't somehow see a woman casting out devils, do you? Nor do I want to go running to some rabbi, having said so often I reject the whole Jewish religious thing. I have a feeling that if we do absolutely nothing, and don't get our knickers in a twist, everything will revert to normal of its own accord. But make up your own mind, Doralee, just get me out of this body. My legs have a peculiar weighted-down feeling – I think it's the varicose veins. And I have a kind of hollow in my middle which feels somehow dangerous, as if it might implode at any time. I couldn't be pregnant, could I? That would be the end.'

The body Peter came through from the bathroom wearing lipstick and mascara.

'Chance would he a fine thing,' he said. 'I'm not in a relationship at the moment. But I never feel too good at this time of the month. I've got a period coming on any minute. I get cramps and my ankles swell.'

The colour drained from the Trisha body's face.

'Don't worry about it,' said the Peter body. He was staring in the mirror and using his finger to clear away little blobs of mascara. He did it inexpertly and smeared black onto his cheekbones. 'I'm on HRT, so it's not too bad. I've left

171

the pills out in the bathroom for you. I'm five days into the new pack, as you will see.'

'I'm not taking those pills,' said the Trisha body. 'They're dangerous.'

'You go for a long life or a happy one,' said the Peter body, 'and give me the happy one any day. I want my body returned in good order, so kindly keep taking the pills. Now tell me about Viagra.'

Doralee left them to make her phone calls. She arranged to meet Dr Paul Otterman the psychiatrist at three p.m. The anthropologist, Professor Simon Edgard was away in Bali developing his thesis that the outbreaks of violent rage that were once such a feature of Balinese society, and could be matched to the berserker rages of the Norsemen, were not a function of drug usage but of the Balinese custom of preventing their toddlers from crawling. Four feet on the ground was seen as too near the animal kingdom for comfort: the frustration of the natural developmental impulse had bad results.

Thwarted in her desire to see Professor Edgard, whom she remembered as having had the most delightfully gravelly voice, which was why she had listened so hard when he talked about the child-rearing customs of the Balinese, it was agreed that the three of them, after seeing the psychiatrist, would drive down that evening to consult Father Bryant. He was the vicar of Ruby's church, the one where Doralee and her sisters and brothers had all been christened. He had signed her first passport photograph.

Trisha and Peter sat on the sofa and chatted. Doralee thought they should be more agitated than they were. She was getting the feeling that it was she who was out of order, not they, and that she was being unduly officious in seeking help.

172

Peter had not been over-zealous in describing what exactly had happened in the hours of his absence. She doubted that it was anything sexual, but perhaps they had smoked a lot of dope which hadn't yet worn off.

'If I go upstairs the balance is okay, but when I go down I have to lean back or I topple. It's the breasts. They're so heavy,' the Trisha body was saying. 'And the nipples are meant to point ahead, I guess, but mine are all over the place.'

It seemed to Doralee that they were regressing. They were losing emotional intelligence; they were turning pre-pubertal. It was as if the burdens and responsibilities of the adult body had not yet struck them. They were curious but uninvolved. Did time flow differently for men and women? Perhaps it did. She wished now she had done a degree in human biology not in pharmacology. Not only was there so much she did not know but she might be married to someone rather different from Peter: someone who had an overview, who was not bogged down in detail as were most of the men she knew. Someone whose grasp on his own character, his own personality, his own moral framework, was more strongly rooted than Peter's. The slightest tug from some inferior soul and he had been lost.

What will happen next?

'Novels have form', said Louis, all those years ago, 'shape and pattern'. I took him literally. I worked out a chart and pinned it to the wall. The movements and encounters of my characters made a formal pattern. I followed their progress with coloured stickers. When their lives crossed so did the lines, curved or straight, seesawing or spiralling, as made by their stickers. When they got a mention, their lives moved forward. If the plot became too complicated I would put a black dot and stop that particular subplot there and then. Death. By the time I was a third of the way through the novel the chart fell off the wall.

I concluded that by now I could do without one. I believed in fate more strongly then than I do now. *Female Friends* is about three girls who were evacuated together in the early 1940s and remained friends through life, when they weren't betraying one another and stealing each other's boyfriends. I had observed that when the chips were down women helped one another, fought for one another, but in the good times they could be just horrible.

Also that women fell into piles of three. You could sort them out like cards from a pack into the erotic, who were in love with their bodies, the maternal, cosy nest-making creatures, and the effective, who loved getting things done. In this scheme of things Trisha is the erotic, Ruby the maternal and Doralee the effective. In the old days, when girls married as virgins, or were meant to, they scarcely knew who they were and married men not particularly suited to them and suffered greatly as a result – the effective type ended up looking after babies, the erotic married a poor man and the nest-maker never got to marry at all. Women are better these days at sorting themselves out. Trisha seduces, Ruby suckles, Doralee functions – look at her now making telephone calls. Just as in time of conflict the mother ant produces more soldiers, in famine more workers, and in time of fruitfulness more nurses, so I reckon more of the functioning kind are born today, though to what end I cannot be sure. Doralees are everywhere, while Trishas and Rubys become scarce.

I finished *Female Friends* in 1973, rising before the rest of the household to work in secret. Understandably children would rather their mothers did not write, but paid them full attention. I used to hate to see my mother writing – she too would rise in the early morning to cover sheets of paper with tiny little words by the tens of thousands, though by now it was accepted at home that I was a 'writer'. I actually had an antique brass-bound captain's desk of my own, and an upholstered wheelchair, of the kind used by eighteenth-century gout-victims who found it too painful to put foot to ground, and in which I am sitting now – these two pieces of furniture must have had a dozen different homes since then, but have survived them all.

I took the completed manuscript to MacGibbon and Kee, who had published the two previous books, but when I got to their offices, behind Golden Square, found that they had shut up shop for good that very morning. I asked a remaining member of staff, left to label the last packing cases, what she thought I should do with it, and she said she believed there was a publisher round the corner called Heinemann, why didn't I leave it at reception there? They did novels, she thought.

So I went round to Heinemann's and left it at reception to see if anyone was interested. Sometimes it is better not to know too much. If you don't look after your manuscript's interests, the Gods of the muses must, and may well make a better job of it than you. A week later I got a phone call from a Mr Charles Pick to say they would be happy to publish it, why didn't I call by. So I did. I signed the contract they put in front of me. I gave away all rights – foreign, film, TV. What did I know? Penguin owns the novel now, and will neither put it on the shelves nor give the rights back to me. It is still in print but doesn't seem to earn royalties, and I never see it in the shops. They just like to own things, I guess, and claim the reward for their initial judgement. It had a very nice pale blue jacket of three Muses, and was well reviewed, and I was asked round to have a glass of whisky in Charles Pick's offices. It was before the days of writer's tours or TV appearances; books sold or did not according to their own merits. Publishing was still a gentleman's profession, and rather dull.

The two earlier novels, *The Fat Woman's Joke* and *Down Among the Women*, have been reissued many times since and are now with HarperCollins, who actually keep new editions on the shelves, all these years later. For which thanks be to them, and the God of short novels and trusting novelists.

Good reviews and public attention did not help my marriage. I had given up paid employment. I say 'given up', but I had, in fact, been fired. Ogilvie and Mather had been bought up, taken over by a US firm. Work methods changed. Our new bosses were trying to whip us into order, turn us into proper professionals. It was their ambition to get the element of chance rooted out from the business of advertising. We, their employees, could spend months working and still fail to make them a profit, might even make them a laughing stock, which mattered to the wives, or on the other hand we could mess about for a couple of drunken hours and make them a fortune and bring credit to their dinner tables. In the meantime we demanded wages, heating, office overheads, insurance stamps. Why could we not get it right every time?

We were now required to write TV ads by rote – so many product-mentions, so many enthusiastic adjectives in the first line, a visual fix within three seconds, and so on, following a strict formula which research claimed had worked in the past. Our masters did not want to subdue our creativity, they assured us, they just wanted an output which would bring predictable profits. We did as we were told, scrupulously. It was an entertaining enough task to write to the new pattern, like solving crossword puzzles, but we knew the new-style ads weren't going to work. Nor did they. They were so dull no one remembered them, let alone the name of the product when it came to point of sale. The more enthusiastic the adjective the less memorable it seems to be.

So they sighed and let us get back to the old hit or miss ways of stabbing at an idea until it felt right, in the hope of netting the zeitgeist. This taught them a thing or two – namely that they were in a high-risk business and always would be and that we 'the creatives' were born ungrateful; and taught me a few things too, including a general rule that the more lip service is paid to the principle of originality and creativity by management, the less attention will be paid to it. And of course the importance of the wives. Those advertising managers from the big companies, though not averse to being dined, wined and night-clubbed, and sometimes more, really liked to impress the wives. Advertising was not done to make a profit, or only so far as profits imply status. Billboard posters never sold a thing but image, but it was image that the old-style wives liked. They wrapped themselves in their husband's glory as in a fur coat. *Go To Work on An Egg, Guinness is Good for you, Drink a Pinta Milka Day.* Now there are no fur coats the fun has gone out of the thing. Wives like their own status: they don't stay home waiting with slippers. They do research at the local university, or run their own chain of gift shops: they have no time to lift their eyes to their husbands' billboards, or if they do so it is

177

only to jeer and murmur feminist thoughts, and wish the menfolk did something else for a living.

The feeling-tone of the passing decades is there to be seen in the vaults and archives where such things are stored. There is Tony Hancock in the late Sixties, that great comedian, on screen selling eggs, in TV commercials written by me, bewailing the fact that he has to make the advertisement, that he had been reduced to this. Advertising eggs!

It was a true enough glimpse of his life at the time, and painful to watch in retrospect. He was to kill himself soon afterwards. The audience was cruel: his contract had not been renewed, Sid James, his on-screen sparring partner, had won the favour of the crowd, and the big parts and all the money for half the brilliance. Hancock's is the humour of desperation. He and I got on: we would just tell the truth, we agreed. We filmed in a studio in Wardour Street, huddling together on the set as if amongst enemies and changing the script as we went along, me dodging out of the way when the cameras started rolling, but his misery was tangible. So indeed was mine. I had had a terrible row with Ron, as I remember. I was tear-stained and abstracted. Hancock would have to nudge me with his elbow and say, 'Concentrate, concentrate!' I would do the same to him. We were both selling ourselves. Hancock's colleagues would jeer and deride and see the film as evidence of his failure, and he knew it. There is no way out, from time to time, yet his colleagues would take no pity on him. '*Sold out!*' they'd say to him. '*Cock a doodle doo! Tony Hancock, reduced to selling eggs!*' At least I hadn't been finally reduced; I was at the beginning, not the end, crawling my way out of this velvet-lined pit, while he was pitching into it. And, being female, I didn't take opprobrium nearly so much to heart.

Trisha, being female, sails through problems – from lottery-winner to seamstress in one fell swoop, so what? – which would have eaten away at Peter's soul and destroyed him. Demoted from deputy head of research one day to clerk in small ads the next – how would Peter have coped? Badly. For one thing Doralee would probably have left him. Status counts when it comes to love. See how now he's in a female body she's going off him at once?

And this was at a time when eggs were a good, healthy, pure kind of product, before research began to prove that eggs weren't good for you at all – they contained cholesterol, and cholesterol and heart attacks were linked, and the more eggs the worse, and the Egg Marketing Board collapsed. Advertising, our egg producers complained, never sold eggs. Wait another twenty years and their image would improve again, the Board would be back in business, the little lion stamp be back on the eggs, and cholesterol divided into two kinds, the good kind, as in eggs, which saves you, and the bad kind which kills you. In the meantime Hancock still lives down there in the archives, and offers himself as a sacrifice to the God of mirth, that ravaged, desperate, quizzical, untidy, un-dieted, un-exercised old-fashioned face staring out of the screen, as intimate and communicative as ever. And without the Egg Marketing Board there was really no need for Ogilvie and Mather to hire me. I charged too much for my services, and took nothing seriously, or appeared not to, and was probably getting on with my own work in the firm's time. But I didn't: I was always honourable in this respect.

Old work is always unsettling. I see in it the confidence of knowing that I am right, all the energy and determination of the young, the insistence that there is something I know which others don't, which will be to their benefit if I pass it on. I wrote what I saw, as best I could through the lens of my own experience, folly, self-delusion, miscomprehension, no doubt, but moving over time as a landscape and noticing the changes.

I don't look at my own early novels if I can help it. Reading them makes me feel uneasy, and envious of my own past. I feel as if I took some unholy leap into places where I had no right to be. My mother stopped writing for that very reason. '*It unsettles people and puts ideas into their heads; false hopes, false expectations*,' was how she put it. '*It's immoral*.' But I think she just thought it was too much responsibility.

I didn't quite get that far. I put my duty to my family – my obligation to feed and clothe them, before my duty to society – and she scarcely did, and she may have been right. Without fiction, without the film, the soap opera, the TV ads, the diet of stories on which we all live today – and without the complicity of the therapist culture which presents us to ourselves as simple narratives rather than the sum of random events – we might be more interesting and individual people than we have become. Trisha and Peter have souls, of course, but they are very loosely tethered; the little cloud above Pooh Bear's head, in that early vision of mine, flimsy and thin and all but dissipated.

Trisha, Doralee and Peter visit the psychiatrist

He was a bent, pale, elderly man who looked as if the juices had been sucked out of him long ago. His skin was like old parchment, fragile, papery-white and crinkled. His bedside manner was impeccable, but his smile thin and evil. 'Miss Thicket,' said Dr Paul Otterman, extending his hand in welcome, 'How good to see you again! How can I help you? My secretary was a little vague as to the purpose of your visit – something about a sex change? You are writing an article, perhaps? My wife is such an admirer of your work. It's all I can do to get her to see her GP, she is so convinced of the efficacy of alternative cures.'

Doralee wondered why she had thought he would be friendly. Perhaps he was seeing her just to get his revenge. People did that sometimes. He had got rather drunk at the charity dinner, felt her knee under the tablecloth, quoted chunks of Wordsworth, tried to arrange a tryst with her to see the ruins of Tintern Abbey, and then fallen asleep with his nose in the little pile of mushrooms served with the chicken. Doralee had tactfully woken him and helped him wipe and straighten his tie, and at the time he had affected to be effusively grateful. But here in his surgery, he was distant and somehow savage. It occurred to her that the events of that evening, which she had all but forgotten until now, were the most dreadful and painful embarrassment to him. He sat Peter and Doralee down but left Trisha standing.
'Can't Trisha sit too?' asked Doralee. 'All three of us do really need to be here. The problem relates to them, but I am better than the other two, at the moment, at explaining what happened.'
'Three of you!' he said, seeming surprised. 'I could have sworn only two people came into this office. But you are quite right, there are three.'

And he drew up the extra chair, and then re-arranged the blind as if to improve the light. It seemed perfectly adequate to Doralee, but she could see his problem. There was an insubstantiality about both Peter and Trisha now, as if it took two to make one. The hard-edged look had gone: they seemed fuzzy about the edges. They were easy to miss. The taxi driver on the way had shut the door too soon and almost caught the body Trisha a blow. 'Sorry,' he'd said in his defence, not sorry at all, 'I didn't think she was there. If there are men, they usually show the woman in first.' Everyone these days felt they had a right to give an opinion, even when not asked.

Now the body Trisha sprawled in her consulting chair, and the body Peter dangled his legs in his. Doralee wished they would sit up and behave. The body Peter had insisted on wearing a kilt, which he wore once a year to a Burns Night dinner, complete with sporran and long red-tagged green socks. Doralee had refrained from asking about underpants, for fear of the answer. She knew well enough, from dealing with her own young brothers and sisters that it was futile to argue about clothes. You just had to go out prepared to be embarrassed. The body Trisha was wearing a green track-suit from Doralee's cupboard, claiming to hate every stitch Peter had brought along with him in the plastic bags, refusing to return to Mrs Kovac's place to get something else, anything more, dropping her own discarded garments disdainfully in the washing basket.

Trisha and Peter seemed to be getting younger by the minute. They fidgeted and giggled. Dr Otterman listened politely. Doralee could see, even as she spoke, that Dr Otterman was going to be a waste of time. He licked his lips with a tiny little pink poking tongue, which flickered in and out like a snake's.

'I think you are describing a *folie à deux*,' he said, 'but a rather remarkable one, since the two parties have not grown into one another over time but apparently have only just met. Or so you tell me. Joint delusions are rare but not unknown. You are sure Trisha and Peter are being honest with you, Miss Thicket? The relationship between them has not been going on for some time, just unknown to you?'

'You don't understand,' said Doralee. 'They don't think they've switched: they have switched. He's in her and she's in him. They have each other's memories. I ask her, and she remembers him. Until yesterday they were perfect strangers. They crossed on the stairs and their souls jumped. That's why people are not meant to cross on the stairs. It's an old superstition.'

'It's true,' they choroused.

'But how could you tell such a thing?' the doctor asked. 'Other than because two people claim that it is true. Perhaps it's a *folie à trois*?'

'Obviously,' said Doralee, 'you could do tests to verify their claim. Look into their backgrounds. Heaven knows what's happened to their DNA. We need a university department to investigate. Probably several. Psychology, I'd say, and philosophy.'

'But to what end, Miss Thicket? Even if there were funds available, even if you yourself are not deluded, there is hardly going to be any course of treatment available. I suppose a wide spectrum anti-depressant or psychotic agent – but I would hesitate to prescribe such a thing.'

'I told you so,' said the Trisha body. 'This is but totally the wrong guy.'

'Nyah-nyah-ni-na-na,' said the Peter body, to Doralee. Dr Otterman looked at them with distaste. So much for wiping his tie and his chin free of chicken and mushroom, so much for believing one good turn would deserve another. So much for putting up with his hand on her knee.

'Go to the authorities,' he went on, 'and I fear they will decide you are in no fit state to be out, and are likely to commit a crime. Under the terms of the new Mental Health Act they may decide to put you in preventative detention. Which I must say would be my recommendation if I were to be involved in the dicussion. People profoundly out of touch with reality can be a danger to themselves and others.'

'Perhaps reality isn't what we think it is,' said Doralee, quoting her stepmother. 'Everything changes. This might be the next new thing.'

Dr Otterman stared at Doralee for a long time. Then his gaze switched to Peter, whose kilt was rucked up.

'Your husband?' he enquired. 'He holds down a job?'

'My partner,' said Doralee, 'not my husband. Yes he does. A very good job.'

'Perhaps you could ask him to cross his legs. I see a little too much of him.'

The Peter body obligingly crossed his legs, showing a length of long male leg with black hairs showing across the top of the socks, which he swung enticingly. The doctor looked away but the Trisha body ogled. Doralee felt inclined to slap her.

'There may well be new drugs on the street,' said the doctor, 'which interfere with the mind's normal responses, and distort the sense of self. I do not know for sure, though I have heard something of the kind, but until the casualties begin to turn up at this office, there is nothing I can do. People who resort to mind-altering substances without proper medical supervision must do so at their own risk.'

'In other words, you don't believe me; if I don't shut up I'll be locked up; I must have been taking drugs; and you haven't a clue,' said Doralee.

Dr Otterman rose to his feet. 'It might be better if you all left. I presume this is some sort of journalistic stunt? I don't take to it very kindly. I have made space in my diary to see you, to my inconvenience and that of others. If anyone has been taking photographs or using recording devices I warn you there will be legal consequences.'

On psychoanalysts, psychiatrists, psychologists and psychotherapists – and how to lose readers

The *Times* was vague about the difference between these various professions when in 1993 it set up a debate as to the value of therapy and put me on a platform to oppose Dr Anthony Clare, the psychologist. We had very little to argue about, both having doubts about the value of the 'talking cure' – so it was not a particularly conclusive or lively debate, though uncomfortable for me. I was certainly unpopular. I had written a novel called *Affliction* in which a couple of wicked therapists destroy a marriage. It had sparked a public debate. The vast Central Hall at Westminister was packed with indignant therapists and their patients, all attesting to the value of their treatment, and determined never to read a thing I wrote again. I was castigated in the press, at literary festivals and in radio and TV programmes for moral and social irresponsibility: everyone knew that therapy was a good thing. I was blaming therapists for my failure to keep my own marriage together. They understood my anger but if only I had sought treatment sooner! In vain to say, *'But look, I was only writing a novel.'*

I had been an analysand myself for eight years, two or three times a week, with breaks for babies. When puzzled and distraught it is nice to have a hired hand to talk to – though a week's silent reflection might do as well. Ron said he would not marry me unless I went into analysis, and it seemed a small price to pay, and I did. Ron's theory was that only those in analysis could communicate properly with others in analysis: it was a closed circle. There was some truth in it at the time. Now everyone knows everything about the inner workings of the mind, the processes of projection, the Cinderella complex, the importance of self-esteem, the tug of obsessive compulsive behaviour (me, apparently), but in the Sixties they did not. These ideas were new. There was a blessed elite of Enlightened Understanders, and this I was invited to join.

For eight years I went on and off, two or three times a week, to visit Miss Rowlands, to lie upon her couch, confess my boring sins, and keep hidden the true ones, hating every minute of it. I never found out anything about her, and she told me nothing about herself, except once she let slip that she had worked with victims of Auschwitz. She was Welsh, older than I was, pretty and stern. She would open the door to me, gravely and courteously, and I would follow her in and take my place upon her couch. She lived in a block of red-brick Victorian flats in Bloomsbury, and it was this block I described thirty years later in a novel, *The Bulgari Connection* – another book which got me into trouble: I had been taking money from commercial sources, and so blackened the Good Name of Literature. Perhaps, come to think of it, I hoped for some kind of absolution from Miss Rowlands.

The custom was for the analysand to lie on the sofa with their head nearest the analyst's chair, so the expression on his or her face could not be read. This I did. She spoke very little and offered no advice. The theory was that if left to themselves the patient would investigate the patterns made by their own statements, come to their own conclusions about the yarns they were spinning to themselves and others. It must have been so boring. I would hear a constant click, click, click behind me and I realised she passed the time by knitting, though what she knitted, and for whom, she never said. I knew nothing about her at all.

When I told her my sister Jane had died – that was in 1969, and Jane was 39 – she wept a little and said, 'She was like a walnut withered in its shell,' which seemed true enough to me, and was the real sentence of death. It came home to me properly then that Jane was indeed dead, had died, was no longer my beloved, tragic, beautiful sister but in a grave, buried in a rural churchyard in Newport, Essex. More, she had left three children behind and they too must be my responsibility. My mother was beside herself. There is nothing worse than the untimely death of children. I must have been in a state at the time, too, I can see.

I had been on holiday with Ron and the three children, in a camp site at Les Sables-d'Olonne on the Atlantic Coast of France, south of Nantes. I knew Jane was ill but not how very ill she was. She had a malignant melanoma, a rarer disease than it is now, and terminal if left untreated, which it had been. I should not have gone away. When the telegram came from my mother saying I must come at once I took the train home from France leaving Ron to pack up the tent and follow me home with the children. He did not alas follow me.

That month men first walked upon the moon: anything could happen. The cosmos became our oyster, but I was dizzy with distress. Like Annette in the novel *Affliction*, unable to believe what was going on.

A friend of mine whose husband had just left her had joined us for comfort and consolation, and had set up a tent next to ours, beneath the pine trees. Around the 16th of August every year the wind turns on the wild Atlantic coast and the hot sands are whipped with cold rain. The summer announces it is over. But this year the turn in the weather was late and Ron's version of consolation took a practical form, and he did not arrive home for another ten days, or phone me, or write, by which time Jane was dead and the funeral over, and Julia – I will call her that – presumably well bedded.

But like so many men of his generation Ron found death embarrassing. He sometimes did not know where to put himself in a crisis except somewhere else. As for Julia, she was a nice, baffled, terrified girl with a difficult husband and I forgive her. She had three small children whom she would drive round in the car between six o'clock and eight o'clock every morning so as not to disturb her husband with their playing and crying. He was a copywriter and needed sleep to fuel his creativity and made a terrible fuss if disturbed. Now he had left. I daresay I would have done the same in her circumstances. Nevertheless it was painful.

Had Miss Rowlands been trained by the Jungians, not the Freudians, had she belonged to some newer, younger, post-feminist school of therapy, I would have been out of the marriage like a shot, divorce papers flying – but the law was not so kind to women in those days, and the current wisdom was that men would be men and women should put up with it. And my children loved their step-father and father, and my niece and two nephews their step-uncle, and, like it or not so did I. And I have had to break the news of enough deaths to enough children in my time not to want to go round rocking any more boats than necessary. I stayed, and had another baby.

Doralee and Peter don't have this kind of problem: the new young are trained to look after their own best interests. They have support groups and are there for one another, and tragedies are only allowed to hang around for so long before acceptance is reached and closure obtained. Though for Doralee and Peter it does seem unlikely that there will be many others in a similar predicament to their own, and 'sharing' they can see may be a difficulty in this particular case.

I do not think Miss Rowlands helped me come to terms with my masochistic tendencies or my low self-esteem, or any of the other neurotic ills that plagued my young life, but it was here in her consulting rooms that I learned to finish my sentences when speaking aloud. I learned to distinguish between what is a feeling and what is a thought, which is trickier than you might think, but useful for novelists. Before Miss Rowlands, feelings and thoughts lay in a viscous muddle inside my head. After Miss Rowlands I could sort them out, put them into the heads of fictional characters, and consider them.

When I started psychoanalysis I lived in a short-term world. This lover, this baby, this profound but passing emotion, this TV commercial – and I could just about manage a thirty-second script but fifteen would be better. After that I would lie back exhausted. Eight years later

I could undertake a television drama, a full-length novel, a radio or stage play. I did not need the gratification of instant results: I could cover more than a single page without pausing to be admired. I preferred to sell ideas rather than products. Was that an achievement? I had the feeling Miss Rowlands thought it was, but she did not say so.

How I hated going to see her, how hard the sofa was, the time went so slowly, it was as bad as being five years old and made to lie down for a nap after lunch. I hated the suspension of real life that occurred in those lunchtime sessions, I hated the sound of my own voice as I searched my past for patterns. I could have been off lunching with one of the colleagues at the Strand Palace Hotel, flirting with my boss, or drinking in the American Bar at the Savoy. Yet I knew well enough the better path was to lie there on the couch, undeserving yet one of the privileged who had found a watering-place in a desert, a tiny oasis of wisdom, and that it was my path and purpose in life to pass it on.

My conversion to anti-therapism came as a bolt from the blue: a flurry of enantiodromia to the head, in fairly dreadful circumstances. Enantiodromia is a Jungian and very useful term for the process of conversion, when someone goes as far down the road of obsession as possible, comes to the end of the tracks, and has no option but to go back the other way. It is the moment when Saul the persecutor of the Christians turns into Paul, the great saint and protector, the flash of light on the road to Damascus.

It was 1991. I had been asked by a group of psycho-therapists to talk to them about the role of the archetype in my novels. I demurred. Not my scene: mine to write, theirs to analyse. They persisted, I went. A large house in North London, headquarters of some kind of association for the dissemination of emotional literacy. Here were courses for policemen, social workers, magistrates, priests, politicians – my, they were busy! Laypersons streamed in, converts flowed out, with the jargon of knowledge, kindness and understanding at their fingertips. Couldn't be bad, I thought. But my audience of therapists seemed to want only to know how to get their novels published. And they were cross with me because without training, without their insights, I managed to do it. And I realised with some alarm that what they did professionally was write their novels in other people's heads, turn their lives into narratives, and give it the end their particular training suggested. The beginning was theirs to define (cold mother, abusive father), the middle (be more assertive, find your self-esteem), theirs to develop, the end (mostly to split with the heretofore loved one) theirs to conclude. Members all of a living creative-writing course.

After the talk we went to a Chinese restaurant. This was 1991. I was living apart from Ron on the suggestion of his therapist. We 'needed time apart', she said, and had done my horoscope and his, to prove how unsuited we were. I could hardly take her seriously, and was surprised he could, but held the general view that therapy was good, therapists were wise, knew what they were doing and it was all going to be okay. But that evening scales fell from my eyes, the cataract was swept away, I was indeed Paul on the road to Damascus. Not only was I wrong, self-deceived, complacent, unthinking, uncritical, I was stupid. These people were dangerous.

Over sweet and sour pork the group discussed patients and cases, using real names, while pondering what should happen next to them. Over apple and banana toffee and bad white wine they decided Jill must leave Jack – he bullied her. That Jack was in the same line of work as his therapist – both were parsons – and both up for promotion in the Church and there was a conflict of interests here bothered no one. Jack didn't want Jill to leave, and she said she didn't want to go, but they reckoned she could be persuaded. I asked how old Jack and Jill were and was told, 'Oh, in their sixties:' They'd been married thirty-five years. 'Mightn't they be lonely apart?' I asked. They turned to me as one. 'We don't talk about loneliness, we talk about aloneness.' And I saw the tall house in North London as the haunted house on the hill out of which streamed the bats of Satan, leaving a blight of sorrow and loneliness wherever they alighted. I went home and rang Ron and said, 'For God's sake be careful.' But it was too late, he trusted her, not me. If his therapist said I was the source of her troubles, why then he believed her. Besides, he was in love with someone else by then, not that I knew that at the time.

His therapist was a new-age devotee, a lover of nature cures and crystals, and saw the family as the source of many evils, and had *Cutting the Ties That Bind* upon her coffee table, and it was her belief that heart by-passes and angiograms were unnatural, and that blocked arteries and all physical ills could be cured by attitude of mind and the right diet. Think healthy and you will be healthy. And within a couple of years of 'treatment' he was dead, from the unblocked artery, on the day of our divorce.

I still get letters from those who have run up against the cruel side of the therapy industry (an industry is what it is, and a powerful one, with influence in high places) and have suffered greatly. My own family has certainly not yet recovered from their father's visits to the therapist. I wrote another novel, *Worst Fears*, vaguely connected to the events of the death, and then felt enough, enough, and left the subject. In this the new widow discovers the truth about the thorny patch she has so blithely and blindly been living in, while deluding herself it was the Garden of Eden. There's a telephone therapist in this one. She's not wicked, not like the ones in *Affliction*, just not very bright.

That was in the early Nineties when the arcane world of psychoanalysis for the few, for those who could afford it, had turned for good or bad into free counselling for those on benefit. But out of the years in psychoanalysis in the Sixties and Seventies, I wrote a series of short stories twenty and thirty years on, tales told to an analyst to whom I gave the name Miss Jacobs, but of course she was Miss Rowlands in disguise. Miss Jacobs sits and nods and knits while lives ravel and unravel around her, and those in denial come to their senses. *A Gentle Tonic Affect*, the PR girl at the nuclear power plant; the good wife with the hysterical paralysis in *Delights of France or Horrors of the Road*; *Moon Over Minneapolis*, title story of a collection, in which twin sisters, one pretty, one plain, visit the twin cities and realise where duty lies; and other stories too, and just thinking about them makes me want to write another one, and resuscitate Miss Rowlands, sitting there, calm and kind. I suspect I had a very positive transference, no matter how I denied it at the time, and since. She wept for my sister, when there were precious few to do it. I think perhaps she saved me from self-pity. She had standards in suffering, after all. She had worked with the victims of the camps.

Trisha, Doralee and Peter
visit the parson

Ruby was disturbed when making jam doughnuts for the village fête by a ring on the doorbell, and was surprised to find her daughter, her partner Peter and a strange young woman on her doorstep.

'Let me guess,' Ruby said. 'You've decided to have a baby after all and this young woman is to be the surrogate mother.'

'Give me a break, Mum,' said Doralee. 'Not at a time like this. I need you to be there for me,' and she sat her mother down and told her the story.

'How does it work sexually?' asked Ruby, taking the plain woman's view, unimpressed by philosophical or medical detail. 'The him-her, the her-him, and you?'

'You mean you believe me?' asked Doralee, surprised. Peter and Trisha were wiping out the mixing bowl with their index fingers. The doughnuts had been deep fried and put aside to cool a little before being filled with jam and rolled in sugar. Doralee hated to think of the wasted calories each one represented. If they were hungry why didn't they eat something good for them? She was not surprised her mother was a size 22.

'Nothing surprises me?' said Ruby. 'The Lords of Misrule are abroad, that's for sure and everything is topsy-turvy in the world. Gay weddings and cloned babies! If these two have had a sex change then that's their doing. Perhaps it's just as well you never married the him-her, though heaven knows who else you're going to find.'

Doralee tried to explain that she was not talking about a sex change, rather a personality change, but her mother failed to grasp the difference. Doralee could see why her father had left. Ruby walked them down to the village church to keep their appointment with Father Bryant, who was rumoured to have successfully exorcised a ghost from the Edwardian ladies' loo in the Market Square and a DVD-throwing poltergeist from a house in Bell Street on the council estate, neither having any potential in the local tourist trade. They walked past the old shambles and the estate agents and the new trendy kitchen shop and the cross in the cobbles where a Catholic had been burned by Protestants four hundred years ago. The Peter body kicked a stone along the road while they walked, attracting looks from passers-by.

'I don't think Father Bryant will be blessing any gay weddings,' said Ruby, 'if your friend is a man in drag, as you say. Little hands for a man and no Adam's apple but you're the one with the education, Dora, and the up-to-date life style, so I suppose you know. I dare say they have hand transplants now, and Adam's apple removal on the NHS.'

'Doralee. Not Dora,' said Doralee, automatically.

'I've changed my mind about that. From now on you girls are going to be Dora, Claudia, Gloria and Mary like anyone else,' said her mother. 'I don't know what I was trying to prove. To upset my mother-in-law, I daresay, and give the fox-hunting set something to talk about. But now she's passed on it hardly seems worth it.'

'Well thank you very much,' said Doralee, bitterly. 'After all that!'

'I can see you're in a mood,' said her mother. 'Your London life does nothing for your nerves. Don't say anything to upset Father Bryant. I warn you he's gone very High Church, incense everywhere, refuses to do signs of peace, keeps using the 1662 Prayer Book in defiance of the Bishop, who is trying to excommunicate him. It was bad enough years back getting you girls christened, he certainly wouldn't put up with it now.'

'Names are so important,' said the Peter body. 'My little boy's called Spencer. I think it's a lovely name.'

'You have a child then?' asked Ruby. 'So at least something works, or did. Or perhaps you mean to have it cut off? Some people do, I believe.'

'A dear little boy,' said the Peter body, 'but I don't see too much of him.'

'You didn't tell me he already had a child,' said Ruby to Doralee. 'He never mentioned it before. You are a dark horse, Dora. I suppose you know what you're doing with your life.'

They arrived at a little stone Saxon church, set amongst yew trees, the other side of a lychgate. A notice said the place was protected by CCTV cameras, and another that it was Grade 1 listed, and pinned up over the board which gave the times of services was a poster headed *Returning the Nation to its Heritage* and obscuring that poster were warnings to countryside roamers to close gates and not to eat yew berries, and not to put up notices which might be seen as offensive to people of other faiths. But the interior of the church was beautifully restored with mock-Victorian stencilling and evening light struck a rosy glow through arched windows. Doralee began to feel quite hopeful.

Father Bryant came forward from the back of the church to meet them, like some amiable, if manic, Friar Tuck. He had a huge double chin beneath a wide face, and astute eyes, and a fine head of light brown hair which looked as if it had been set on rollers before being brushed out. He carried a bag of boiled sweets in his hand but offered the others none. He thanked Ruby for the doughnuts which he said he would give to the fête-organisers in the morning. He wore voluminous white robes draped with a purple sash, and big walking boots.

'Talk about cross-dressing!' whispered the Peter body, too loudly, and the Trisha body kicked his ankle and he squealed. Ruby went home to deep fry another batch of doughnuts.

They sat in the vestry. The Trisha body wriggled in the orange feather stole so it slipped from her pale, sloping shoulders, and she did not bother to pick it up. The Peter body directed flirtatious glances at the priest, looking out from under long lashes. Doralee had not realised before how long they were. Doralee got them settled as best she could. Thus in her childhood she had settled her little brothers and sisters. She told her tale as if she were talking to her editor, in measured and civil terms, and the priest listened attentively.

'It is my opinion,' Doralee concluded, 'that the two of them won't revert of their own accord, but need some kind of cosmic help, and as soon as possible. They're regressing. I don't know how these things work but I would imagine the longer they are out of their bodies the more somehow diffuse they become: they won't fit back properly and that could be disastrous for my relationship. I don't want to share my life with someone who's got a strange woman inside him. I'm the one with the oestrogen. I want a full return to normality. But if you do bring this about I would be happy for Peter and I to go through a marriage ceremony. It would be the least I could do.'

'Thank you,' said Father Bryant, 'but bribes are not necessary, pleased though I would be to welcome you back into the Church. I was there at your christening – the power of

197

the Church reaches out and draws its children back. I am not sure however that the regular exorcism ceremony is appropriate. The unfortunate couple you bring to me, Trisha and Peter, hardly seem to me to be instruments of the devil's malice. They may rather be implements of God's blessing, a miracle, though it would take a convocation or so to get to the bottom of it. They are not lost souls waiting to go to heaven or afraid of going to hell, for whom the ritual has been devised. They are not loitering in public lavatories the better to frighten the living. They are not wandering energies with disturbed spirits, throwing the crockery about. The man is in the woman's body and the woman in the man's. What can this be but God's visual fix? Time and time again my parishioners come to me and tell me their boys are behaving like girls. It is the boys who are modest and sensitive and easily hurt; it is the girls who are forceful, energetic, predatory, notching up sexual conquests while the boys do what they can to preserve their virtue. The transmigration of souls, which seems to me what we have here, was bound to happen sooner or later, and I am most obliged to you, Doralee, for bringing it to my attention. God sends his messengers in the most surprising way. He speaks not from out a burning bush but on the back stairs of a dry-cleaning shop and domestic employment agency!' He was quite excited. 'I will raise the issue with the General Synod at their next meeting in two months' time. That should stir them up a bit. One in the eye for the Bishop, in fact, who, as you may have heard, is not on the traditionalists' side.'
'You mean you're not going to do anything?' Doralee was horrified. 'Not even pray? Surely this counts as possession. Surely you invoke the Archangel Michael? What about bell, book and candle? It worked for the ladies' loo, it worked in Bell Lane for the poltergeist. You have to help!'

Father Bryant said he worried about the validity of trying to perform an exorcism when a miracle might be involved, rather than a curse from hell, and when there were two parties involved, neither of whom were demonstrating any particular distress or showing any signs of diabolic possession. It was without precedent. Doralee said there had to be a first time for everything, and that she would write the exorcism up in her columns. That persuaded him, though he first asked for picture approval, which Doralee promised. She would argue about that when the time came.

Father Bryant led Doralee, Peter and Trisha into the dimmer light of the church, Peter and Trisha whispering and giggling unabashed the while. All were required to kneel. The priest asked for the intercession of the Archangel Michael. He asked for the banishment from these people here present of all spells, black magic, witchcraft, malefics, maledictions, the evil eye, diabolic infestations, oppressions, possessions by all that is evil and sinful, jealousy, perfidy, envy: all physical, psychological, moral and spiritual ailments. The abjuring went on for some time.

When the good Father paused for breath the Peter body made a fuss about the state of his knees and demanded the right to just sit on the pew and bend his head. Father Bryant pointed out that a state of humility was desirable when supplicating the Almighty but conceded it was okay. The Trisha body pointed out that she was half Jewish, and the Peter body said he was as Christian as anybody else, it was just that all this grovelling got up his nose. The Father said that exorcism was well accepted in the Jewish tradition. He asked if either of them had drunk from rivers or lakes the previous night because that was when, traditionally, the hazard of demons was acute. The Trisha body said in horror that she'd taken a swig from

199

some bottled water the night before, she hoped that didn't count, but it did describe itself as spring water. Father Bryant, who was beginning to show signs of annoyance, said it well might. The Peter body sobbed and gulped a little, and actually knelt and prayed a little, but the Trisha body said this was all a waste of time and wouldn't it be more sensible to go to the police. To which Doralee replied sharply that that was fine, if he wanted them all to be locked up and certified, or used by the CIA for research. Surely prayer was safer. The Peter body recovered from its fright and complained to Father Bryant that it was the first time, and he hoped the last, that he'd heard that bit about not being worthy to pick up the crumbs under the table. 'They'd have a fit in my self-assertiveness class,' he said. 'I am just not going to say that. What have I got to be humble about? I won the lottery! Surely that means I'm God's favourite!'

Doralee shushed them and calmed them down and Father Bryant was able to continue. He seemed more prepared to believe now that the couple were not just possessed but that the devils were intractable. He asked on Doralee's behalf that the healing waters of her baptism now flow back through the maternal and paternal generations to purify her family name of Satan and sin, and for calling upon powers that set themselves up in opposition to God, which Doralee thought was unnecessary. Surely, of all of them, she was the innocent party here, and certainly the most likeable.

The rosy light faded. A dim sepulchral light suffused the chapel. Father Bryant's white and purple robes moved in front of the altar. He now had bell, book and candle. He asked for the breaking and dissolving of all curses, hexes, spells, snares, lies, obstacles, deceptions, diversions, spiritual influences, evil wishes and desires, hereditary seals known and unknown, and any dysfunction and disease and any and all links with astrologers, channellers, charters, clairvoyants, crystal-healers, crystals, fortune-tellers, mediums, movements and occult seers, palm- and tarot-card readers, satanic cults, witches and voodoo.

Doralee thought guiltily about the times she had filled in on the astrological feature in *Oracle*: was it worse to make it all up or to report – as best she could, not being an expert – on the state of play in the heavens? The Peter body yawned, and the Trisha body seemed to be asleep.

'I rebuke you,' cried Father Bryant suddenly in a loud voice, so they all jumped. 'I command you to go directly to God without harm to me or any here present!' It was at that moment, and probably fortuitously, since the pattern of light in the church changed as a cloud moved off the face of the sinking sun, and a rosy light shone in through stained-glass windows for an instant, only to be gone again, leaving a denser gloom behind, that a flock of black-winged creatures took sudden leave of the rafters. They circled the air above Father Bryant's head, flapping leathery wings, making an impatient, angry sound. Father Byrant waved them away, protecting his hair, for which they seemed to have a fascination. Then as one they rose, and streamed out into the dusk through one of the arched windows in the tower, which Doralee could see had been left without glass. Doralee gasped in shock. Peter and Trisha were suddenly wide awake and transfixed, clinging together.

'Only bats,' said Father Bryant, when the church was quiet again, and his hair was safe. 'I thought they'd gone but I see they're back. Take no notice. Long-nosed, alas, a protected species. They won't let me get rid of them. Only last week I had an e-mail from the Bat Preservation Society forbidding me to play the organ in case it disturbed them. We may use a piano and sing, however, since it is a place of worship and if we can produce a performers' licence. But I shall now have to bring in Health and Safety because of the danger of verminous infection to the congregation. Let them fight it out between them. Now, about the interview?'

'Well?' asked Ruby, when they got back to the house.
'Nothing has changed,' said Doralee. 'Except they seem to be growing up a little,' and it was true. On their way home from the church the couple seemed quite adult and serious, as if the bats had taken at least part of the spirit of entropy with them. But Peter was still in Trisha, and Trisha in Peter, the ropes of reality that had bound soul to body – the image of the fluttering clouds would not leave her – having worn so thin, or been so badly tethered, that they had cast loose. It could happen to her too, now, at any time, and she was alone with the fact, and where was she going to find help?

Her mother was making things worse. Doralee needed time but there was to be none.
'Darling Dora,' her mother was saying, 'I had a brainwave and called Peter's mother and asked her if she could drive up to join us for dinner. You will be staying, I suppose. So long since we all got together – everyone's so busy these days. Claudia and Gloria say they can come: they'll be thrilled to see you.'
'I expect they will,' said Doralee. 'We can all discuss our new names.' The name change had shaken her more than she thought. Perhaps souls were wandering entities anyway:

like a lot of party balloons drifting by, strings dangling, you could grasp whatever one was nearest, and it would do, only normally male kept to male and female to female. It only became noticeable when you got the wrong gender.

'Damned if you do,' observed Ruby, tartly, 'and damned if you don't,' and went back to the kitchen.

Doralee wanted to make excuses, any excuses, and go back to town but the Peter body and the Trisha body said they were hungry, and promised to behave. They would simply act one another. The Peter body reminded Doralee that she had played Polly Peachum in *The Beggars' Opera* and the Trisha body talked about when he had played Ophelia in the school play – his adolescent growth spurt had been late and he had stayed short while everyone around him had been giants. Doralee capitulated.

Dinner was served as formally as could be managed in the panelled library where once Doralee's grandfather had written his sermons. The tablecloth had been her grand-mother's, and was of heavy, yellowed linen. Graham had bought up the lot before her grandparents had moved off into an old people's home, rather sooner than they had hoped to go, where there was space for very few personal belong-ings. They had simply, and kindly, moved over to make room for Graham's new young family. He had been a late and only child, and they wanted their son and his line to have everything they held so dear. Graham in his turn had waited until encroaching Alzheimer's meant they scarcely noticed when he went off with his yoga teacher. Ruby had wept bitter tears in front of them for a while, but they had mercifully got in into their heads that it was because the labrador Rex had died.

It was on this table that all of Ruby's six children had done their homework and carved their unnecessary long names (the girls) and peremptory short ones (the boys). Much of the grandparents' original dinner service had been lost or broken – with Graham's departure Ruby had become something of a butter-fingers, as if the material world itself was a source of indifference to her – so that very few of the pieces on the table now matched. The table was cheerful enough, however, since Ruby had got first choice at the bric-à-brac stall at the village fête over the years, and always picked the brightest and best.

'Nice and cheery and homey,' the Peter body said, as Ruby brought in a tureen of thick green pea soup with a knubbly, crusted brown surface into which the serving spoon had trouble breaking. The tureen itself was Limoges and porcelain, an ornamental crouched hare on its lid in pink and green, and was very hard to clean, nor did Doralee suppose that Ruby had made much effort so to do. Doralee kicked the Peter body's ankles and the Peter body said, 'Why did you kick me under the table?' to which Ruby replied 'She wants to draw your attention to the tureen. It is a very good piece and worth a lot of money and the stains on the bottom are not dirt, Dora, but a flaw in the making, as you know very well. Please do not try to show me up in front of Peter's mother.'

Peter's mother Adrienne, having driven up from London at the last moment, and protesting that she hadn't been allowed time to change properly, only throw on a couple of scarves and pull on some rings, had still turned up with a city elegance seldom seen in Ruby's village. The scarves were Dior and the shoes Blahnik.

'Cheery and homey?' she asked her apparent son. 'Whoever taught you to use words like that?'

'Well I think they're nice words,' said the Peter body, 'and I really like that rabbit on top of the tureen.'

'It's a hare,' chorused Ruby, Claudia and Gloria. The Peter body was the only male, if such he could be called, at the gathering. He seemed to be very conscious of the fact – a parody of a male, indeed – and was looking Doralee's sisters up and down appreciatively, bending a little forward over his bowl of pea soup to see down Claudia's cleavage. Claudia was a make-the-most-of your-assets person, who worked as a TV actress and sometimes made commercials. Gloria was a social worker and came in a woolly jumper and jeans. But all the Thicket women were strikingly good-looking.

'Actually,' said the Trisha body, 'new research suggests that the rabbit and the hare are so closely related genetically it is legitimate to refer to one as the other. There is even a suggestion that they are the descendents of a fertile chimera.'

Doralee could see this was not going to work for long. She could claim sudden illness and leave the dinner party but then who would drive? Trisha had never learned and she could not trust the Peter hands, or even the Trisha hands under Peter's control, to take the wheel. Having children must be like this. A constant anxiety that they would disgrace you in company, an inability ever to relax and enjoy your dinner. Terror as to what was about to happen next.

Adrienne was looking at her apparent son as if puzzled by something. 'Do you have a sister called Thomasina?' the Peter body was asking Claudia. 'I have a good friend on the stage called Thomasina. She's so like you it's amazing. She's appeared on the Edinburgh fringe.' Trisha had assured Doralee that her lesbian days were over but Doralee could see that they were not. The Peter body was now fingering Claudia's sleeve. Another kick under the table from Doralee, and the Peter body desisted, saying brightly, 'I do so just love good old-fashioned velvet like this.'

The company looked confused but Ruby was bringing in a boiled gammon, roast potatoes and green peas and carrots mixed. Both Claudia and Gloria looked at the meal askance – Claudia was on the Atkins diet and Gloria was a vegetarian, but it was their mother's custom to ride rough-shod over sensibilities of which she did not approve. Doralee was too distracted to engage her mother in reproaches on her sisters' behalf.

'Surely you know how many sisters your partner has?' asked Adrienne, drawing the edge of a chiffon scarf out of spilt soup. When the spoon finally went through the crust there had been quite a splash. 'I know there are quite a few, but even so. How many years have you been together?' and the Peter body answered gamely 'Lots. And every one a delight.'

'High time they actually got married,' said Ruby, finally saying it. 'Don't you think so, Adrienne? Then we two can be the mothers-in-law and have some status. Will you carve, Peter?' and the Peter body took up the carving knife and with inexpert, albeit, male hands and no knowledge of how the thing was done, began, carving the wrong way of the grain and still paying attention to Claudia's cleavage which he could now see to advantage.

Claudia raised the top of her dress a little and said pointedly it might be just as well, it might help to grow Peter up a bit. Everyone knew marriage made for a stable partnership, whereas being a partner was just asking for trouble. She was dedicated to her work and so wasn't going to have either, and certainly no children.

Ruby said she would change her mind when she got to thirty and at least Dora was trying, and with any luck hadn't left it too late, didn't Adrienne agree. Gloria said on the contrary, probably Claudia would not, the latest statistics showed otherwise. Podding off was simply not what people in a modern society did any more, wasn't that so, Peter? The birth-rate was dropping and a good thing too. The Peter body said he didn't have the slightest idea about that kind of thing.

'I hope you're not getting depressed, Peter,' said Adrienne to the Peter body. 'You have such a good job there it would be a pity to lose interest. That's what your father did before he died – got depressed and lost interest. That's why the cancer got a hold so easily. And if you lost your job, what would Doralee have to write about in her column?'

'I expect I could find something,' said Doralee.

'I didn't mean it like that,' said Adrienne. 'You know I didn't. But I would like a wedding to look forward to. It can't be a proper Jewish wedding because of Doralee, but I'm reconciled to that by now, and Christian weddings can be quite nice, if things are done properly. I'm sure you'd conceive quite soon, Doralee, once you were legally married.'

'Well said,' said Ruby. 'Well said!'

'I would like to have things settled before I pass on,' said Adrienne. 'When your grandmother was my age she died of cancer of the liver. We're not a long-lived family, I'm afraid. I haven't been feeling too well lately, but don't worry about me. I expect it's just neurotic. Shall we say in the autumn? September is such a pleasant month for a wedding. High summer and it's difficult to know what to wear. One doesn't want to look Ascoty, but one does like to look as if one had made an effort.'

But the Trisha body had pushed back her chair and was

207

now crouched by Adrienne's side, and was taking the older woman's hand in her own soft little one.

'You must stop thinking like this,' said the Trisha body. 'And I have never seen you look so healthy.'

Adrienne pushed the Trisha body off, and hissed at the Peter body.

'You just sit there and do nothing! You will be marrying into a very peculiar family, and I don't think much of your new friends, but you will do what you will, I suppose. Carving pig! What point exactly are you trying to make?'

'Oh my God,' said Ruby, mortified. 'I am so sorry!'

Ruby had served boiled gammon so often in her life, she said, such an easy dish to prepare and always popular, she had quite forgotten what animal it came from, and Peter always ate bacon when he came to stay. But she was so sorry, she would make Adrienne a nice tinned salmon salad this very moment, and Adrienne said not salmon, it would only be farmed and full of little worms. She apologised for her outburst: she thought it was because her metabolic balance was disturbed, and perhaps that was the cancer. And it was really hypocritical of her to be worried about eating pork, since she had given up kosher when Peter's father had died. What kind of God was it that allowed such things to happen? Everyone waited until she had finished the food on her plate. Doralee wondered what it would be like if she and Peter had a child and it turned out to be like Adrienne. It would have a minimum of twenty-five per cent of her genes.

One way and another attention was diverted from the odd behaviour of Peter and Trisha, until the serving of tinned peaches and ice cream during which the Trisha body, who had drunk far too much, began to laugh hysterically and said to the Peter body, 'I could have another son and call it

Thomasina,' and the Peter body reacted by tweaking Claudia's nipple, at which Doralee burst into tears and said she had terrible stomach cramps, probably a miscarriage and she wanted to go home right now.

Everyone crowded round, offering to call ambulances and saying she couldn't possibly drive, and having to pull her back from the driving seat, and Claudia said Doralee had always been insanely jealous, and Gloria that Doralee had always stolen her boyfriends what was she complaining about, and Doralee pushed Trisha into the driving seat and got into the back with the Peter body and they drove off. Though when they were round the corner she made Trisha stop the car, and got in the front and drove herself, cool as a cucumber, and pain free, all the way back to London.

Doralee parked in her allocated parking space in the court-yard of High View as the Kleene Machine van was leaving from outside the front door. George was just locking up. 'You're late,' he said. 'I thought you were off for the night. The cleaners left some stuff for you,' and he handed over a couple of hangers, well draped in plastic covers, which Doralee removed and binned as soon as she entered the flat. It was her black dress, deliberately slit in many places from hem to neckline, falling from its thin straps like black streamers.

Doralee stared at it for a long time. It is horrible to be hated, and cursed, when all you have done is demand your rights as a consumer. She even cried a little.
'I don't see why they should take it out on you,' said the Peter body, 'just because I gave you the mattress-cover without asking for the money. I quite forgot, what with one thing and another.'

'What exactly,' asked Doralee, 'was the one thing and the other?' and the Trisha body said that after they had realised what had happened, that they were each other, and had tried passing and re-passing on the stairs for a bit and it hadn't worked, they'd had rather a lot to drink and gone down and trashed the shop.

'It was great,' said the Peter body. 'It seemed what my body was made for. What's the point of muscles if you don't use them to bash about with? I smashed the chairs and the computer and found the mother board and stamped on it and destroyed all their stupid records. I swung from the light fittings and brought them down. I poured all the carbon tetrachloride down the sink and kicked their piles of mending stuff around and tangled their embroidery threads.'

'It was great, just great,' said the Trisha body proudly. 'And I wedged a fifty pence piece in the ironing machine so when I turned it on it overheated and burned. And I got all the stuff from the racks and muddled it up on the floor. That'd serve her right, the old bitch.'

'Nobody treats me like that and gets away with it,' said the Peter body. 'Nobody speaks to me as if I was nothing. I'm a lottery-winner; I am accustomed to respect.'

'It might be that the fumes got to her brain and destroyed some brain cells,' said the Trisha body. 'That might even have triggered the swap.'

'But nothing *happened*,' said the Trisha body, who was not interested in causes, only in consequences, to Doralee. 'She's not my type. Only ever you, darling, only ever you.' And the Trisha body put her arms round the taller woman and stared up at her with Peter's sweet look but smirking, and smelling of the peppermints she had eaten in the car. Doralee distanced herself as best she could.

'And I'm the one who gets the voodoo object or whatever it is,' said Doralee, crossly. 'From the sound of it I'm lucky to have got off so lightly.' She bundled the fragmented dress into a plastic bag and put it down the rubbish chute. She just wanted it out of her home.

'I don't imagine they'll try anything worse,' said the Trisha body. 'They're bound to be illegals. They won't want to risk drawing attention to themselves. And it could have been anybody. They're bound to have enemies.'

Doralee felt immensely tired, all of a sudden. 'Time for bed!' she said, putting the Peter body in the bedroom, the Trisha to sleep on the couch in the office, while she herself slept on the sofa in the living room, the better to keep an eye on everyone. She checked first that the doors to the outside world were all properly locked.

Feminist!

In the mid-Seventies, my publishers, aware of the sudden and insatiable market for books by women about women, labelled me a feminist and the label stayed. I did not fight it, I certainly would not deny that was what I was, but it was not why I wrote novels. I was not a propagandist. Sonia Land of my then agency, Shiel Land, a brilliant enough woman and at one time Rupert Murdoch's right-hand woman, shook her finger earnestly at me one day, when my sales were drooping, and said, 'You write consistent product, we sell,' but I could only ever write what I saw, and then produce a stream of alternative realities, of the kind the real world failed to provide. I set novels in the society I saw around me, and still do, and it changes all the time. If the world would only produce a consistent face, I might be able to do better myself. It is my job to report it, not unify it.

I realised one day, in about 1970, that celebrity was a peculiar process, slow moving but inexorable, which had very little to do with oneself, or talent, or actual achievement, but something self-perpetuating. Every press cutting fed upon the last. Get to a critical mass and there was no stopping it. The less one did the more one's renown grew. It flourished in one's absence. I never sought out publicity, never employed a PR person, never volunteered an opinion unless asked to. I wrote what I was asked to write and spoke the exact truth when asked a question. Only latterly did I so much as have my hair done for a photograph: I thought I was 'meant' to appear as I did in real life, and only when a friendly photographer explained that this was not the case, you were allowed to take measures to ensure you looked your best, and even gave you friendly tips, such as not putting your chin in your chest or lying back in your chair when they clicked, and that bare forearms leaning into the camera look enormous, and if you prop the side of your cheek into your hand you will get a fold of flesh – better to just touch your cheek with your finger tips and not actually lean – and that it was all part of a complex game of perception, did I learn to present myself in the best light. And once discovered it seemed to me a vast and greatly entertaining game – I assumed with journalists that we were all somehow in this together, all in the world of communication, with deadlines to be met, jobs to be done, money to be earned, reputations to be preserved, and fun to be had, so the quotes flowed and the articles wrote themselves and were usually kind, especially in the early days.

I did not make the mistake of believing that the person interviewed was 'me'. The public figure was a fictional character. From the beginning I did not watch myself on TV, would switch off when I heard myself on radio, or read any article about myself other than with half an eye. This was partly because of my awareness that publicity brought endless trouble into the home, partly for my own peace of mind. I would tear articles out of the paper before Ron saw them. I was meant to be the port and lemon girl, vulgarly employed, with few brains, without artistic or aesthetic sensibility, whom he had married, not a literary figure. And up to a point that is what I wanted too: anonymity is a great pleasure and it is hard to give it up. Success is something others observe, seldom the successful, and so it is little comfort. The path towards it is littered with minor failures, rejections, bad reviews and tax demands, and that is what one notices. Ordinary wives are spared all that.

We went out to dinner the night the pilot episode of *Upstairs Downstairs* was screened – to universal acclaim, as they say – and our hosts insisted on switching on the television and watching, to my apologetic discomfiture and Ron's fury. He thought it was trashy, popular, down-market stuff. That was mid-Seventies. Mid-Eighties, I took the fuse out of the TV plug just before the BBC version of *The Life and Loves of a She-Devil* was screened. 'Oh dear,' I said, 'the TV has broken down,' and we had a peaceful evening. Otherwise there would have been tears before bedtime. And anyway I wanted to be a private person, not a public one.

'Good Lord,' my mother said, when I once said this to her. 'You! You've no idea what it's like out there. You go into the fish and chip shop and they give you the best piece of fish.' I daresay that is true. Mothers are like that, as in

Ruby with Doralee. You think they see you from the inside out, then suddenly you realise they too see you from the outside in, and the ground shifts beneath your feet. It can happen at any age.

By and large, if you get bad reviews and a hard time in the press, turn from a national sweetheart over night to a hate figure, which can happen, people are immensely kind to you, if a little patronising. There, there, my dear – you tried, and failed. We love you all the same. If the reviews are good, they feel free to take you down a peg or two.

You don't win. But whoever was trying to win, anyway? I was only ever trying to find time to write.

By the mid-Seventies I had become accustomed to the table vanishing from beneath my pen to be sold to the highest bidder. But the shop was not doing so well: punters knew more than once they had. They too read *Miller's Guide to Antiques* and watched the *Antiques Road Show*, and knew the proper cost of everything if still the value of nothing. The supply of undiscovered, unrecognised antiques was drying up. Skips which once were full of Dutch tiles and Georgian washstands for the taking were now piled with nothing but old bricks: the demolition industry had discovered the value of the past and gone into Reclamation. Being a shopkeeper, not an artist, had its drawbacks. Saturdays were the worst, Ron would complain. Customers came in to have their domestic quarrels in front of him: they would wrangle over a piece of furniture – she wanted it, he didn't, or vice versa – and the quarrels would be bitter and nasty. Others took their power freakery out on my poor husband: he would be asked to take down the highest, heaviest piece of furniture to ground level for closer inspection: twenty minutes of hard toil later they'd say, 'Oh I don't think so, after all. Junk!' and walk out.

He felt it was demeaning, and it was, and not what he wanted from life. The old art-studenty world was going, a new one, far more status-conscious, was coming in. A man was valued by the money he made, not by the books he read, nor the paintings he liked. Class was increasingly determined by income, not education. Worse now, when the front-door bell at home rang, or the phone, it would be for me, not for Ron. It was uncomfortable. We had terrible rows.

The house became full of unsold furniture, overflow from the shop. I had small children and I could scarcely find room for them. To navigate even the stairs was a problem, so cluttered were they and so upset Ron was if anything was moved from one place to another. From the mid-Sixties we'd had a series of au-pairs to help – good, grateful, hard-working, principled, diligent, virtuous girls from Europe, who helped in the house, went to English language classes and then went home. We had been so lucky. Now the spirit of freedom and rights was everywhere. It was the age of flares and sideburns and LSD – the au-pairs had boyfriends, lives of their own and well-developed temperaments. They were as likely to park the baby outside the pub in your absence as look after it.

The whole world was in uproar, not just our house. The price of oil soared as OPEC found its claws, rationing was threatened, a three-day week was imposed, it snowed in June, feminists stalked the land in Doc Martens boots, refusing to smile and demanding their rights, and it was all my fault. I was, Ron reproached me, spending too much time writing popular rubbish; if I must write – and I wasn't exactly Dostoevsky – shouldn't I be looking after the children better? We would quarrel: Ron would go and sleep in the shop – or I hoped that was where he was. I was insanely jealous (his story): he was stubborn and cruel and drank too much (mine.) Heaven knows, in retrospect, what it was all about.

One day, in protest, small children in tow, unable to find a space even to put down the bag of shopping, Ron carousing in the shop (or so I saw it), I started removing things we could do without from the house and putting them in a row along the elegant railings, while the neighbours raised their eyebrows. I put out nine very heavy aspidistra plants, I remember, in their robust Victorian planters, three occasional tables, an ancient olive-wood bench, the head of a Roman emperor and some glass decanters. Ron got to hear, came round to collect them in the back of the Volvo, took them to the shop and sold them. Too late to say but this was not what I meant, not what I meant at all, I was only registering a protest. To this day I regret those aspidistras. You had to dust them leaf by leaf, and what giants of plants they would be now, but spectacular. And that night he did not come back: he set up house in the shop for at least a week. How I wept, until he came back. I did not do it again. I should have.

Even as I write this, Mrs Kovac is putting Trisha's furniture out into the street, for anyone to take who might pass by. Mrs Kovac knows well enough who trashed her shop. There was something about the tangling of the embroidery thread that clinched it. Angry, niggling female fingers, plus the muscle no doubt of male friends. Part of her knows Trisha was right to be angry. She even respects Trisha a little for fighting back. All the same she throws Trisha's chattels out, family photographs and all, onto the street. Thirty years later it will go at once, or will by morning: only Spencer's comfort blanket, worn thin by washing, the one he clutched to his toddler chest when his mother was Trisha and not the economist, will be left on the pavement to rot and disintegrate, finally. In those days even good furniture, flung into a skip, could stay where it was, unclaimed for days.

At Kleene Machine

Everyone was so busy these days it was easier for the authorities to diagnose insanity or criminality, or to postpone judgement to the next meeting of the synod, than get to the bottom of anything. They must not move without caution, as Doralee pointed out at breakfast the next morning, and the Peter body and the Trisha body agreed. They had slept well in their new bodies and seemed more settled in their selves, more adult in their behaviour. Apparently you could get accustomed to a consciousness change very quickly. Of the three, it was Doralee who seemed most aware of their changed state, acutely aware of any confusion in gender behaviour, alarmed at the notion that there was not to be a quick solution to their predicament.

She slipped out herself to bring in fresh croissants: she no longer trusted the Peter body or the Trisha body to go out by themselves. Their account of how they had conducted themselves at the Kleene Machine had alarmed her. It seemed that the new bodies were impulsive, as if the social restraints which operated on one gender did not apply to the other.

In the current climate, if they ended up in court, their pleas of switched consciousness would simply be ignored. No one would have time to attend to them: a great number of those before the courts were on drugs anyway, and as like as not hallucinating. So far, thank God, the couple's sexual impulses had been muted: perhaps sex cut in when basic identity was more established. What she was seeing in Peter and Trisha was the hot-wiring of the personality before the urge to reproduce, and all its attendant passions, took over.

'No work today?' George the doorman asked her. Doormen kept you safe but also under observation.
'A day off for both of us,' she told him. 'A touch of the flu.'
'All right for some,' he said. 'I'm seventy-six years old and never had a day's illness in my life.'

Doralee had once been in an earthquake, and had felt the ground shift beneath her feet. She had been terrified out of all proportion to the actual event, which was quickly over. It was one of the tenets of existence – that the ground stayed still and you did the moving. If it were otherwise, you could predict nothing, be sure of nothing. She felt the same now. What George said was patently untrue. When he wasn't claiming perfect health he was talking about his ailments. She had visited him in hospital once to do an interview, on the subject of out-of-body experiences, which he claimed to have had, under anaesthetic. This George was not the one she knew. He was a simulacrum who had picked up the wrong script by mistake. The body-snatchers had invaded and she was the only one who didn't know.

'Only kidding,' said George. She must have turned white. 'I only wish it was true. I'm getting older. I get these flashing lights behind my eyes. I ought to do something, I suppose.'

218

She murmured sympathy and bought a dozen croissants from the paper shop. Both the bodies had big appetites. Give people permission to gorge, and they would, that was evident. She bought some butter as well, and some home-made lemon curd. If they wanted to clog their arteries let them get on with it. She crossed the road casually and took a look back at the Kleene Machine. It was closed. There were boards over both windows. With any luck they had closed up for good and gone away. But she could see it was not likely. They would re-open once the place was cleared up and she would not only have to use another dry-cleaners, but if matters escalated she could see herself having to move house. Peter, when he was back to himself, would probably want to do something idiotic and go round and apologise, saying he'd had an adverse reaction to medication, or some such, and offering to pay damages. But it didn't do to show weakness. Better to bluff it out. She could see it was a pity that she had thrown the ripped dress out: it might have been useful as evidence.

She felt she was thinking with unusual calm and clarity. Could this be the effect of having fallen out of love with Peter? She had to accept that she had, or at any rate that these emotions were in abeyance for the time being. At yesterday's dinner the thought of getting married to Peter had seemed even more alarming than that of having a baby. Perhaps love was an emotion which ruled out common sense and self-interest? Yesterday she had wanted only to get the despoiled dress out of her home as quickly as possible – today she was thinking of it as evidence.

There was another rather alarming possibility, of course, which was that mood swings were nothing to with hormones, but with a temporary switching of soul between one person

219

and another. All women were really the one woman: the variations were in circumstance and IQ, not in essence. Religions which believed in reincarnation, that you got the body you deserved every time you changed, saw time as linear. You had to die before you moved on. But perhaps the body, whose memories were perceived as 'yours', housed forever changing souls, which were registered as changing moods? Like in the earthquake, the ground, believed to be steady, moved. You were the one who stayed still.

Her sister Claudette – that was her name, no matter how often her mother called her Claudia – always complained she was another person when pre-menstrual. Perhaps she was. She would have liked to have discussed this with Peter but he was too busy chattering away to Trisha about their physical states to be interested. She was afraid she rather slapped down rolls and butter in front of them, and did not provide a spoon for the lemon curd. They used their knives and the globby yellow substance in the jar was soon messy, and full of bits of butter and pastry flakes.

'I'm not against breasts in principle,' the Trisha body was saying, 'it is quite nice the way they go before like the prow of a ship, but they spoil one's balance. Or are you so used to it you don't notice? And there's a perpetual sense of unrest inside one, a feeling you ought to be doing something, not just sitting about. I feel guilty all the time, but what about? And this cyclical business, connected to the moon like the tides? It's unbelievable. No one talks about it.'

And the Peter body just said he felt great as a man. He loved flexing his muscles. He loved the straight up and down feel of his body, he loved the flatness of his belly, the way he could see sharply and clearly again. He loved the way his thing went twitch, twitch, if he thought of Kylie Minogue, how he had the sense of a future that went on and on as if in a straight line into eternity: as a woman looking ahead there was nothing but hills and bumps and the feeling that the other side of the next hill the road would run out altogether. 'Women expect to die,' he said. 'Men don't.'

It seemed to Doralee that they were becoming altogether too contented in their new shells. The Peter body had taken up the inside pages of the newspaper and was actually reading them. The Trisha body had decided to paint her toenails. Perhaps they were beginning to merge? She made notes. She took photographs when they weren't looking. She would trace the process, however it ended, with integrity and honesty, for a book which would make her millions and help others at the same time. It would be called *SoulSwitch*. She couldn't decide whether that should be one word or two.

She called Peter's office and got through to a colleague who said it might cause problems if Peter did not come in that day. There had been developments on the weapons of mass destruction story and Peter's expertise would be useful. It flashed through her mind that the Peter body could go along to the meeting and play dumb but realised almost at once that she would be wiser not to suggest it. As well send Polly Peachum along to pass judgement on Emmanuel Kant. It would be the family dinner party but worse by a hundred times. Her family were a pretty dozy lot but those in Peter's office were bright, inquisitive and quick. She did not want them breaking her story. She said she was sorry but it really was flu and she could send a doctor's note and he backed off.

She called *Oracle* and got through to her own extension. But it was Heaven who lifted up the receiver and said oh, poor Doralee, I guessed you must be ill, you're usually the one who's in first. Hurry up and get better. There's all this stuff come in on your e-mail about the new miracle drug, the one which cures wrinkles: I don't know why it came to you, I thought that was my area. So I'll just stay on your desk if you don't mind and deal with it. It's a big story. They want it for this month so it needs to go to press right away. You were really missed at Heather's baby shower but everyone knows how you loathe all this baby stuff: she went into labour this morning, so she's not in either. Did I tell you I was pregnant too?

Normally Doralee would have been straight round to the office to make sure Heaven didn't establish some sort of lien to her desk and e-mail – but how could she? She had to nursemaid the bodies. She had to write *SoulSwitch*.

She found the magazine *Spiritual News* on the Internet, looked up the Services columns and made appointments for the following day for them all to see a hypnotist and a medium, chosen more or less at random. She would do what she could to make things better; that was the least she could do, but after that it was each of them for themselves. If the worst came to the worst she would go to Australia and publish the book from there.

Doralee caught them mid-morning lifting their jumpers to study each other's navels, as if trying to discover the root of some mystery. It was a sexless curiosity, at least so far, as if two six-year-olds were examining each others bodies to compare differences. She wondered how long that would last. She feared it would not be for long. The thought of sex with the Peter body was somewhere she, for the moment, simply could not go. Kylie Minogue! It seemed as if the new Peter still contained Trisha's aesthetic sensibilities.

Trisha Perle, for all her lottery win, was a walking disaster area. It could do the Peter body no good at all to contain her. There had been a child, it seemed, but even that had apparently been given away: there'd been more than one husband, a series of unfaithful lovers, a lesbian interlude, too much drink and drugs, and she had managed to lose a fortune and end up working for the Kleene Machine. Translate that into male terms and what did you get? If the initial Trisha make-up had the X chromosome and not the Y in the womb, and been fed testosterone not oestrogen from the beginning, what then? A forty-year-old hippie with a pigtail, perhaps; a determinedly out of work actor with a drink problem and a couple of unsupported families to his name? She wondered if it would be possible to get pregnant by the new Peter: it probably would be but what would she produce? A hermaphrodite? Just because Heaven was now pregnant didn't mean she had to panic.

And as for the Peter soul, it might well have done better in a female body. It would have married a banker and been a brilliant dinner-party hostess and had a part-time job running an estate agency, like his mother. But so dull!

'If Jesus Christ,' said the Peter body now, sententiously, 'came down from heaven today he would be locked away as a madman.' A Trisha sentiment, thought Doralee, though spoken with a male voice to which the listener automatically granted more authority than had it been female. She must keep it steady in her mind that it was not the bodies which had switched, but the consciousnesses; what happened was that the bodies carried trace memories and hormonal tendencies. The Peter body was primarily Trisha, but with little bits of Peter still hanging around, like little scraps of mitochondria around the nucleus of an ovarian cell, of the kind which prevent even a clone from being an exact reproduction.

Of course the Peter body would retain trace memories of swirling skirts and choose to wear a kilt to visit the psychiatrist. Of course the Trisha body would enjoy bashing things up at Mrs Kovac's.

'I think you're wrong about Jesus,' Doralee responded, not without some bitterness. 'I think if there was a Second Coming people would be only too anxious to believe. Then they could go round giving all their worldly goods to the poor, leaving the State to support them.'

Strange things do happen

Last week I got a letter from a reader. 'I met you once,' she wrote. 'In a field in France, in 1971.' And so she had.

The Nineteen Seventies. The middle classes trooped off to France with their children and their tents for their holidays. Now they own real houses abroad, but I liked it the way it was, when like a snail you carried your house on your back. We took everything with us, pepper-grinders as well as sunscreen. 'When you are part of Europe,' as a French shopkeeper said to me, triumphantly, 'you English will all have to speak French.' We still try, but out of politeness, not necessity.

That year, like so many of our compatriots, we went off in our Volvo to the South, with Dan aged twelve, nephew Benj aged eight and Tom aged not yet one. It was hot, hot, hot, the beginning of the French holiday, the great August weekend; we circled and circled the Paris ring road as in a comic film, with its furious, unstable drivers, unable for hours to find a space to leave it. We ended up exhausted fifty miles out of Paris, in the middle of a great wheat plain, in a field used for overnight campers on their way South. A tiny shop, a tap, a smelly earthern loo, a brilliant, beautiful night sky. Ron got out of the car and lifted the tent from the roof rack and slipped a disc in his back and lay on the ground.

The baby howled, the children ran round looking for bats, Ron lay beside the car. I did not drive, I didn't know how, I had never learned. There were other overnight campers there: a whole bus load, even: a football team, their trainer. The trainer looked down at Ron and said, 'I am an ex-army doctor. You must lie where you are for two weeks and not get up and you will have no more trouble with your back. Otherwise this will plague you all your life.' So Ron lay there. The football team moved the car, put up the tent around him. The doctor was right; he never had back trouble again.

But it was so hot, and there was no telephone, just thunderstorms which frightened the wits out of me when the heavens clashed and crashed their vengeance for everything I had down wrong in my life; there was a wasp's nest in the tree overhanging the tent. How they buzzed. I guarded the children as best I could. The shop sold baked beans and Jaffa Cakes for the English tourists, and Coca-Cola, but what about the baby? He needed milk. And Ron demanded ratatouille and bouillabaisse and complained when I could not provide them. He was half mad with pain and the pills the overnight campers provided. I would beg for them; as their cars drew into the field I would be waiting: I would feed them into his open mouth, wash them down with the wine they'd generously given.

That year all the car radios played the same song. '*Chirpy chirpy cheep-cheep. Last night I woke and my momma was gone – oh! oh! Chirpy chirpy cheep cheep.*' By night the field was crowded. People from all over France, so far as I could see, came to visit the man on his back in the field, and his poor wife, and provide pills and baby milk. This was real fame, the kind that counted, nothing to do with writing. I managed an hour or two with my pad and my Pentel, while the baby slept and even Ron quietened in the noonday sun. That year I think the novel must have been *Remember Me. Chirpy chirpy cheep cheep.*

After ten days Ron got up and played a game of *boules*. And three decades on a letter from a reader who's just read *Auto da Fay* and told how she'd visited the field and remembered me and the baby and the children and pitied me, and was that me?

Nothing surprises me any more, not even Trisha and Peter switching, to Doralee's inconvenience, so she's put off having babies for fear of hermaphrodite births. Daniel as a child lived half in one world, half in another magic one. He bent spoons like Uri Geller; he watched the magician on TV one day, and within the week the cutlery drawer was full of forks and spoons bent so they could no longer be used. Not just the thin cheap ones, but really expensive heavy ones. Real silver too, from the shop, some of them. But silver is soft and easy to bend, so we didn't count those. He was nine – there was an epidemic of spoon-bending amongst prepubescent males. Perhaps they could always do it, but why ever would they think of trying if it hadn't been for Uri Geller? Producers tried to show them do it on TV but when the cameras were rolling nothing happened. The cutlery stayed useable.

If Peter and Trisha switch why should I doubt it?

But people do doubt. Dan would rub the cutlery gently with his childish fingers – table spoons and carving forks would twist and turn and writhe. He did it once for Hetta Empson at the dinner table, put the spoon down, and we all watched the metal handle bend itself gracefully backwards of its own accord. I took a photograph of it on that occasion. Hetta denied that it had happened at all, refusing the evidence of her eyes. She just shut them and said it didn't happen, and shouldn't happen and would someone please remove the spoon before she opened her eyes. Dan found his school friends reacted in the same way. 'Didn't happen,' they said.

Then he took to his bed and wouldn't get up. Between the ages of ten and twelve he grew pale and thin. He got dreadful sore throats which would not go away, and which various doctors were convinced were psychosomatic – this being the favourite, and indeed the cheapest diagnosis at the time for any ailing child. They were in as much denial as Hetta when they looked in his throat and saw pink healthy tissue, not what he described as red, inflamed and sore. Taking out tonsils was seen at the time as something which belonged to a superstitious past, old-fashioned and unnecessary.

White as a sheet Daniel lay in bed, declining to get out of it. Friends were convinced it was because I had let him bend spoons. But I finally found a doctor to do the operation, for a fee – facing out the disapproval of friends and family, who thought privatised medicine was wicked – and once done, Dan leapt out of bed and started organising the students' union in his school. But he never bent spoons again and does not like to be reminded that once he did. Better safe than sorry. Should Trisha and Peter get out of their fix I don't suppose they'll cross other people on the stairs again. They'll be very careful.

Mid-Seventies, and the city we knew seemed to be collapsing around us. We were not accustomed to foreigners, other than West Indians; suddenly the Middle East was with us, our institutions were being bought up, not to mention our race horses, and the West End bars were full of blondish girls for sale. The price of petrol went up to nearly fifty pence a gallon, and tights were available, even in Harrods, in only one choice of colour. The former much alarmed the men of Primrose Hill, and the latter the women. What, was even the privilege of the wealthy to be no more? Terrorists were active, bombs were going off in London, too close to home. They reached as near as next door, to No 1 Chalcot Crescent, where the Minister for Ireland, Lord Donaldson, now lived.

Lord Donaldson was a cheerful man, who got very drunk with my husband the day they moved in to their new home. They drank whisky together and ended up dancing on our dining table – refectory, old and solid – and letting down their trousers, to the horror of his wife, a serious academic and historian, and the delight of all our children. Our relationship with the Donaldsons thereafter was distant if polite. And Ron never drank whisky again, only wine

The police asked for permission to run through our house and into the Donaldsons' back garden should there be reason to suspect an assassination attempt or a hostage-taking

situation arose, and how could we refuse? There was a difficulty: the handle of our back door was missing. To get it
open you had to use the end of a pair of scissors. The alarms
next door would go off, our doorbell would ring, the police
would rush in and pile up in our corridor like the Keystone
Cops while I went to find the scissors. It was always a false
alarm, mostly the cat, and if Lady Donaldson had vanished
it was because she was round at the launderette, which she
favoured above a washing machine. But it made you nervy.

Dan, sitting in a local café, overheard a plot to blow his
lordship up. We told the police who told the Bomb Squad.
It turned out to be a conversation between off-duty security
guards outlining scenarios of possible attack, but it was
disconcerting. Dan could scarcely leave home without untoward events occurring. First spoon-bending, now this.
When he got in a car with Ron the sturdy Volvo engine would
start to fizz and blow out sparks. Dan would have to get
out before it would behave normally. Clocks and watches
would stop if he went near them. He was seldom home on
time: there had been a bomb scare or someone had jumped
under a train. He played the trumpet like an angel: he went
to Pimlico Comprehensive, a tough school with a good music
department. He stopped off the bus to watch the Norwegian
Christmas tree go up in Trafalgar Square, left his trumpet
behind, and went back to retrieve it. He found the Square
cleared and cordoned off and the bomb squad about to blow
up his trumpet case. They were not amused to discover it
was his. No one was amused. We were all too frightened.

I took Dan to a psychoanalyst, I remember – I must have
been well into the grip of Freudian fervour – and asked him
what to do. 'This child is event-prone,' he said. He was calm
and wise and saintly. 'It is a recognisable condition. You are

229

lucky. He could be accident-prone, and then you would be in real trouble. This kind of child attracts events in the same way some rare people attract lightning. They are catalysts for change: he will walk through clustering events without being touched himself. He will grow out of it, with puberty.'

And so Dan did, by and large. But I never grew out of my belief that anything you can think of actually happens somewhere. I wrote a passage in a novel, *The Hearts and Lives of Men*, in which a three-year-old survives an air crash, because she is sitting in the tail and it floats rather than falls. Soon after in real life a three-year-old survives just such a crash over Chicago. The writer invents, real life follows suit. The world is so crowded with people that if you can think of it, someone, somewhere, is doing it. Somewhere in India, or Malaysia, or China or Mexico, even now, two people have crossed souls like Peter and Trisha: it's just when it happens in Wilkins Parade that denial sets in.

Doralee is tired

Even now that she understood better what was going on, trying to sort out Peter and Trisha was a nightmare: it was like umpiring at tennis – one makes a mistake, the other one gets a point: that one moves, yet that one speaks: it exhausted her. She wanted to be able to cuddle up to Peter for comfort and warmth and reassurance, as she was used to, but there was no proper Peter around. She was on her own. And then the Trisha body would turn and stare at Doralee with a kind of yearning which reminded Doralee of Peter so that she almost wanted to hug her. But she despised the Trisha body. Trisha was too fleshy and too soft and not young enough: the idea of too close contact with her breasts, especially her naked, floppy breasts, was horrible. Yet she was beginning to think about it as a possibility. She had had lesbian leanings towards other women – she had inner stirrings towards Heaven Arkwright, if the truth be known, alongside the antagonism. Heaven had a kind of lean, muscly, dark-skinned smoothness that called out to something in Doralee, who felt pathetically white and soft by contrast, a little mewling creature battering fists against something more significant than herself, but about to be swept up and enclosed, which she half wanted, and half didn't want. It was incorporation that she was after. Yet Doralee, in the same room as Heaven, always felt unentitled in some way, perhaps by reason of having a church-going mother and a father who worked for an NGO; or perhaps it was just because she'd done something she knew was wrong, reading Heaven's e-mails and snaffling a job from under her nose. Well, now she was punished.

Doralee said she was going to lie down for a little, yet still hovered by the door, while the Peter body and the Trisha body played Scrabble, and took no notice of her, Doralee. They had left her behind, and now used her to look after them: they saw that as natural. They were a more perfect form than she, who was a mere heterosexual. Like snails they carried both male and female inside them.

She left the room and lay down on her and Peter's bed, and then found herself wondering what the Peter body might be like sexually when moved by Trisha's spirit. She, Doralee, was being offered the best of all worlds, surely. What was she doing, turning her back on experience? She was a journalist. It was her duty to find out. She slept.

Selling up and moving on

Come 1975 our front door too was sold, along with the other antiques. Ron wanted to live in the country: I could not see that it made any difference to me where I lived. One green field was much like another. I assumed he wanted me to come with him. In retrospect I am not so sure. The house was put on the market; a buyer came along, the deal was struck, and Ron put the contract under my nose and meekly I signed the papers. It was midwinter, and very cold. Now we had nowhere to live.

The house was sold to a banking family – in the fifteen years we had been there the Crescent had gone up in the world. How could it not? Central, airy, just down the road from the zoo and Queen Mary's rose garden, pretty Georgian houses – of course it had. A dream of a London house. Yet I'm sure I complained about it at the time – too small for our needs, too narrow, too tall, too many stairs – yet how sorry I was when it was gone. I pass it sometimes now, and never without a pang of nostalgia for the past, for the days when the future seemed to go on for ever.

I went back to Chalcot Crescent last year with a film crew – pad, pad, pad, they go, obsessively, in one's footsteps, recreating – but the magic was gone. Just another house. Plain, white-painted in the new style, no paintings, spruce and clean, too narrow, too tall and too many stairs. Could the walls have forgotten us so soon? Yet nothing is ever really over. Shut your eyes and stretch out your hand, and there it will still be: friends, laughter, the music of the Sixties, *Sergeant Pepper* heard for the first time, Joni Mitchell, veal roasted in lemon, endless bottles of wine, the warmth of the Pither stove, dinner parties, birthday parties, family Christmases, the voices of children, the crying of babies, new goldfish in the pond, the back door that wouldn't open – and all those emotions which surged from room to room, the gestures of love and affection, the wildness of sex, the anxiety of jealousy, the tears, the murmurings – and the sheer work of it all: the taps that in your time you've wiped behind, the surfaces cleaned, the washing baskets filled and emptied, the ironing you haven't done, the sheets folded, the stairs you've climbed, and climbed and climbed again, the domestic running to stand still, that intrepid almost religious female fight against chaos and entropy – it all goes on the same in some other parallel universe. Fifteen years must imprint themselves somewhere, somehow, upon eternity. You can't just shut the door on it and believe you've left it behind.

But of course there's a relief in it too. Too many years in the same place, and awkward events accumulate: there are public scenes you'd rather forget, neighbours who took offence, whispers behind hands, dreadful things the children did – now all left behind. All embarrassments conveniently solved by leaving familiar streets. It was always my mother's way of dealing with difficulties. Pack up and move on. And the house was indeed tall, and my legs were tired from carrying babies and shopping up the narrow stairs, and Ron didn't want the pitter pat of journalists' feet outside the door – *Upstairs Downstairs* had been screened and they were out in force – and he just wanted out of there. I signed, there was no argument and pretty little discussion.

Mid-sentence, mid-thought, it is true I tend to say anything, sign anything, just to make people go away and let me get on with the next piece of writing. I try not to but I do. And we had nowhere to live, and Ron showed no signs of actually looking for anywhere, though we bought *Self Sufficiency*, a book about living off the land, and I was busy writing.

Mantrapped! How can I explain to you, in these talkative days, so full of instruction from the wise to the foolish, the recommendations of experts and TV therapists and counsellors, and quizzes as to what makes a good marriage and what doesn't, and the insistence on talking things through, the attraction of the silent, troubled marriages of the day? Man proposed, and man disposed. Or perhaps it was just assumed that after so long, fifteen years, we would just read each other's minds. I fear I read only what I wanted to read.

The shop meanwhile had been sold over Ron's head. The new landlord, who lived above, wanted to charge a full fifty pounds a week rental, instead of the customary ten. Monstrous! And somehow my fault. The whole modern world, with its galloping inflation, its admiration of the trivial (me), its refusal to recognise the true artist (him) was my fault. Eve-like, I accepted blame. And he was quite right: I should not have taken so many taxis. I should have saved money, not spent it, and when the time came there would have been enough in the bank, in cash, for him to buy the shop outright. Everything had to be sold, everything, including the roof over our heads, in particular the roof over our heads, and all my fault. Thunder and lightning crashed around. But I was writing the last pages of *Remember Me*: yes, yes, I said. Anything. Whatever. The country. Yes.

In the novel, a ghost story, Madeleine the rejected first wife is killed in a car crash but can't die, because she has a child to look after. When, finally, her work done, she is at rest, the eyes consent to close. She is buried.

'*Oh my sisters, whispers the memory of Madeleine to still troubled air,*' I wrote, '*and my brothers too, soon you will be dead. Is this the way you want to live?*

'*Which at least seemed to create some kind of consensus, for or against, because after that there was nothing but the wind to ruffle the grasses, and disturb the little pots of dried flowers on the more recent graves, and whatever trouble there was dispersed, and there was peace.*'

I was very child-centred in those days, I can see. But I'm glad that even then I gave a mention, although a little grudging, to the brothers. I came to the end of the book, and looked around. I had two children at home, one aged twelve, one aged five, a restless husband, a house to pack up and the new owners were patiently and politely knocking at the door. The contract was signed. There was nothing I could do other than what was under my nose. I packed.

But it was daunting, and a hard winter and the central-heating broke down. Ron was too busy in the shop to help. I noticed he was still buying stock – there was no sign of it closing down – I thought perhaps he could not stand the trauma of leaving. He had been in the house for longer than me, more than twenty years, and I lived in my head and he lived with the aesthetic of made objects: it was easier for me. How could mere things carry so much emotional weight? But they did. And so much of it. Every surface, wall and shelf was covered with treasures, bits and pieces, Georgian chamber pots, Victorian knick-knacks, French pottery brought home from holidays; the cupboards stuffed with raccoon coats –

Edwardian, prime pieces in good condition, only a little moult – rusty tin boxes of assorted buttons, ditto broken jet jewellery, photograph albums of other people's holidays, everyone long since dead. '*Oh my sisters and my brothers too, soon you will be dead. Is this the way you want to live?*'

Into crates and boxes went the mad yet wonderful collection of what to Ron represented both his own past and all civilisation, and I did not doubt for one minute but that everything must be looked after and properly packed; newspaper mostly, it being in the days before bubble wrap and foam. And I even gave the furniture one last coat of beeswax before it went to store – the Etruscan olive-wood table, the carving in elm of Edward VII (why? Why?), the carved-oak Jacobean blanket chest, the noble Welsh dresser, the staid Victorian chairs, the doubtful ancient-Egyptian frieze, the gracious bentwood chairs, the late Victorian lace-covered cushions. And the battered first editions of Somerset Maugham and the complete works of H.G. Wells – and all the books that Ron had ever read or bought. I seldom bought books and still do not: I was too poor until my late twenties to afford them, and after that I had lost the habit. Books were things you wrote, or borrowed from libraries, or found in the post.

And then the artwork. Cynthia's upsetting paintings, down from the racks in a cloud of dust: and then Ron's – rather gloomy, heavy colours; later, when he started painting again and was more miserable, the paintings were to became inordinately cheerful and distinctive – bright colours, fauvist, full of appreciation and generosity of spirit – I notice the same thing in myself; if I am miserable I get really funny: it is the search for balance in all things, no doubt – but then untouched for years (all my fault), finished and unfinished, all the stiff unusable brushes stuck to the bottom of jamjars, the glass

236

now multicoloured, from which the turpentine had evaporated. A couple of Sheila Fell landscapes, the two sandstone Gaudier-Brzeska sculptures I had bought for two hundred pounds from a passing scholar, who told me he had rescued them from Violet Hunt's garden in Camden Hill. Ron kept them as doorstops; only after his death did I feel able to rescue them, set them on marble pedestals and admire them. A massive collection of Ron's 78s – mostly early jazz – and yet more accumulated aspidistra plants. And *objets trouvés*, pale bits of tortured wood, and mastheads, and copper pans from every century, Victorian lace-trimmed underwear: nothing could be discarded or thrown away. I tugged at string and labelled everything. I bound boxes round and round with sticky tape. I remembered every lesson ever taught me by my mother, who so believed in packing up and moving on, and had thrown so much of my childhood overboard, when we left New Zealand for Britain in 1946. '*I can't go on lugging this stuff round the world for ever.*'

I gave Trisha an easy time, when it came to packing up her lottery-winner's house. I chose an easy way out for her and let her put everything into auction except what was required for her immediate needs.

Making good

Mrs Kovac had had to close the shop for a day, and put off some of her best customers. She'd had to throw out skein after skein of paint-splashed embroidery thread, which was these days hard to come by. That hurt. Her records were gone, her lists of customers: also the names and addresses of former contacts in the people import business. She was not in that business any longer: it had got too dangerous and she had gone straight, but you never knew when you might need to recall favours. She had not wanted to involve the police. Mr Kovac was legally in the country but a man in his position was easy enough to frame. There were informers everywhere you looked, and he had friends who were very sensitive and might get nervous if a police car was seen outside the premises. You sometimes had to pay a heavy price for having a man in your bed.

The repair man for the ironing machine had promised to turn up but hadn't. That meant finishing would have to be farmed out, at extra cost. She was tempted to ask Mr Kovac to hurry him up with a hammer over the kneecaps but stayed quiet. This was no time to be stirring up trouble, however aggravated you were. She should certainly not have cut up the black dress and sent it back just because a customer had been rude. There were laws against that kind of thing now – and her business-college tutor would have been horrified.

The damage done to the shop had been more than you would have expected from a little thing like Trisha, no matter how angry or drunk. The yuppie she'd sent up the back stairs to collect his repairs might have had something to do with it. She wouldn't be surprised. He was cheating on his wife – or partner – that was clear. They'd left a bottle of vodka behind them and the nasty bits of card and debris dope-smokers used for anyone to find. It might not have been dope, of course, there were all kind of unpleasant new drugs out there which you could smoke. Mr Kovac only dealt in the old-fashioned kind which had known results, or so she hoped. These sudden outbreaks of uncontained and irrational violence worried everyone. If Mr Kovac dealt at all, of course. There were other reasons than drugs, these days, for having pockets full of cash. She had stopped bringing girls into the country because the field had become professionalised, and there was no room left for the amateur.

She, Mrs Kovac, had put her past behind her, was a good citizen, paid taxes, did her accounts, had a grant from the Small Business Office, and was doing her best to make it in the new society. Anti-social elements made it difficult, but when did they ever not? The shop needed redecorating anyway.

She called up the Chinese person who'd been after the flat before Trisha Perle had turned up with her grumpy ways, false promises and crude stitching. She'd never seen worse buttonholes. The white races had no idea any more of fine work. They left it all to imported labour. She was gone, leave it at that and put it down to experience. The new girl's name was Anneping Lin. That was pretty. She sounded a nice person. Perhaps they could be friends.

First thing she'd thought, when she saw the damage, was that Mr Kovac would not make too much of a fuss. Men so often did. Mr Kovac had called by around lunchtime, to find the shop closed, the glazier's van taking up his parking space, his wife still working on the damage, he unable to deliver because even after the muddled tickets had been sorted, little bits of glass still had to be vacuumed out of shoulder pads and belts. He had indeed overreacted. He had thrown her teapot through the glass window. The window would have to be replaced yet again, but at least the glass had already been measured up. And he kissed her in apology, which was nice.

Mrs Kovac thought it was wise to suggest the perpetrators had been a couple of tripping youths she had seen hanging round when they closed up the night before. She also let slip that the new tenant had been thrown out for sloppy workmanship and for being on the game. She didn't want Mr Kovac turning up at High View and making trouble. She had a lot of good customers there, and she was more interested in profit than vengeance. She doubted that the same could be said for her husband.

Trying to get out of the city

The cities were falling – only in the country, next to nature, would anyone be safe. Rural fervour swept the land, and our family was not immune to it. We, or at any rate the self-aware middle classes, would live on food from the fields, nettle soup and dried herrings, and be the better for it. We would live next to nature and clasp trees and be restored in spirit and mind. Self-sufficiency was all the rage and John Seymour was its high priest. Hetta Empson went to visit him on the banks of a muddy river and came home to report that she had never been so hungry in all her life. Quarter of a kipper for dinner, she complained, albeit served with ceremony. John did nothing, she complained, while his wives toiled, up to their elbows in mud.

Time was running out. The new owner, a famous banking name, was waiting to move into Chalcot Crescent. Ron thought perhaps we should buy a country rectory to live in – the Church Commissioners were selling them off cheap. We went to see one or two but he did not think they were suitable, on unspecified grounds. I could see his heart was not in it. Perhaps all he wanted was to get away from his analyst, Mrs Warburg, and could see no other way of doing it other than sell the house over his own head, as it were; he said as much, once. Now terror had struck his heart as it had mine – nettles in winter are tough and stringy, Dutch elm disease had swept the Southern counties: the fields, without their tall green hedging, did not look so pretty now. The threat of rationing had gone, the increased price of petrol had not brought the world to an end, the bomb scares were fewer than they had been. Business in the shop was good: perhaps a negative transference to Mrs Warburg had switched to positive, who was to say?

I rang Mrs Warburg once, only once in all those years, and complained and said, 'How can I ever have a conversation with my husband, he only ever talks to you. All things intimate belong to you; I want him to stop.' And she thought a little, and then she said, 'My dear, you will be sorry when he stops,' and it was true, I was.

Homeless! I put down the opening page of *Little Sisters* – '*We are all within spitting distance of millionaires. Spit away, if that's what you feel like . . .*' and bought us, in haste, and from friends, and without consultation with Ron, because there seemed nothing there to consult with, a small new square modern concrete house, an in-fill between two big houses round the corner in Belsize Park. It was there, and it was somewhere to go, with our suitcases and our minimum of belongings. It had two rooms up and two rooms down and two bathrooms, and was neat and small and trendy, and confirmed Ron's view of me that I had no aesthetic judgement and given a choice would choose a kidney-shaped dressing table over a Queen Anne cabinet any day. 'It will be a *pied-à-terre*,' I said boldly, 'because if we are going to live in the country we still both have business in London.' But even I could see he was bound to hate it. It was brand new and had no history. It smelt of the seaside, there being a fan above the cooker which belched out ozone to freshen the air, but was quickly to be taken off the market as a danger to health.

Some twenty years later, after Ron died, it fell to me to pack up Orchardleigh, the Somerset farmhouse we eventually moved to in the August of 1976. Another two decades of accumulation to sort. I found some of the Chalcot Crescent boxes in the barns, still unpacked. I thought everything was done: I stretched up and opened a hatch in the ceiling of the bathroom lobby and a large wicker basket from the holiday camping days – tent, metal tent poles, camp beds, folding chairs, waterproof sheets – disintegrated and tumbled down on top of me in a cloud of reddish powder. Rust and moth had got in to corrupt; and time, the great destroyer, sneered at me. I was cast off the stepladder into a heap on the lino floor and beaten about the head with falling objects. *Take that, and that! Let this teach you to value the past! It is over, gone . . .* Something had got into that house. It lurked on a corner of the stairs, hulking, evil, foul and menacing. I dreamt the taps ran blood. Professional cleaners came: they make all the difference. Whatever it was left its haunt on the stairs and I could go up and down in peace.

These days I have less patience with things. I take them round to the charity shop on the slightest excuse. I try not to accumulate objects and speak harshly about the evils of the consuming society. If I had to pack up all my worldly goods I don't say they'd fit into the back of a car but a couple of vans would do it. I like to be ready to run. It feels safer like that. My archive, the proper sum of me, is contained in the shock-proof, bomb-proof, temperature-controlled vaults of an American university.

When I visit my children I notice they serve dinner off plates that were once mine, on which I served the lemon veal joints from the Elizabeth David *French Provincial Cooking* recipe, and the glass bowls for the chocolate mousse. We sit upon sofas that once I bought, sleep on mattresses familiar under the weight of flesh and bone, and were not the row of copper saucepans hanging on the wall once a source of anxiety? (Ron found them in a skip back in 1961, and they were never properly tinned.) The pottery vase in which the pot plants sit was once my salad bowl – I remember the very shop where I bought it, in the main street of Cahors, the year Tom was bitten by a viper.

The final decree of my divorce from Ron in May 1994 came through the day he died, and it was unclear whether I was divorced or widowed. It still is not. I remarried a week later: the date had already been set. As I say, you see what's under your nose and go ahead and do it, if you can. Then everyone settles quicker.

Trisha had an easy time of it, indeed: I did not make rotting wicker baskets full of rusty metal poles fall upon her head and shroud her in slimy waterproof sheeting: I am writing a comic strip, not a horror tale. A story about swapping souls, not moving house. Mantrapped.

Doralee adjusts

People can be good at adjusting to new situations, especially when they are young. On the Monday Doralee was living a happy and successful life, by Wednesday it has fallen to pieces. By Thursday it is true she is in quite a state, and it is getting worse not better as the implications of her present plight become obvious. She finds herself out of love with her partner, whose body is inhabited by an older woman she does not admire. When either Trisha, who is really Peter, or Peter, who is really Trisha, attempts to so much as touch her, she tends to pulls away. She is confused.

She must face her responsibilities. She must give up thoughts of running away to Australia. She might well get her book *SoulSwitch* published, and it may even cause quite a stir but it is unlikely to make her a fortune. No one is going to believe something so profoundly unbelievable. She will still need her job. Rescue needs to come soon, before the new personalities harden into their bodies and turn into just more people, but people without much hope of earning a livelihood. Will she, Doralee, be expected to support all three of them? The Trisha body is of course qualified to do the Peter job, but who will employ her? She has Peter's intellect and store of memories, which includes everything there is to know on weapons of mass destruction and so forth, but no certificates to her name, and no qualifications other than an unfinished course in embroidery and patchy employment on the stage: lottery winning is not a recognisable craft. The Trisha body could settle down to winning pub quizzes, but there's no money in that. Peter might just about manage a job as a male model but he's already in his early thirties, well over the hill.

And where is rescue going to come from, Doralee asks herself. It is she who has squeezed the orange juice and run round for the croissants. She left them to make the coffee and instead of grinding it and using the percolator they have spooned instant powder into their mugs. Peter in the new

Trisha body seems to like to just sit and accept what happens next. He does not think of the medium and the hypnotist, Doralee must do that. Not that she has many hopes of them.

Trisha in the Peter body is making Peter slovenly. She has lottery-winner standards of idleness but has lost the lottery knack of being lucky. Or perhaps not? Was it not Trisha's luck and Peter's unluck that led them to the change? Perhaps Trisha is a witch and is not as innocent as she appears and has stolen Peter's soul: but Doralee dismisses that thought. Doralee does not believe in witches.

But what is she to do next? She hates the feeling of being at an impasse. She can consult other authorities of course and probably will. There must be other, better psychiatrists, wiser priests than the two she has so far encountered. She could, and perhaps should, hand over Peter and Trisha to the police or the intelligence services. They might be one of the first of an alien infestation from outer space; the authorities might be looking out for such specimens, she has no way of knowing. Really it is nothing to do with her, she is just an innocent bystander, and she has no legal responsibility towards Peter. He is not even her husband.

She took a shower. That cleared her head a bit. She was a perfectly ordinary person, living the life someone with a middle-class background and a proper education could be expected to live, with a loving partner and a pleasant home. It was true her parents showed signs of eccentricity, but that was not unusual in the elder generation, as the reports of friends suggested. Her anxieties at work she could now see were trival – whether Heaven Arkwright was taking advantage of her absence, whether Heather would actually come back to her desk after maternity leave, was unimportant.

And now suddenly out of the blue, this. Nor were the ordinary agents set up by society to return everything to normality as soon as possible – police, fire, ambulance – of any use to her. She could not claim on insurance: there was no victim-support group in place to help.

She could hear the low murmur of Peter and Trisha chirruping away over Scrabble and it annoyed her. Neither had bothered to have baths. They seemed too happy in themselves to want to do anything. They were not anxious about the future. It was as if being female permanently entered by the male, and male permanently embedded in the female, brought great benefits to the individual but none whatsoever to society.

She sat at her computer and wrote her next week's column on a report that David Beckham had performed a miraculous cure on a deaf child at a football match. As David scored the first goal of the match the child's hearing had been restored: he had heard the roar of the crowd. Doralee called various press departments for their comments. The Archbishop of Canterbury's office said the whole matter of miracles was currently under review, and the girl at the Archbishop of Westminster's office, who was on work experience, said it was a lot of old rubbish. She didn't herself go along with Mother Teresa being canonised, the old witch hadn't been dead long enough, and personally she loathed football. But she'd go away and find someone who knew. She went away and no one returned to the phone. Doralee hung up after five minutes.

She then called the BMA who found an expert who said that in rare cases, mostly in children and when the incapacity was hysterical in origin, hearing could indeed unexpectedly be restored, but obviously they would need documentary evidence before they could make a proper comment. Doralee wrote a thousand words suggesting that deafness in itself was not really a disability, rather a different state, and that the silent world had its own pleasures, and look at the deaf couple who had chosen to give birth to a child who would inherit the genes of deafness.

And then she wrote about the real miracles all around, the growing of the seed into the flower, the rainbow, the smile on the baby's face and so on. Then she deleted the whole thing. It was nonsense. You could believe in Trisha and Peter swapping, indeed you had to, but if you did there was nothing else you could take for granted. Write an article today and by tomorrow the whole world might be changed. The ground had shifted beneath her feet.

Then she went to her recycle bin, thankfully unemptied, and restored the article. There was nothing wrong with it at all. It read perfectly well, so long as you looked at it through yesterday's eyes, not today's. Science just needed to come up with an explanation, and the terrible feeling that the world was falling to pieces would depart. It must have been equally terrible when word got round that the earth wasn't flat but round like an orange. Life might not continue as normal but work could. She put up *SoulSwitch* on the computer and wrote up her notes.

There was a small argument that evening about toothbrushes, which Doralee solved by going out to buy two new ones. The Peter body didn't want to use the one in his tooth mug, but the one he'd brought along with him from Wilkins Parade, along with a nightie, some face cream and some hormone replacement pills. The Trisha body wasn't sure that she wanted him to do so. The inside of the body, the mouth, was apparently still an area of indecision. Whose was it? And which one of them was going to take the hormone pills? Doralee thought the Peter body should because it would increase the chance of a transfer back, but the Trisha body got panicky at the thought of not taking them.

In the end they both ceremoniously took an orange pill, though the Trisha body disliked the fact that now the succession of pills in their foil sheet, marking the passage of the menstrual month, would be disrupted.

Before they went to bed, encouraged by Doralee, who surreptitiously made notes, they spoke about their new bodies, their new selves.

The Trisha self in the Peter body liked the feeling of being young again, and healthy, and without the little niggling aches and pains, which could only get worse over the years, and being able to see so sharply, and not have dots swimming in front of her eyes, not having breasts and being flat down her front, and never having to have a period again, but on the other hand always worried about having genitals which were on the outside and made you feel vulnerable.

There were benefits to being a man, the Peter body said, like pissing standing up, and feeling you could batter your way through anything that stood in your path, and the kind of underlying grey cloud, which he guessed was guilt, simply not being there any more. But he acknowledged Doralee's right to have her partner's body back, and he wouldn't try to keep it if he felt it going. But he could do with a little financial help to set her on her feet again, as Trisha. She had no money, nowhere to live, and no job.

And how was she to earn a living, if she stayed in a man's body? Too healthy looking and too tall for a rent boy, no memory, no good at facts and figures, and not temperamentally suited to physical work.

'I could just have babies, I suppose,' the Trisha self said – he was changing out of jeans and T-shirt into a long pink designer dress of Doralee's in which he planned to go to bed – it just felt right, he couldn't explain it, but it expressed his personality. The dress looked quite good, Doralee realised, the delicate hem revealing black-haired male ankles, and black chest hair sprouting through the fine material which had once shown Doralee's dainty breasts to advantage. His body seemed to be compensating by a rush of testosterone to the glands. It was as if the body had decided the time was ripe and was beginning to flower.

'There's always the State,' said the Peter body. 'I could just have babies, couldn't I, be a single mother and get benefits?'

Doralee said women who lived off the State were pathetic and she hoped the Trisha body would do nothing of the kind. At which the Trisha body raised her eyebrows in a particularly Peter-ish way, and reproached her for being uncharitable. And Doralee felt a pang at being thus betrayed by her partner. It must have showed in her face because the Trisha body first tried to take Doralee in her arms and hug her, but the arms were too short, so she gave up and said why didn't they all open a bottle of wine. So Doralee did.

They sat and drank and listened to Johnny Cash – the only music they could all agree upon; sad songs about mortality – and looked out over the city, and Doralee was almost content. The sky was blue and pink around the edges, and you could see Canary Wharf in the distance, and the light on its top winking like a steady heartbeat, and a plane coming down into the City Airport, and the hum of the city, if you listened hard, pulsing first loud, then soft, all around. But that might just be your own blood surging through the arteries next to your brain. It was a wonderful place to be, all agreed.

The Peter body chattered on about how she had once had an affair with a woman, Thomasina, and how nice it had been, soft and gentle and safe, only they'd such terrible rows, they had to part. Trisha had been black and blue.
'And I'm a mass of scars,' said the Trisha body. 'Look!' And the Peter body pulled up the Trisha body's skirt to show the shins, which were indeed dotted by little white patches. 'Cigarette burns,' said the Peter body. 'It's how she'd punish me for saying the wrong thing. And she was very jealous. I'd explain and explain how I was bisexual but she didn't want to listen. Perhaps it's all my fault this has happened. I should have been more one thing or the other.'
'Not necessarily,' said the Trisha body. 'I've always rather liked dressing up in women's clothes. Sometimes when Doralee's out and I'm stressed I wear her knickers. If you put them on back to front they fit really well, and the silk's comfortable.'

A few days ago, thought Doralee, she would have been horrified, perhaps even asked Peter to go to counselling, but now it was trivial, nothing. And what support group could ever help her through this?

The Peter self had more to say about the female state. He loved the underwear, and was coming round to the breasts, a sort of decorative optional extra, even though they were far from perfect, and he actually quite liked having this kind

250

of closed-up neatness between his legs, which gave him a moral superiority over men, whose genitals hung indecently as appendages. Those seemed to have a life of their own, and to be a kind of second self, not totally under the control of the rational brain. A built-in disapproval factor of the male seemed to go with the knowledge of containment and neatness, which compensated for the untidy whooshiness of the womb. He could think of no other word . . . And the Peter self liked the lightness of being Trisha, of having such tiny feet, but he did think she should go on a diet. The Peter body said that was fine by him, it was up to the Trisha body. If when she got back to being herself she was a stone lighter, she could live with that. The Trisha self, whom Doralee suddenly felt quite affectionate towards, undertook to eat well while in Peter's body and try to stay off the junk food. Whether it would happen of course was another matter.

'But the great disadvantage of being you,' said the Trisha body to the Peter body, 'is the age thing. Otherwise there might be some point in calling it a day and you and me getting together. But I want to have babies and I had hoped that Doralee would finally come round to it, but the Trisha body might not be able to do that, might she.' If he stayed a woman, and added the two disparities up, the fifteen or so years lost by losing his own body, and the seven years by which women normally outlived men, the original Peter would lose out on more than twenty of life. He would have the worst of both worlds.

'What about me?' asked Doralee, pained. 'Am I of so little account? Don't I come into the equation?'

'I care about you very much,' said the Peter self in the Trisha body, 'but you must see I am not much use to you as I am. And statistically the odds always were that without children we would split apart. We were not married, after all.'

Doralee stared out at the darkening sky and thought of life alone, without a man, back to dating and socialising, and thought it wouldn't be too bad. She had allowed herself to get stuck in a rut. She should probably look for someone in science or philosophy. Peter had a practical brain: she needed someone with more imagination, more capacity for speculation. But she did not want to think of the Peter body in bed with the Trisha body.

The Peter body said he'd take a raincheck on that if no one minded. God had given him this great opportunity and a great body and it would be a sin not to go out there and use it. He wouldn't be true to himself if he didn't go out there and play the field. Nineteen wasn't too young for him, was it?

'Nineteen will need to be in a position to support you,' said Doralee snarkily. 'I don't see you doing it yourself. And I certainly won't be.' Well, she was hurt. The Peter body, which housed Trisha, took Doralee's hand and stroked it.

Doralee withdrew her hand and said briskly you never knew, the new selves might not age at all. They could be anything. They could be immortal. They could be from some other universe: astronomers now accepted the fact that there was most likely to be intelligent life on other planets, it was just a matter of finding it. Or of course if there were alternative universes, which lots of nuclear physicists now claimed there were, what with string theory and suchlike, some bug thing might have slipped through – and brought a soul-swap infection with it. Or it was intentional, a deliberate Mars, or even Venus, attack?

But the others looked at her so reproachfully she apologised. That was a horrid idea, and should not have been suggested. There was no more talk of Peter and Trisha getting together, but when she went out to the kitchen for more wine, she wrote down *Soul Swap, the Sars of Outer Space.* It had a terrible ring of truth.

Doralee brought back more wine, and had to open it herself, of course. The pink in the sky grew vivid, the blue faded, the sharp shapes of towers and spires faded, like Trisha's eyesight with encroaching age. The moon was up, a couple of days beyond full, just a flattening out from perfect roundness. 'Gibbous,' said the Trisha body. He would.

Normally prudent herself, Doralee drank less than the others, and kept filling their glasses. She needed every minute of this experience, however it pained her.

A home to go to

Winter, 1975. Removal vans came and went. Our worldly possessions went into store.

Jane Bown came to photograph me. I was honoured. Jerry Bauer, too. Lord Snowdon as well, though I think that might have been later. I remember the good and talented Lord rifling through my wardrobe to find something suitable for me to wear, and finding nothing but a quilted coat in a pretty sprigged material fashionable at the time which would do to wrap around me. He set me under a tree and put a dog beside me, so I daresay that was indeed later, in a more rural phase of life. Wind swept through my hair.

A film crew making a documentary about the new feminism came to the house and found the electricity switched off, no furniture and me with scrubbing brush and mop. I take care to clean all the houses I leave as best I can, as evidence of my willingness to be a good citizen, earn the respect of others. That was one of my mother's legacies. She moved house as often as she could, always in search of something better, and always left them spotless and herself exhausted. I knew it was the thing to do. But it was so cold.

The day came when the new owners moved in. Ron went off to the shop as usual with a few things thrown in the back of the car. I wrote another sentence or so of *Little Sisters*. It was about a nineteen-year-old girl off on an illicit weekend with an antique dealer.

Elsa is abundantly lovely. She weighs twelve stone four pounds and is five feet eight inches tall. Her swelling bosom and rounded hips give promise of pneumatic bliss . . . Ah, she's beautiful, lush but not louche. 'You would have forgotten these,' says Victor, handing her the pink sachet of contraceptive pills. He'd picked them up from where they were hiding between the claws of a nine-foot Yogi bear.' 'I wouldn't,' she protests. But she would if she could.

I went to the new house and turned on the heating. It did not work. I went to collect Tom from his infants' school on Primrose Hill, and we went home to our cold new little concrete house. When Dan came back from school it was here he had to come. And the white cat got out and ran away and we looked and looked but couldn't find him. That evening Ron came home. But without his accustomed house around him he seemed denatured; I had never known him without it. I could hardly recognise him as having anything to do with me and I daresay he felt the same when it came to me. We went out to dinner with our friends Evie Williams and her new husband Anthony Perry and came back to the freezing house and Ron stayed the night. And in the morning he said he could not possibly live in such a place, what had I been thinking of, it was made of concrete and he was going to live in the shop until there was somewhere proper for us to live. We looked some more for the cat but couldn't find it.

So I found a house to rent in Rothwell Street, No. 5, which backed onto 3 Chalcot Crescent and was similar in every way, except it was not ours. We left the concrete house empty and moved in. My mother, my sister and the children moved in to take our place. From Rothwell Street I could see right through our old house to the Crescent beyond. It was so nearly home. But Ron said he did not like here either, he could never feel at home in such a place, the paintings on the walls were bad and of the African veldt, he would stay in the shop. Three months passed: I fretted and grieved; Tom and I walked into a lamppost on our way to school and we both knocked ourselves unconscious. It was snowing so hard I could not see. Indeed, I could not see. I went on with the book. *We are all of us nice, charming enough people*, I wrote, *until tried by circumstances and hard times, and then, and only then, do we find out what we really are.*

But I still did not find out. I wore a watch fashionable at the time. It defined your mood. I consulted it as if it were a charm. If you were unhappy or depressed the face was black: if you were cheerful it turned green or blue. I would go down to the shop and spend the night with Ron on the futon on the floor between the refectory tables and the marble washstands and the face of the watch would turn from black to bluey green. I liked to see that. I took it as a clue from fate that true love would win out in the end.

I caught a glimpse through two sets of windows of a white shape sitting on the Chalcot Crescent pavement and ran round to No. 3 as fast as I could. It was our white cat, toothless and thin and ragged: he had found his way home over railway lines and busy roads. I held out my arms and he leapt into them. I took him back to Rothwell Street. But he kept trying to get back into the Chalcot Crescent house, where he was now not wanted.

I could see Ron would never come to Rothwell Street, because of the bad paintings, so I rented the top floors of a house only six doors down from No. 3 Chalcot Crescent, where the cat consented to stay but Ron did not. Now I was paying one mortgage and two rents. I could no longer avoid it: it was nothing to do with any of the houses, I was the one Ron did not want to live with: I had just been very slow in realising it. I shut my eyes to dawning realisation. I went on with the novel. I give Elsa a happy end. She escapes from would-be murderers.

Elsa walks a good half mile down the road, unkempt, barefoot, and distraite, before a garage van going in to London picks her up. She is home by half past eleven, in time for the epilogue on television, and cocoa with her brothers and sisters.

But where was home? I'd told a story in *Down Among the Women* of a ship's magician on the *Titanic*. Every day he gives a children's party, does his tricks, makes a parrot disappear.

'Where did the parrot go?' cry the children. 'Here!' cried the magician, and there the parrot is, on his wrist. The *Titanic* strikes an iceberg and sinks, the magician and the parrot drift alone on a raft, day after day. For three days the parrot says not a word. On the fourth day it speaks. 'All right. I give in. Where'd the bloody ship go?' I was the parrot. Ron, Ron, I finally said, *where'd the bloody home go?*

Had he planned it in advance? How to unhook yourself from a clinging wife, old style? He told me once a friend said the way to let a woman down gently was to be so horrid to her she'd finally be glad to leave of her own accord. That shocked me so greatly I had wicked Angie and her even nastier lover Clifford do just that to sweet Helen in *The Hearts and Lives of Men*. In *The Heart of the Country* the antique-dealer has a room at the back of his shop where he entertains passing lovers. Easier to write it than to live it. In retrospect I see I spent a lot of time writing missives to myself which I then failed to read. 'Oh,' I say, 'I never go back to any of my books after they're written.' Pity.

Yet though often suffering acute fits of jealousy, they were, as it were, unspecific. I believed in Ron's fidelity, in his good sense, and in his standards. I thought that the normal rules of conduct did not apply to me, and that I was somehow special and would be saved. That once you have found true love it will be yours for ever. I was like a girl who chooses to believe, because she wants to believe it, that you don't get pregnant 'if you do it standing up'. I believed that all the fame stuff – and it was after all a very minor fame, and you were only ever as good as your last book – was of no real importance to anyone and that Ron would see it the same. That he had married me for better or for worse anyway, and if his musician friends addressed him as Mrs

Weldon, and they would do that, meanly, sometimes, he would simply ignore it, because it couldn't be helped and what I did earned our living. And actually I was right.

Come August, and Ron wrote to say he had found an old farmhouse on the side of a hill, and had bought it, and needed my signature, and would I and the children come down and join him. The house was called Orchardleigh, it had a garden and fields and was in Somerset, and you could see Glastonbury Tor large and clear if you lay on your back on the attic floor and craned your neck to see past the roof ridge to the skyline. His choice. That was all it needed.

Twenty-five years later, in *Worst Fears*, I was to raze the house to the ground. Passing it a month or so back I was surprised to see it was still standing. I had thought I would see nothing but a rectangle of charred ground, with a garden and fields. But real life is stubborn: its nature is to persist. *Worst Fears* was only a book, words on paper, for once about what had happened, not what was going to.

Temptation

That night Doralee had trouble sleeping. She looked in on the Peter body where it lay sleeping, just as usual, on its back, arms flung wide and welcoming. The Trisha body lay curled foetus-like on the office sofa, making snuffling noises. Doralee sat at her desk and found the Internet and kept the volume down. The Trisha body did not wake. She looked up the nature/nurture debate on Google as it related to gender and found all kind of interesting things about the hard wiring of the species nature, about woman the nestbuilder and man the protector of the nest, and how human babies are the only creatures along with birds who call the parents back to the nest when in need, and at what time gender-specific behaviour cuts in – and made a note or two of background information for the book that would make her fortune and career. But there was nothing directly to the point. How could there be? Vast masses of ill-digested and agonised guff on transsexualism, and transvestites, and rather more lucid stuff on hermaphroditism, all on the nature side, totally ignoring nurture; and how babies can be born without the mother's DNA because they have absorbed from a lost twin's inheritance, not the mother's. But a whole personality transfer, memories and all, and only the sympathetic nervous system left, as if the actual brains had shifted from one body to another – nothing. It was in no one's experience. She marvelled. Peter and Trisha might indeed be the only people in the world to whom this had happened, even if you included the vast populations of China. It was a frightening feeling, thus to be the lone witness to the future, walking on glass in a kind of drug psychosis which would never end, and yawning chasms of nothingness underneath, yet awesome. She would be on so many TV programmes it didn't bear thinking about. The cover of *Time*, even – of course they might try to use Peter and Trisha but they wouldn't get much sense out of them, and she, Doralee, was certainly more photogenic than Trisha.

She got through to alien abductions: perhaps sometimes people were swept up as one sex, and returned as the other? But there was nothing there either. A note came up on her e-mail. It was from Dr Otterman. He was sorry he had been unable to help but he had passed on the relevant details to the Department of Neurology at UCH, where there was a specialist department devoted to phenomenology and the study of consciousness, and giving her a phone number. Doralee deleted the message. Later, when the book was published, when she was the one who knew everything, and the whole world was aware of it, others could investigate all they liked. She would not be dog-in-the-mangerish. She opened a new file. Doralee/ *Soul Switch*/ *Work in Progress*.

Her body was restless, full of vague desires; it missed Peter's body, even if she didn't. There was no real Peter. But she kept flicking back to wanting him, as the caps lock key on an overused keyboard will flick into uppercase unasked. She could join him on the bed easily enough. It was her bed. But was this a permitted exercise? Because it was Trisha really and would count as lesbianism. It would be being unfaithful to the real Peter, who was stuck in Trisha's body. They had none of them really discussed the matter of sex, just skirted it. She couldn't think why: it was enthralling.

If she were Trisha and had a man's body the first thing she would do would be to try it out: if she were Peter he could be excused for wanting to see what it felt like to be a woman. Perhaps in this new state of existence the sexes didn't get together: they did it to themselves, like snails, which everyone knew were hermaphrodite.

Doralee heard a female voice talking from the bedroom. Had someone broken in? She hurried in but the Peter body was sitting up in bed, bare-torsoed, and seemed to still be asleep, other than that he was talking in a high, chattery little voice. 'I'm not the kind to take advantage,' the Trisha voice was saying out of the Peter body. 'You know what I'm like. I'm just going to see it as a holiday, do all the things I want to do, eat what I want to eat, stop feeling bad about little Spencer, not worry about going with other women's husbands, be a man, in fact. I might go and beat up Rollo because he's a complete shit.'

Doralee ran her hand over her partner's familiar shoulders and felt the tenseness in them, and dug her thumbs into knotted muscles to relax them.

'That's lovely,' said the Trisha voice. 'Don't stop. Do you know what I think happened? I think that man who hangs around Kleene Machine, and Mrs Kovac says is her husband, comes from werewolf country, and there is a full moon. I reckon he's put some kind of spell on us, and it might be wearing off. But I suppose it's better than white slavery.'

'Just because people are immigrants doesn't mean they're white slavers,' said Doralee, primly. 'I hope you learn a thing or two from Peter while you're in there, Trisha. You've got some really odd ideas.'

It was obvious now to Doralee that Peter's penis, familiar though with a new driver, was rising and making a little peaked mountain under the sheet. She made a movement to lift the fabric but the Peter body pulled it down again and said in the female voice 'No, I'm sorry, Doralee, I don't want you to do that. And you'd better stop the massage. Why won't this thing just do as I ask? I don't want it to stand up and twitch like that. It's stupid. How can a man stop himself being a rapist? No wonder such terrible things happen in the world.'

'But I'm your body's partner,' said Doralee, seeing a chapter in danger of vanishing. 'And there's an almost full moon, and it was such a fabulous evening. We ought to celebrate.'

'Peter wouldn't like it,' said the Peter body, and the vocal cords were back in his charge. Another change was settling in, hardening, not weakening. The voice was even deeper and louder than Peter's own. Another flood of testosterone, presumably. 'Just go away and leave me to sleep, for fuck's sake.' This from Peter, who never swore.

The sound of the TV came from the living room and Doralee was glad to get away from the bullying stranger in her bed. The Trisha body sat with her short arms clasped round her legs, dinky little toes with the chipped orange varnish matching the henna hair. She was wearing one of Peter's white T-shirts, in which Doralee thought she looked very fetching, and watching a ball game on TV. Doralee felt twin surges of affection. One because the Trisha body suddenly seemed soft and kind and a source of comfort, and she wanted to be close to it, and the other because the expression on the Trisha face as she raised it to Doralee's was so like the Peter she remembered and loved. But also because she wanted to write her book and must not miss these opportunities.

'Tell you what,' said the Trisha body, 'I have to redo these toenails. Do you have any varnish? Can you show me how? I don't suppose for one minute it's easy.'

Doralee sat close to the Trisha body so their bodies touched, and she picked up the little Trisha foot – it was white and pretty in spite of the little cluster of fine varicose veins at the ankle – and admired it. Feet are so personal, she thought. They contain all the character of the owner. She would write an article on the subject of feet: there were probably people out there who read soles as well as people who read palms.

Doralee made a quick note in what she now in her head called her SSS (Switched Soul Syndrome) notebook, then went to the bedroom, removed the T-shirt she wore to bed, found the cream silk negligée with lace trimmings Peter had, rather to her surprise, bought her the previous Christmas. It was just not her kind of thing. Now she understood better why it hung near the front of the cupboard, and why although allegedly never worn there were a couple of coffee stains down the front. The Peter body watched from the bed, scene of so many passionate couplings, without apparent affect.

Doralee, seductive (she hoped) in cream silk, returned to the office with her little box of nail accessories – remover, pale pink varnish, clear second coat, cuticle cream, scissors, clippers, cotton buds – and sat at the end of the couch. The Trisha body stretched a leg flirtatiously but went on watching the ball game, as Peter would sometimes do if he woke in the night and not even sex could get him back to sleep. Doralee took the little foot in her hand and stroked it. Trisha took no notice. Doralee took one of the big toes in her mouth, and gazed up at Trisha, using the sort of gawping, goggling expression that girls used in the porno films she and Peter would watch in foreign hotels.

Trisha did not react, other than to seem vaguely irritated, but Doralee felt hurt, rejected and humiliated. She made herself try some more, hoping for a response, taking the flesh of the nipple between thumb and forefinger and tweaking, but there was no denying it, the breasts against her forearm felt flabby and collapsed and old, not full and firm, as her own were. She felt revolted by herself, rather than by Trisha. Trisha was just human.

Doralee gave up and went back to bed, taking off the negligée so it fell to the floor, a pale silk circle of fabric which bore witness to thwarted hopes and lost love. Trisha went on watching TV, having lost interest in her toenails. Doralee cried softly under the bedclothes, but then got up and made notes on her iMac. She must not let personal humiliation stand between her and her future. Tomorrow she would put Peter and Trisha in the same bed. It would hurt but it had to be done. It might be that Soulcrossers – was that a good word to describe this new breed of people? could she compare the first switchings to the arrival of humans in the Neanderthal world? – were hard wired for fidelity and could only do it with each other. They only mated and bred with their own kind. If so, as more and more of them evolved, or transpired, or came from outer space, or whatever they did, and took over, the planet could look forward to a more tranquil future. But it would, she supposed, be the end of art. That could be a chapter to itself.

The next morning everyone behaved themselves. The Peter body refrained from smoking. The Trisha body ate the vitamin spread and abjured the lemon curd. They laughed and joked about mediums and hypnotists, but seemed prepared to make the outings, to wear conventional clothing, and even to hope that the treatments would work. No mention was made of Doralee's nightly visit. The morning sun shone from a clear sky: it seemed a day without pollution, and the city spread out below was sharp and clear and detailed, like an aerial photograph developed just right. Doralee called the domestic agency to say she did not need a cleaner that day: she was told she would have to pay for the missed appointment, since so little notice had been given, but for once she did not argue. She would be rich enough, soon enough, not to worry.

She nipped out for the morning paper and saw the Kleene Machine was open again, and the customers coming and going. That was good. She went back up and settled down with the paper. Unplanned time off like this was precious and rare and she meant to make the most of it.

George the porter called up from downstairs. He had the driver from Kleene Machine there. He'd left a pink shirt for Mr Brandon at No. 5. But George was sure it was one of Peter's. Could Ms Thicket check her cupboards to see that she didn't have No.5's shirt by mistake? A Canadian plaid? Not George's favourite, but dear to Mr Brandon. Then everything went to pieces. The Trisha body grabbed the phone and squeaked, 'That bastard from Kleene Machine! Do you know what he did to my wife's dress? Don't let him get away! I'm coming down!' And the Peter body lurched to his feet with a roar, spilling the coffee all over Doralee's supplement so that she squealed in surprise.

The Trisha body leapt for the door and the outside world and Doralee could almost feel the sudden burst of energy which went with her like a current in the air, leaping from the Trisha body to the Peter body, and back again, like short-circuiting electricity. The Peter body followed. Doralee could see she should follow, though oddly, as their energy increased, hers seemed to deplete, as lights will dim all over a city when there is a sudden call on power.

She could see she needed to follow them down, but she was reluctant to do so. She could not face any more trouble. She mopped up the spilt coffee and checked that she had her key before she left the room. She dreaded what she would find. Perhaps they would trash the lobby as they had trashed the Kleene Machine. Then she would certainly sell up and move house. Another chapter, perhaps. *Soulcrossers, berserkers and me.*

She took the lift down and came out on the lobby and was met by a tableau which was to be engraved in her memory long after the notes for the book which was never written had been deleted from her computer.

George stood beside the desk, as if paralysed, holding a shirt on a wire hanger in his hand. It was pink and button-down, with red splashes down the front, and was not Peter's. Half the plastic wrapping had been torn away. Mr Kovac was lying on his side on the floor, a splodge of red growing on his very white shirt, the friendly smile still on his face. Perhaps it was painted on, thought Doralee. But he was dead. You could tell, though she had never seen a dead body before. They had a kind of completed, over, look about them. Unmistakeable. The Trisha body was dead too. She lay on her back, hands flung up above her head, in the same position Peter slept at night. Half of her head had been blown away. Bits of red spattered George's desk as well as the shirt. A van was driving off. A shudder of bullets clattered across the tall, wide windows of High View's lobby, bursting and exploding glass. The Peter body stood next to George, with his mouth wide open, swaying. The crashes, pings and tingles of falling debris died away. The three left living were untouched.

Doralee was the first to move. Everything was very quiet. No one came running from Wilkins Parade to help. No doubt they knew which side their bread was buttered. When trouble came they kept out of the way. She called the emergency services from the landline on George's desk. She had left her mobile upstairs. No one answered for two long minutes. Peter pulled himself together and took his watch out and began to time the delay, tapping his foot. A few passers-by stood as if paralysed, staring.

'Can we check your number please? This is in the customer's interests and in case of hoax calls.'

The Peter body grabbed the phone and shouted, 'Give me the fucking phone.'

It was evident to Doralee that body and soul had been restored to one another, but leaving Peter rather more forceful than when he had begun. Perhaps he would end up editor. And that was the real Trisha lying dead on the floor. Doralee felt tears well up in her eyes. Poor, valiant, unlucky Trisha.

'There's been a drive-by killing,' Peter was now saying, out of call-centre mode, and to someone he seemed to take seriously. 'All three services, please . . . two dead, no one else hurt. Drug-related, I would assume . . . that's the man. But there's a woman here too. No, I don't know who she is. An innocent bystander. A stray bullet, would be my guess.'

The paramedics came first and were impatient to take the bodies away and get on with their busy schedule, and would have done so before the police arrived if they could. They were anxious to save paperwork. Doralee and Peter gave the police their witness statements, as the ambulance drove off to answer another call, promising to return when they could, and the police set up their crime scene.

'Poor woman, poor woman,' said Doralee. 'I think she lived above the dry-cleaner's. She must have called by to deliver my mattress-cover, and then this has to happen!'

She was sorry to have to abandon the book, but it would seem like pure fantasy now and not marketable. But being a witness to sudden death could keep her in the public eye, and in copy, for quite a while. The police would not take too much time on the case – gangland killings were frequent. And at least she had Peter back. They went back to finish breakfast, just the two of them, shocked and shaken but together. Doralee shoved the butter plate towards him. 'Eat what you like,' she said. 'It's your body.'

Home and normality is restored

We went to live with Ron, husband and father. He'd asked us and we went. Of course we did. He loved us after all. He'd missed us.

That was 1976, one of the long hot summers of the century. An anti-depression had settled over the country, bringing with it endless still days and blue skies. The sun set warm and secure each evening, orange light glowing against the old brick walls of the barn. *Red sky at night, shepherd's delight.* I thought this would be home for ever.

The house, which was set amongst parched fields, had been left empty for years. It had nearly fallen down altogether but now we were building it up. We plastered and wall-papered together, making good. Ron and I slept on a mattress on the floor: one night in that first week we heard giant thump thump thumps down the stairs. I thought it was some ill-omened monster, ghost of past and future, but it turned out to be only rabbits, mistaking our home for their burrow. The children slept safely upstairs. I had never been so happy. The moon shone through windows fringed with creeper.

The white cat came with us, of course. But she never quite forgave me. I had failed to look after her properly. She went to live next door, where there were carpets and no chil-dren, but sometimes she would come and sit in our garden in a friendly fashion, and stare at me as if she had a great deal to say, a great tale to tell, if only she had the words.

P.S.

Ideas,
interviews
& features ...

About the author

About the book

Read on

Split Personalities

Louise Tucker talks to Fay Weldon

The first volume of your autobiography, *Auto da Fay*, is a much more classic example of the genre. What made you switch for *Mantrapped*?

It's the next stage on. Autobiography is interesting but so is fiction-writing and one day it occurs to you that the gap between them is not so large as you suppose. How much of the autobiography is fiction? None of it – though one or two people tell me differently. I think of the novel as totally fictional so I chose, rather deliberately, something which hadn't happened and which couldn't happen. There is certainly a relationship between what you remember and what you put in a novel, though barely consciously. Tiny things surface and that becomes interesting.

With *Auto da Fay* and *Mantrapped* did you feel you had to wait until most of the real-life protagonists were dead before you could write about them?

Oh yes, decidedly! There are quite a lot still alive but they didn't mind. Family and friends get used to it over the years, I'm afraid, perceiving themselves in what I've written even though I didn't realize I had included them.

Did anyone complain?

They've done very little complaining since too often their income depended on my earning power. I certainly discouraged my children from reading anything I'd written if only because I don't really want to discuss it with anybody. What's done is done.

And have your children read your books?
We all go on pretending they've never read anything. For example I've done a treatment of *Puffball* with my son Nicholas, for which he composed the music and I read extracts, and we went round the festivals but we still went on pretending that he hadn't read it! And my son Dan has been working on a screenplay of the same book and he also pretends that he hasn't read it.

Do you think as a writer that you have more than one self?
Of course, yes, as a writer one does tend to have a split personality. In my case the writer part is two people, writer A and writer B. Writer A is female, creative and wakes up in the morning with these amazing ideas; B is male, an editor with a red pencil, and he keeps on saying, 'You can't say that, it's absurd. How revolting.' If you get those two married, if they get on, you can then write a book. One will not do without the other: they're interdependent whilst resisting each other every moment of the way. There's also a C personality who gets the writing paper, organizes the mail and does the secretarial stuff. (She's hopeless.) D lives the day-to-day life and does the shopping and the washing. Then there's E, the public speaker, a mode I can go into quite easily. (I love her.) They're all different, quite separate and distinct. ▶

❛ There is a relationship between what you remember and what you put in a novel, though barely consciously. Tiny things surface and that becomes interesting. ❜

Split Personalities *(continued)*

◄ If you're writing fiction you have a sense of these divisions; if you're writing non-fiction you think you're just a person. No such luck!

You describe how having written your first book you realized you'd found your métier. But have you ever had writer's block?
I haven't had writer's block as such. I've gone through patches where I've thought that what I was writing wasn't as good as it should be or was not inspired, but then you can't always be inspired. So I've never stopped writing but I've gone through patches where I haven't enjoyed writing. Some of those novels were written with B predominant: actually it works better if A is in charge. Fortunately readers don't seem to notice this.

There's a real sense in your early career of downplaying your abilities, that you should have been scrubbing pans, not writing. When did you start to feel proud of your work and why?
I still think I should be scrubbing pans. I think women never grow out of the feeling that one day they will be discovered as presumptuous and an impostor, that I have no business to be doing this. One bad review and you believe them. Found out at last!

Do you think you'll ever stop? Has it become life to you now?
If I stopped it wouldn't be because I wanted to stop but because I got too tired. It's what I do; it's like breathing.

6 I certainly discouraged my children from reading anything I'd written if only because I don't really want to discuss it with anybody. What's done is done. 9

Psychoanalysis played a big part in your marriage to Ron and you yourself spent many years in analysis. Do you think it helped or hindered you and your writing?
I think it helped my writing but I don't think it really helped me. Before I began I could write only advertising copy: it was all short-term quick results stuff, whereas after analysis I had the courage to go on and write longer things and wait patiently for publication or production.

Is there anything you wanted to be when you grew up?
I wanted to be a ballet dancer. I was quite good but then it started to hurt and once we moved to England it was out of the question. But I remember those ballet lessons – I could bend backwards, walk on my hands – I can still touch my toes with my hands flat on the floor in front of me, but that may be because I have short legs.

Do you have any influences as a writer?
Every book I've ever read. Quite early on I had a furious letter from a professor in Spain who said *Remember Me* was a direct rip-off of Dylan Thomas's *Under Milk Wood*. Man's mad, I thought. Then I read the first page of it, and he was right. The whole rhythm of it – though not the characters, not what happens – was exactly the same. Then I remembered I heard *Under Milk Wood* on the radio when I was 14 and thought it was the most wonderful thing I'd ever heard. And there it is, back again … I've always been very ▶

6 When a book is finished you realize it wasn't the book you meant it to be so you write the next one. You go on in the hope of one day getting everything right. 9

Split Personalities *(continued)*

◄ sympathetic towards any writer who is
accused of plagiarism because how can you
help it? If you like something, if it appeals to
you, then in it goes: you regurgitate it later
on. In terms of the stealing of plots, this used
to be what writers normally did. Look at
Shakespeare. It was seen as rather vulgar at
the time to provide your own plot. It was how
you dealt with the story, how you presented
your characters, the moral sense you made of
it, which was interesting, not what happened.

**What advice would you give someone
starting out in writing now?**
I wouldn't advise them at all. It is not a career,
it is something you do. If you find yourself
writing then lucky old you. You write what
you want, you finish it, you don't ask anyone
to publish it before it's finished and it takes
an enormous amount of courage because
you might be totally wasting your time. But
you have to have something to say; it is no use
trying to write if you haven't, so you may
have to wait. One day you may well have
something to say – it might be early, it might
be late – and then you do it. You have to set
up the page, your first page, with more than
you can possibly chew in the next three
hundred pages and then you start chewing. If
you find yourself wondering how many pages
you've done so far or padding, then give up
because it's obvious that you have nothing to
say on this particular subject. Find another.

You also need to have an urge not to be a
writer but to write a book. People want to be
writers and it is now seen as a career option
which it never used to be. It was just

something you did and if you did it often enough people would refer to you as that writer; otherwise you would be referred to as that milkman or that layabout, if you delivered the milk or never did a decent day's work. By your results will you be known.

Ron is described in *Mantrapped* as preferring vision to fulfilment, 'but then a painter often does'. Do you find that of writing too?
No, you have a vision and you try to reach it but you never get there, you always fail. When the book is finished you realize it wasn't the book you meant it to be so you write the next one. If you did it properly, if you thought you had done what you wanted to do, then you probably would stop because why go on, just for the sake of it? You go on in the hope of one day getting everything right. ■

7

A Writing Life

When do you write?
All the time unless I can't, unless there's
something else I have to do. In my head I
write non-stop, in real life days go by and I
write nothing!

Where do you write?
Before I had a computer I could write
anywhere, on the stairs and in bed, but now I
write in my office. A pity.

Pen or computer?
Computer. I used to do a first draft with a pen
and then type; now I type and then do a
second draft with pen on the printout, then
somebody else types that.

Silence or music?
Silence.

Why do you write?
Because I want to persuade everybody to
agree with me about everything, for their
own good.

**Do you have any writing rituals or
superstitions?**
It used to be A40 pads and Pentels, lined,
wide-spaced paper and a soft-tipped pen, but
the modern Pentels are too soft and I have yet
to find the right pen after ten years of
looking. And I like writing out of sleep, as I
get up. Now I go straight to the computer but
I used to wake up and start writing in bed
which was very annoying to anyone else who
happened to be in the bed.

Which living writer do you most admire, if any?
Hilary Mantel, she's quite amazing. She seems to have extra antennae planted in her as to what goes on in the world.

What's your guilty reading pleasure or favourite trashy read?
Thrillers, though I'm not sure I'd call them trashy. I've just read a Gerald Seymour and he is very far from trashy: I bought another title for the train and then discovered I had already read it. I all but cried. He holds you, he really does. A good thriller is hard to find but once you've found one they're extremely satisfactory. There is no need to read anything guiltily. Though I admit back in the sixties I used to tear the lurid covers off *Amazing Science Fiction* before reading them in public.■

The Real Me?

By Fay Weldon

One of the problems with being a writer of fiction active over several decades – I have some thirty-three novels, plus various other works to my name – is that you tend to forget who you are. You become the sum of your fictional parts, with a *soupçon* of characters to come, waiting in the wings to pounce. So how can I describe myself to you, as my editors require, with any hope of getting it right? I would first have to 'discover the real me' which many people these days go to therapy to find out, though I am never quite sure what the advantage is. Supposing you found the 'real me' and really disliked it? You can usually leave it to a spouse or partner to do it for you anyway, and report back from time to time in unflattering if, one hopes, forgiving terms.

Ask me what I am like and all I will say is this person sitting on an office chair in front of a computer making things up: or else ask my husband, and please don't tell me what he says. There are all kinds of things I don't want to know: at the doctor I don't want to know my weight, my height (you lose inches over the decades, apparently: though I like to think this is my characters stealing my very life statistics from me, rather than age). I don't want to know when I stand in front of the stationery cupboard that I need more paper clips, typing paper, bulldog clips and sticky tape that won't break my fingernails: I would rather close the cupboard and think about it some other time and get back to the people on the page. I am so conscious of the loose connection between the writer and the 'real me' that it is easy enough for me to envisage a couple of people crossing on the stairs and switching gender, identities and souls, as happens in *Mantrapped*. Really one could be anyone, depending on whom you happened to meet on the stairs.

It was in trying to focus the fictional identities back into myself again, and show them who had the upper hand – me, me, me! – that I felt obliged to intersperse the fiction with sections of autobiography. So you have this hybrid of a book, which makes librarians and booksellers tear their hair, because where in the classification system does it reside? Some of it's plot, some of it slips into me, and vice versa. Some prefer the story, some prefer the memoir sections. I like them both, obviously, or I wouldn't have written the book.

But I have been preoccupied with identity for some time, I realize. *The Cloning of Joanna May* (1986) was the story of one woman inhabiting four bodies, against her will. *Splitting* (1996) was about four personalities sharing one body. *The Life and Loves of a She-Devil* (1983) was about a woman trying to change her body into that of her husband's mistress. In *Mantrapped* I return to the problem of identity. What is it to be male? What is it to be female? Are we the sum of our hormones, or the sum of our souls?

It occurred to me a long way back that if you were to be a novelist you had to give up ▶

6 One of the problems with being a writer of fiction active over several decades is that you tend to forget who you are. You become the sum of your fictional parts. 9

The Real Me? *(continued)*

◀ any idea of yourself as a 'nice' person. You had to lose your good opinion of yourself. One of the problems that young novelists today find is that having done so few truly awful things in their lives and being trained anyway in the avoidance of guilt and the pursuit of high self-esteem, they can see themselves as victims easily enough, but seldom identify with the perpetrator within. Things get a bit placid.

I too – this is a confessional – used to argue from the platform at literary festivals and so on that what I wrote was purely fictional. 'Why,' I'd say, 'if I did everything my characters did I'd be in prison or dead!' and the audience, who are always incredibly trusting and supportive, would nod kindly and approvingly. After reading *Mantrapped* I can see I lied. I am not so much inventing as trying to find the real me – a worthless preoccupation but clearly compulsive – by extrapolating from one remembered event to another and making leaps in between. That church where Doralee, Peter and Trisha meet the bats: that ray of sun cutting through the doom: that rush of unseen wings: I'm pretty sure I've been there, seen that, heard that. What false pride to claim 'I made it up.'

The rabbits who come thumping down the stairs in the house I went to live in when once again reconciled with my then husband – they were true enough. If I'd taken a photograph I would have had proof that the rabbits existed. But then I remember a photograph my first husband showed me – taken by him, in 1952, when visiting Versailles. It was in these same gardens that in

> ❝ It was in trying to focus the fictional identities back into myself again that I felt obliged to intersperse the fiction with sections of autobiography. ❞

the thirties two lady schoolteachers famously walked into a time warp, emerging to describe in great detail the court of Marie Antoinette. They were much derided at the time. When my husband took his photograph, of an elegant rotunda amongst greenery, the rotunda was empty, the gardens deserted. When the photo was developed the rotunda was full of laughing people, in stylish period dress, hands outstretched towards the camera. Well, if you can believe that you can believe anything. But I saw them, and it wasn't a trick of the light or the camera. They were there in the photograph, as clear as the egg on your face, those people who weren't meant to be there. What's true, what isn't – we can only make a stab at it. ■

6 It occurred to me a long way back that if you were to be a novelist you had to give up any idea of yourself as a "nice" person. 9

Have You Read?
Fay Weldon's other books include:

Auto da Fay
In this, the first volume of Fay Weldon's
autobiography, the author takes us from the
1930s to the 1990s, from New Zealand to
London, from being an unmarried mother to
a CBE. Young and poor in London,
unmarried mother, wife, lover, playwright,
novelist, feminist, anti-feminist – there are
few battles Fay Weldon hasn't fought. An icon
to many, a thorn in the flesh to others, she has
never failed to excite, madden or interest.

The Bulgari Connection
Take one wealthy businessman on his second
marriage to an avid, successful young
woman; one ex-wife who happens to be a
saint; one artist, and a portrait for sale; two
women wearing Bulgari necklaces: add a
touch of the supernatural, a big dose of envy,
stir, and see what happens.

Puffball
Richard and Liffey, a young married couple,
follow their dream of moving out of London
to a country cottage in the middle of
Somerset. Richard continues to live and work
in London, coming to stay with Liffey at
weekends. But Liffey's pregnancy, the odd
neighbours and Bella, Richard's lover in
London, all threaten the rural idyll she has
imagined for so long.

Remember Me
Madeleine, ex-wife of Jarvis, wants revenge.
Hilary, their daughter and witness to the

wrongs her mother suffered, grows fatter every day under Madeleine's triumphant care. Jarvis, happily remarried, fends off his ex as best he can but she is determined to be remembered ...■